The room was cold with night air. My stomach hadn't recovered from the acid burn I felt when Deputy Michaels had said I wanted Ray Tantro dead.

I couldn't let Michaels or Paolo see the shame on my face, the pettiness that had betrayed me down in Star Valley, the greed, the blind avarice, the sudden need for riches and fame through the paintbrush of a dead artist—who wasn't quite dead then but definitely was now.

I hadn't killed him but I was guilty, guilty of everything I despised.

I hadn't even known him. I wanted to, I did. I heard his voice in my dream, indistinct and low. *We went down the same road, Alix.* But he kept dying, and dying.

———————— ★ ————————

Also available from Worldwide Mystery by
LISE McCLENDON

THE BLUEJAY SHAMAN

LISE McCLENDON

PAINTED TRUTH

WORLDWIDE.

TORONTO • NEW YORK • LONDON
AMSTERDAM • PARIS • SYDNEY • HAMBURG
STOCKHOLM • ATHENS • TOKYO • MILAN
MADRID • WARSAW • BUDAPEST • AUCKLAND

PAINTED TRUTH

A Worldwide Mystery/December 1996

This edition is reprinted by arrangement with
Walker and Company.

ISBN 0-373-26222-1

Printed in U.S.A.

ACKNOWLEDGMENTS

Thanks to everyone who helped in the process,
including Larry McCann of the Billings, Montana,
Fire Department; Tom Minckler of
Thomas Minckler Galleries;
Evan and Nick for the comics;
Marvel Comics and everyone at the Mighty Thor;
and as always, Kipp.
May you always have heroes.

HE LIES WAITING. It is coming, he knows. His eyelids are too heavy to open. He tries to remember where he is. Not home, no. There is his mother then, in the kitchen of the house on Fremont Street, the white one with green shutters, and his dog, a wrinkled mutt named Hitch. When he remembers Hitch he feels like crying. But no tears come.

In the dark he smells things that frighten him. He wants to run, to go far away, to go home. But his legs won't work, his arms lie leaden and useless at his side. The fog in his brain keeps the thoughts from connecting. Then he smells the smell that scares him the most, and the scream that he tries to make sticks deep in his throat.

He wishes his nose couldn't smell, wishes he could just lie back and sleep. How he wants to sleep, a soft bed, a pillow. God, what he would give for a pillow. But instead the hard floor makes him listen and smell, his only senses that work. The eerie silence is punctuated by muffled voices and the cry of a baby far away. A dog barking fills him with sorrow. It could be Hitch.

The odor makes no sense. It reminds him of a birthday once when the candles made green puddles on the cake. Sweet like sugar, it's comforting. For a minute the fear subsides. He is young again, eight or nine, and can smell the waxy leather of a new baseball glove.

Then a pop, a whoosh, then another louder pop. The heat closes in like a suffocating blanket. His face feels shielded from it but his legs and arms get hot, hotter. He wants so badly to run; the scream builds inside his chest. With enormous effort he tries to move but even his mind refuses to obey. As his clothes burst into flame he is confused. This didn't happen at his birthday party. He isn't here. This is a dream, a bad, horrible dream. Just before he slips into unconsciousness he hears one last sound, strangely near yet far, far from him.

It sounds like the end of the world.

ONE

LATE JULY, a Thursday. The kind of day when you make deals with the weather gods to never again complain about February if July could just stretch out ninety days long. The first truly summery day we'd had in Jackson Hole. June had been rainy and cold, and July had only just begun to bounce back. The wildflowers along the riverbanks broke hibernation in pink and blue. A striped-faced badger washed his lunch in a clear green eddy, while in a sky so warm you wanted to wrap yourself in it and sleep, a bald eagle let the wind lift his wings as he glided over the river. The kind of day where you expect birdsong and moments of penetrating contentment. Not twists of fate that make you mistrust your instincts.

Instincts don't come easily. I have to listen hard. I tried to listen to the river today; results were mixed. A snapping turtle with a brain and a bra, one boyfriend called me, right before he left me for a raven-haired tootsie. A left-brainer, I know it, even though I own an art gallery in one of the most beautiful valleys in the West, in the world. The irony hasn't escaped me.

We were in Pete's car, the three of us, driving back through the Snake River Canyon into town, rehashing the white-water run, when I realized we'd been lulled into believing the day could be perfect. Driving was Pete Rotondi, my kayak instructor, a lanky, athletic guy, not my type but appealing in a rugged sort of way. Eden Chaffee, friend and witness to today's escapade, sat wedged in the back among the gear, chattering about the photographs she'd taken. Pete was kidding me about the alabaster quality of my tan-resistant body, saying the only way I could get any color at all was to let a paddle flatten my nose. Which I had done today, upside down in my kayak. I could thank Kahuna, the Snake's meanest wave, for giving my face color, although two black eyes weren't exactly what I had in mind.

The river run had been such blessed relief from the mid-summer madness that was Jackson Hole, Wyoming, that I didn't even mind the black eyes. My lungs ached from all the river water I'd sucked down. My nose felt fat. But I was thrilled to have done the Snake River Canyon, a mean bronc-busting stretch of white water that attracts serious kayakers and intrepid vacationers from all over. I was glad to have had a break from the Second Sun Gallery, to be able to give the problems there some perspective.

I had spent the morning trying to find the truth of our troubles. My partner, Paolo Segundo, had refused to discuss them. Part of the mess was the promise I'd made, a promise I would have to break. The poor season, bad sales, and the rock we'd gotten through the front window hadn't helped.

The truth, of course, is a slippery thing. Take, for instance, the truth of who you are at any particular point in time. Today I am Alix Thorssen, semiprosperous art dealer, so-so kayaker. Single girl, thirty-something. Tomorrow I might dye my hair purple, kayak the Amazon River, marry a half-naked native hunk with creative body paint, and live in the jungle forever. It's doubtful, at least the marrying part, but anything is possible. So who am I? Who is anyone? Some questions float around us like clouds of confusion, grabbing our attention when we least expect it.

The truth of a place is subject to the same confusion. And when a land has been mythologized as much as the West has, as a place of desperation, freedom, and majesty, the waters are plenty muddied.

Some people see the West the way Albert Bierstadt did, as a hidden paradise where sunlight tastes like honey and rainbows remind us we're only human. But that's only one truth. For other folks it's Indians or loneliness or the smell of latigo. Whatever your view of the West, you can bet it is right—and wrong. The truth isn't necessarily what you see, but how you see it.

Eden Chaffee leaned forward. "I got a great shot of you upside down in Kahuna, Alix."

"Yeah? My best side." I flipped down the visor to get a look at my face. Below my Norwegian blue eyes were their evil twins: tomboy, brackish as a primordial backwater, I-can-do-anything-you-can-do-better, all-American shiners. I had only been blessed with basic Scandinavian looks, no candidate for the Swedish bikini team. God, wasn't I gorgeous now.

"What's that?" Eden said. She was a tiny person with a high voice that annoyed me when I first met her. "Shit."

Pete was craning his neck forward as I flipped the visor back up. "Looks like the square," he said.

Black smoke hung ominously over the town as we reached the Teton Pass turnoff and dissolved into the lines of traffic headed into the heart of Jackson. The sky darkened and the smell of burning reached us. I watched the smoke intensify, wondering what the hell was going on.

"You can't tell from here. Can you?" Eden asked. She didn't want to believe Pete. She owned an art gallery too, opposite mine on the town square. She had come to me for advice when she first moved here.

"Could be anywhere," Pete said. He exuded trust-funder sass, a ski-and-river bum more interested in a good time than money. His bleached-out brown hair hung over his forehead. He was at least a few years older than me, with crow's-feet around his blue eyes. "Could be a grass fire."

The smoke was too black and concentrated for a grass fire; even my untrained eye could see that. Besides, it was in the middle of town.

Eden leaned forward again, gripping my shoulder. "Jesus God, it *is* the square."

Jackson's town square is a grassy park framed by arches on each corner built years ago from zillions of elk and deer antlers, lit up with twinkle lights at night. Boardwalks crisscross the grass. A bronzed bronc rider is installed in the center, with names of war veterans below, just like any small town. The square is the part of Jackson that changed the least, and because of that I liked it the most. The city planned to cut down a tree for purely aesthetic reasons last year and I made six urgent pleas to the city council before they reconsidered. I would have strapped myself to the old elm before they would change the square.

I bit my lip hard and tried hard not to envision flames licking the corners of the Second Sun Gallery, my home for the last eight years. All the problems at the gallery disappeared. The precarious checking account seemed manageable. My apartment over the gallery was dry and secure, even though the roof leaked, and I installed extra locks last winter after a break-in and stashed the handgun my mother sent from Montana in a kitchen drawer. And, of course, Paolo still loved me.

In my years in Jackson Hole, the Teton Mountains weren't the only peaks and valleys I'd seen. Business had a way of slamming you down just when you were getting ahead. This summer had been particularly difficult, with slow sales due to the recession in the East and who knows what else. Just plain consumer reluctance to buy art, I supposed. There were so many shops in Jackson now competing for the tourist dollar: souvenir shops, factory outlets, sporting goods, T-shirts, posters, jewelry, junk, you name it.

"Could be the pyro again," Pete said.

"What pyro? A pyromaniac?" Eden squeaked, running a hand through her unruly brown curls.

"Everybody hoped he'd given up. Or moved on." I turned toward Eden in the back seat. She had lived in Jackson just two years. The traffic around us had slowed to a stop about a half mile from the town square. "There were a bunch of suspicious fires in stores. About four or five over that many years. Nobody was ever arrested."

"And now he's back," Eden said, frowning.

"Let's just wait and see what's happening." I heard my voice, the calmness in it, and tried to reconcile that to the feeling in my gut. What if it was my gallery, my apartment above? What would I do? I pushed the thoughts aside and felt my nose, approaching zucchini squash status.

Pete looked over at me. "Nice shiners. They're coming right along." He smiled, as if the fire meant nothing. He didn't live in town. "Kahuna counted coups on you today."

I touched the bags under my eyes and frowned at him. My bangs hung in wet hanks over my thick brown eyebrows. I had forgotten to comb my hair after the aborted Eskimo roll in the Snake River. I doubted I even had a comb on me, patting the pockets of my damp river shorts helplessly. Instead I pulled on my Ray-Bans to cover my eyes and my olive green slouch hat to cover the river-whipped mess of almost blond, shoulder-length hair.

"It must have been my instructor's fault," I said.

Pete shrugged. "You can blame me if you want. I thought you looked great. What about that war whoop you let out just before Kahuna sucked you under?"

I opened my mouth to answer, slightly embarrassed at my exuberance on the river. On the other hand, I liked that kayaking brought out my wild side. Sometimes the art business was too sedate for my taste. Maybe that was why I'd been concentrating on insurance and fraud work for the past few years. It got me out of the white box gallery into the real world. Last year I had stared down the barrel of a jealous lover's pistol and tripped the light fantastic with a wacko medicine man. Maybe Big Kahuna's right hook was as much violence as I'd have to face this summer. But something about the smoke told me Kahuna was only the beginning.

The car hadn't moved for ten minutes. I looked back at Eden. She sat with her knees pulled up to her chest, her khakis rolled up over black rafting sandals. Her short, dark curls were wild and the delicate features of her face were pinched with worry. She was twisting the ring on her finger round and round.

"I think we should walk," I said. "What do you think, Edie, hon? This waiting is killing me." I've never been a patient person. It was one of those things I work on now and then, but this was no time for self-improvement. I put my hand on the door latch. "Park the car, Pete."

We hurried along the wooden boardwalks of Jackson, dodging baby strollers, ice cream cones puddling, gray-heads in small flocks, until we reached the edge of the crowd. It was dense and large, filled with cowboy hats, ball caps, porkpies, and big hair. We were still half a block from the corner of the square, and everything was obscured by dark smoke. The sky disappeared. We pushed through the crowd, my hands on Eden's shoulders, guiding her along since she was so short she couldn't see her way through.

I kept moving, blinking furiously from the smoke. Eden and Pete were coughing. I could see the commotion on the near side of the square, not near the Second Sun. It wasn't until I stopped, dropped my hands from Eden's shoulders, and let loose a "holy shit" that she looked up at the landmarks and realized that we were in front of the corner where her gallery, Timberwolf Arts, stood.

All four county fire trucks, a full contingent of our local cops, and every tourist who remembered the song about Smokey the Bear filled the square. Beyond the excited crowd, crying children, barking dogs, and a whole lot of official mayhem, stood Eden's gallery, ablaze. The building, a blue frame two-story with a square front facade and yellow awnings on two upstairs windows, was, as they say, completely involved. Flames licked at the tops of the windows. The roof had disappeared in smoke and thin air. The sign that read "Timberwolf Arts" with a howling wolf was half burned and hanging off the facade. We stood, speechless, watching what was left of Eden's dream go up in smoke.

Eden Chaffee had come to Jackson two years before from upstate New York with her inheritance to invest in a gallery, her first. She had romantic notions about art and galleries, the same ones I once had of bringing beauty to the masses, of brightening the ugly workaday world. Maybe I felt the need to recover that old passion; I took her under my wing, taught her a few things about art, about the business, about the tourists and rich and not-so-rich art buyers.

Despite my efforts and her warm personality, Eden was not a great businesswoman. She didn't have a feel for what would sell, what people wanted. She had become discouraged lately and immersed herself in photography. She often took off in the afternoons to catch the sunset over Mount Owen or the Grand, or frame up an elk against the aspens. She usually hired someone to fill in for her on the days she went off shooting pictures.

A confusion of yellow-slickered firemen had strung hoses from the red pumpers parked haphazardly in the street. Thick smoke poured out the windows. Above, attic insulation was exposed and wiring hung over the once-blue wood siding. The firefighters wet down the facade and roof of the neighboring café. I could see Billy, the grill cook, nearby in his greasy white apron, biting his nails. Arcs of water poured from gray canvas hoses into the broken second-story windows of the gallery. As I watched, a fireman wielded an axe and broke down the front door. The sound tore through me physically.

"Oh, Alix." The tiny words escaped Eden's small, ashen face, a reflection of the grayness around us. I put my arm around her shoulders and tried to think of comforting words. None came to mind. None ever came to mind on the spot, the curse of the Norwegian. To be stoic, calm, rational in the face of chaos and tragedy: that was the ideal growing up with my mother. If the possibility existed for something awful, she would become rigid and start to clean. By the time the outcome was clear, good or bad, the baseboards were wiped, the kitchen floor shining, and the simple pine furniture rubbed with lemon oil. No time was wasted on emotion that might not be appropriate and certainly was unwelcome and embarrassing.

Eden turned to me and began to cry. I held her, the only thing I could do. Pete touched her hair briefly, looking down on her childlike body from his height, and shrugged at me. Around us, tourists bored of the spectacle and filtered off, thinking, of course, that the worst was over.

Pete gave Eden a polite hug and said good-bye, begging off because of a dinner invitation. The firemen scurried into and out of the frame storefront, windows gone, gray smoke belching through the holes. Timberwolf Arts had never had as much attention as it did today. Despite Eden's hard work, my experience, and a great corner location, something never clicked. When she was not out taking photos, Eden stared out the window and sighed, "They never said it'd be like this back in Lackawanna."

AT LEAST THE Second Sun had its good years. Eden just had no sense of style, no flair for choosing art. That was evident in her current show, a comeback for a once-great artist. She thought he was a big enough name to rescue Timberwolf Arts. But once gain, she was wrong.

Eden pulled away and wiped her face with the sleeve of her sweatshirt. Her eyes slowly moved from the chaos of the fire to my face, then back. A crash inside the building made her lurch forward, blinking her big black eyes. I put my arm around her shoulder again, and for ten minutes we watched the firefighters move into the building, knocking down walls, dragging hoses and debris. The fire was out now. The stench of soggy, smoldering wood blew over us in a cloud.

Inside the building the firefighters suddenly began shouting. One ran out, his long yellow coat slapping against his black rubber boots. A new siren split the air, whining, raising the hair on my neck. The couple in front of us chose this moment to leave.

"'Scuse, please. 'Scuse," the husband said. Since no one opened up around us, I dropped my arm to let them wedge between me and Eden. A well-matched elderly couple, Indiana or Michigan, I guessed. His porkpie hat, weighed down with hundreds of pins, flashed in the late sun breaking through the smoke as he pushed his blue-haired consort ahead of him. "Keep moving, Thelma. Keep moving," he mumbled.

By the time the remaining onlookers had reassembled, I was behind Eden. A surly teenager with overgrown shoulders had squeezed into my spot. I peered over Eden's head in time to see Charlie Frye emerge from the crowd. He stood out among the well-built firemen with his ever-present gray suit, baggy and worn, white shirt, and black string tie. He looked more like the stoop-shouldered insurance agent that he had been before his appointment to chief of police. I had done plenty of work for his agency, appraising art, stolen, damaged, and just insured, before the mayor had elevated Charlie to crime fighting.

Frye followed two firemen into the Timberwolf's dark interior. At five forty-five in late July plenty of daylight remained. But between the smoke and the charred interior of the building we could see nothing after they disappeared into the gloom.

Eden opened her mouth to say something. Nothing came out. Ash sifted down on her dark curls, giving her a powdered look. I felt so bad for her. She had lost her inheritance. She had paid too much for the building two years ago, coming into the market unaware, then spent more fixing it up. She had sunk her heart and soul into Timberwolf Arts. Her dreams—and her finances—were reduced to a pile of ash.

At last Charlie Frye appeared, talking rapidly and gesturing in a group of men, some of whom were firefighters. Others looked liked cops, or at least public officials. I recognized Danny Bartholomew, a reporter for the *Jackson Hole News,* who had somehow infiltrated the official circle. I watched them for a moment, saw that the boundary deputies had gone, then grabbed the yellow plastic barrier tape.

"Go, Eden!" I pushed her under, shuffling and stiff, and followed. She hesitated, clutching her camera bag. "Come on," I said, pulling her. "It's your place. You have a right."

Frye saw us coming and conversation stopped. The faces of the firefighters were blackened and weary. The policemen's expressions held a curious mixture of excitement and repulsion.

"Alix, please. Behind the line," Charlie Frye said. A fireman took my elbow.

"This is the owner," I said, tugging Eden's sleeve. She stared at them, a horrified look on her face. "She wants to know what's going on."

The men's eyes bounced from face to face. The fireman dropped his hand. Danny, slight and dark with a scratchy beard, scribbled something in his spiral notebook, leaning forward to catch every word. Eden stood up straighter. She cleared her throat, the most conversation she could muster.

"Did you have an employee working in the building this afternoon?" Frye said. He glared at her with drooping gray eyes "Miss Chaffee, is it?"

Eden nodded.

"You had an employee?" he said. Another nervous nod. "Who was it?"

I stepped back, glancing into the black depths of the gallery. The cause of the commotion inside was suddenly clear. My breath caught in my throat. On the same wavelength, Danny B. scribbled furiously. Eden stared at Frye, then at the firemen in their yellow slickers and helmets, their tired, smudged eyes.

"Who?" I whispered to her. "Who was it?"

She looked at me, blinking furiously. "Ray."

"Ray Tantro?" She nodded. He was the artist whose pieces she had been showing for the last several weeks, horrible, abstract stuff that hadn't been popular, hadn't sold at all. I kept my opinion of his work to myself, which may or may not have helped Eden. It made no difference now.

"The artists," I told Frye. He frowned at me, the gray stubble on his head moving forward to meet black eyebrows. "The artist who was showing at the gallery," I explained. "Ray Tantro. He was big in the seventies. Trying to make a comeback."

"But he didn't come in," Eden said, her voice cracking. "He was supposed to show up at three so I could go with you, Alix. I was taking photographs of Alix on the river. But he didn't come in."

"You didn't see the employee, this Ray?" Frye asked.

"I just locked up," she said, looking guiltily at me. "Business was slow."

"What is it, Charlie? Was he...?" I glanced at the burned hulk of the building.

Charlie's face was a flat, controlled mask. "Looks that way," he said.

THEY BROUGHT OUT the body zipped into a black plastic body bag on a stretcher. We couldn't see it, thank God. Frye said he was burned pretty badly, not much left. He figured Ray Tantro showed up late, opened up with his own key, and proceeded to burn the place down. A dramatic way to kill yourself, Charlie mused, but effective. Probably drank himself unconscious in the process, from the looks of the debris.

We watched as the ambulance crew loaded up the charred remains of the once-great artist. Slowly, without fanfare, the ambulance pulled away.

RAY TANTRO did not leave this earth in a pleasant way. The old Norsemen would say that human existence is a difficult, painful thing, followed by destruction. That man must struggle, with the help of his gods who control his all-too-certain fate. Odin, the benevolent father, even tested poor Thor, making even gods prove themselves worthy of Valhalla.

I wasn't sure, as I held Eden Chaffee on the evening of the destruction of her dreams, whether the old Norsemen knew what the hell they were talking about. There had to be pleasure, didn't there? The Norsemen, for sure, never experienced the thrill of Kahuna in a little purple kayak. They were more practical. Their lives weren't concerned, as mine was, with the pursuit of beauty and truth, two of the most illusive and spectral worldly elements. Life was more simple to the Norsemen, more black and white. Existence had no silver lining. Maybe Ray Tantro felt the same.

At any rate Tantro probably would have agreed with my cantankerous big brother, who once during a family reunion while well lubricated with aquavit and lutefisk summed up the Norse mentality in his inimitable fashion: Life's a bitch, then you die.

TWO

As NIGHT FELL, Eden and I hunkered down upstairs over the storefront of the Second Sun Gallery, in the apartment I call home. For a while after Paolo moved out it seemed too spacious. But the space is only two rooms and a bath, with a main room that includes living, dining, and kitchen. When we first moved in I painted the walls indigo blue and stenciled silver stars and gold suns up by the ten-foot ceiling. I am sick of those stars and the gloom of the dark blue walls, but the thought of getting up on ladders again and repainting makes me tolerate them. A thrift-shop sofa is slipcovered in a wrinkled natural linen that I let my decorator friend Darlene talk me into; the verdict is still out on the home grunge look.

Behind the sofa stands the only bookshelf I have room for. The low pine case is filled with my collection of books on Norse mythology and the Mighty Thor comic books I have collected since I was nine, kept clean in plastic cases. When my father died I retreated for one summer into the world of the Norse gods, spending long days in the hammock lost in Asgard. I played fantasy games all by myself against invisible foes, with me playing the courageous and brave heroine—the Mighty Thorssen. The bimonthly installments of the comic held me together that summer and I continued to collect them, always with a soft spot in my heart for the blond superhero, the Thunder God, Thor. In some way they connected me with the real life-hero I lost that year.

Lately I'd been looking out my tall Victorian windows at the wooded hills that ring the Hole we call Jackson and thinking about a cabin. The close proximity of the gallery downstairs, the tension and anxiety it had been producing, made me want to escape. Somewhere open and sunny and private, with trees and flowers. It wasn't just the mess with finances in the gallery, although like in any business when the money's bad, nothing else really matters. My partner cut me no slack just because we had been lovers once. And then there were the tourists, thick as fleas on a dog's butt at high summer, and just as much fun.

I tucked Eden in on the couch, her small, sunburned face flushed with wine but peaceful at last. She began to snore, musically at first, then in earnest. I turned from the window and looked at her in the pale light from the half-moon. I should complain. What would she do? All she could think about was Ray Tantro, her client and friend.

"I should have saved him," she had cried as we made our way across the damp, ashy grass of the square to my apartment. The crowd had gone home, all but a few die-hard voyeurs. "I should have been there." Tears streamed down her cheeks. I put my arm around her shoulder again, at another loss for words. Nobody cried like this at home. My mother never shed a tear in front of me.

"I knew he drank too much," Eden sobbed. "Just last week I saw him at the rodeo, hanging around the stands with the cowboys drinking beer. He yelled at me, something obnoxious, you know. I didn't know what to say so I just ignored him. Pretended I didn't hear." Her cries deepened, her face contorted. I took her hand and led her through the gallery and up the back stairs to the apartment, the hollow sound of our footsteps on the wooden stairs making me lonely.

"Did he seem depressed or anything?" I asked.

She shook her head. "He sometimes got down when he drank. Usually he wanted to go dancing." She started to cry again, squeezing her eyelids together as she sat on the edge of the sofa. "I think I kind of loved him."

"Oh, hon. I didn't know," I said, sinking into the armchair facing the couch.

"I'm not sure, you know," she said through sobs. "And now I'll never find out."

I covered my battered eyes with my hand, careful not to press too hard. Ray Tantro, burned to death. Lost love. Lost gallery. I didn't see how it could be worse.

"You didn't know he was going to do this. And even if you had, what could you do? You can't save somebody who really wants to kill himself. I'm sure you made him happy, Eden. I mean, you tried." I heard myself talking, talking, just saying anything to stop the tears.

To my surprise she sniffed hard and stopped crying. "You think so?" She blew her nose on a tissue. "I guess you're right. What could I do? He was a strong man."

The crying was over as fast as it began. Then her face reddened and she pounded the arm of the sofa. "I just wish he'd talked to me. About the gallery and everything. I only wish I knew..." Her voice trailed off.

"... Why he burned down the gallery too?" It did seem odd. Most people commit suicide in the privacy of their own homes. "I wonder. Maybe it was those new paintings," I said. The paintings he'd done twenty years ago were exquisite masterpieces compared to this crap. I was trying to picture his early works, thinking of shows I'd seen and articles I'd read, when I remembered the small Tantro oil I bought back in the seventies. I had it stored away. I'd forgotten all about it.

Eden was glaring at me, her dark eyes red-rimmed but fierce.

"What's that supposed to mean?"

I shrugged it off. "Nothing. Just that maybe his comeback wasn't, ah...coming back?" Eden looked like she was going to cry again. "Only a thought."

She pulled a cigarette from the box in her purse. "Got any matches? Oh, never mind." She took out a matchbook and lit her cigarette. "Jesus, Alix, what a day."

I watched her face as she drew on the cigarette and tried to calm herself. Then I moved to the sofa and sat next to her.

"I'm sorry about everything, Eden. It's terrible." There, I felt a flutter of nerves, then relief that I had finally said how I felt.

She looked at me, then blew smoke the other way. "It's a piece of shit, is what it is. Not just the gallery. I did like him but..." She slammed her fist on the arm of the chair. "It makes me so mad. That bastard Ray Tantro. What the hell was that all about?"

I shook my head. "I don't know. But I promise you, Eden, I will find out."

Her eyes held mine, clear for a moment. "Your eyes just turned that steely blue color they get when you latch on to something. Like when you latched on to me, and whipped the Timberwolf into shape." Her anger had disappeared. She bit her lip, slumping into the chair. "I'll never forget that, Alix."

It had been a long day. I was still wearing my swimsuit and river shorts under my yellow chenille bathrobe. The pizza box sat gaping on the coffee table, the pizza barely touched. Eden smoked, angry and exhausted. She drank three glasses of wine and passed out. I covered her up with a goose-down comforter, stubbed out her last cigarette, and turned out the light.

FROM MY BEDROOM window I can look out across the town square. Through the tall pines and elms that shade the grass and antler arches from the moon's glare I made out movement in the light in front of the blackened hulk of Timberwolf Arts. They would be digging around in there all night, I supposed. I wondered what changes the fire would bring to the square, if a fancy new structure would fill that corner. I was missing Eden's charming old building already.

I peeled off the swimsuit and got into old sweats that provided security on cold or lonely nights. (Okay, yes, I wear them just about every night.) I pulled my arms tight around my ribs. The evening was still. I could hear the faint sound of the honky-tonk band at the Million Dollar Cowboy Bar across the square. It had been months since I'd straddled the saddles that doubled as barstools there.

Jackson can be boisterous and rowdy and then turn around and sleep for weeks, a town of mercurial fits of energy. During slow months you could spit across the square and not hit a soul. When summer starts the locals slap on their "Bring Back Off-Season" bumper stickers and both curse and rejoice in the mayhem. On summer nights flatlanders roam in packs, searching, laughing, spending.

I looked down on the deserted streets. No flatlanders tonight. The events of the day had put a reality-crimp into vacation bliss. No airing the baby, no necking couples, no cruising for trinkets tonight.

Ray Tantro, once a wunderkind in the art world, a man destined for greatness before he dropped from sight, was now just an unidentifiable carbon form, roasted like so many marshmallows. Had he been despondent about the new paintings? Sick about his lost affinity with the lucid light of morning? Maybe I was romanticizing his suicide. Who knows, maybe he wanted to go out like a martyr. I wondered about his last years, his last thoughts.

I hoped Ray's ride down life's big river had its rollers and curls and thrills in the heady days of his early fame and glory. I had to believe it did.

THE PHONE on my desk rang early the next morning, before opening. Eden had been up with the birds, showered, and dropped off the film of my kayaking run at the photo shop before I emerged from the bathroom. What I'd seen in the bathroom mirror hadn't cheered me. My nose was still swollen. I could hardly breathe through one nostril. And my eyes had gone technicolor, greens, blues, and yellows. I did what I could with makeup even though it hurt to rub it on. I took three aspirin and cursed Pete Rotondi for good measure.

I thought that going to work early would take my mind off my rearranged face. I put on my sunglasses and settled into my cubbyhole office, a former walk-in closet in the back of the gallery. The Second Sun occupies a storefront in the middle of the block facing the square, with a glass-filled front wall and a porch overhang above the boardwalk, and cream-colored side walls in the undivided front gallery. Paolo and I had sanded and refinished the wood floors several times over the years and put in new track lighting last winter. We were due for a new paint job when the summer season ended, but the place looked good: clean, warm, minimalist in the best sense, with a focus on Art with a capital A. Despite our fondness for Bierstadt and Russell, we favored more affordable contemporary art with modern techniques and styles—stylized landscapes, impressionism, graphics, ceramics, and weavings.

I arranged the piles of messages into two groups, In and To Do, scanned the blotter covered with phone numbers, and dusted the old brass piano lamp before the phone rang. My old wooden desk with its scratched-in names—Bus, Tony 43, Laura, Go Tigers—was like a member of the family. I bought it from an old rancher who said his father used it in a railroad office back in Ohio and brought it west with him. In my office I kept no clock, no radio, no stereo, no television. Last year I had given in to a fax machine, but it sat expectantly idle most of the time, like a wallflower waiting for an offer to dance.

Above the desk two bookshelves are filled with reference books, directories, and art books: my library. Next to the books a giant Rolodex holds all my contacts in business.

Under the shelves, the only decoration, hangs a framed silkscreen print by Bill Schenck of a cowgirl in sunglasses with shirt agape, a pretty sneer on her lips and a six-gun up by her shoulder ready to blast the next guy that looks at her cross-eyed.

I had been expecting an hour of quiet—time to think about the events of yesterday, dab extra makeup around the eyes, and rub my desk—so when the old black telephone rattled at me I was annoyed.

"Good morning," a male voice said on the line. I hesitated, too long. "It's me."

By this time I recognized both the sexiness and the slight irritation in the voice. It was Carl Mendez, my on-again boyfriend and Missoula cop, whom I talked to on the phone almost enough to recognize his voice.

"I knew it was you," I said. "No one else would call this early."

"Are you ready to run the river?"

I groaned, not softly enough.

"What's that?" Carl asked. "You're not backing out?"

Carl had been taking kayaking lessons in Missoula so that we could run the Snake River together. I'd been doing the same here, putting in numerous hours at the high school pool with Pete. And of course yesterday's river run.

"Of course not. I'm just busy. I got a new roommate and two new shiners yesterday. There was a terrible fire at my friend Eden's gallery. And on top of all that, I got caught in Kahuna." I took off my sunglasses and gingerly felt my sore nose. The Ray-Bans were too heavy, I was just going to have to brave the questions about my new battle scars. "I felt the raw power, I can tell you that."

"The Big Kahuna? Oh, man. I've heard about that one, and Lunch Counter. The waves up here are nothing like that. I can't wait till I get down there." He paused, whistling through his teeth.

His enthusiasm was catching, despite my bashed face. I had to remind myself that I had a lot of work to do before he arrived. Carl had scheduled his first-ever two-week vacation, saving up all winter to spend it kayaking with me. It began in a week. Eden should have her finances and insurance figured out by then. Last summer's backpacking weekend with Carl had been wildly adventurous, at least inside the pup tent. It would be good seeing him again.

Then I could see that wave again, feel the thrill and surge of its rollers. "Listen, Carl—"

"I know you've got to work," he interrupted. "Captain's staring at me right now too. I just had to talk to you for a second. Can't wait to hit the river! Call you later and we'll get the details figured out." He hung up.

The receiver was heavy in my hand. One of these days I'd have to get a neat, slim portable phone like everybody else had. But now there was no money for telephones. I hung up, making myself concentrate on my immediate crisis—I pulled out the account book and pawed through it. It was the third time this week I'd stared at the figures, trying to make them change.

The problem was simple: Expenses exceeded income. We had a decent reserve to tide us over the lean months, assuming there weren't too many of them. The big problem was a mess of my own making and its name was Ditolla. Martin Ditolla was a local artist I had been bringing along and felt was ready for the big time. I had agreed to buy four of his paintings that we would both sell and make into posters for the gallery. If we paid him the $10,000 for the four originals as agreed, plus went ahead with the lithography so we could recoup our money and hopefully make a profit, well, we'd be scraping bottom. Broke. No groceries, no electricity. It wouldn't matter if we had a telephone or not.

I rubbed my forehead, trying to erase the headache centered around my nose. How had this happened? This was

July, supposedly the busiest month of the year. I tried to imagine what we had done wrong. Were the Ingrid Wistmiller pastels too weak, too strong, too cold, too overpriced? Did we have too many expensive bronzes and not enough pottery? Not enough western-theme stuff? Too much? I was ready to tear out my hair. Paolo had always been so good at his "mix," a delicate blend of contemporary and traditional, exotic and familiar, high-priced and affordable. Had he lost his touch, or was I just hopelessly out of the loop?

I took a deep breath. It wasn't going to help to start blaming Paolo—or myself. Or to panic. Maybe things would bounce back. Maybe we'd have a buying frenzy of oil-rich Texans even though the oil business had gone to hell in a handbasket. The Texans who still came to Jackson weren't shelling out the derrick dollars like in the old days.

The lock turned in the front door. That would be Paolo. I closed the account book, since nothing I could do would help there, and rolled my office chair across the floor to look into the gallery proper.

"Morning," I called.

"Did you hear about the fire?" he yelled back. He was starting coffee on the counter behind his desk. I could hear the water running.

"We were there. Eden and me."

The bell rang on the front door then, and I saw Eden step into the gallery. I got up and joined her. She smelled of baked goods, which she carried in two white sacks.

"I brought breakfast," she said, smiling.

Paolo frowned at her and at the chocolate muffins she was extracting from the sack. "I ate already."

"He's kind of a health nut, Eden," I said. "But I'll take a muffin."

Paolo had turned back to the coffeemaker and was pouring three cups of coffee. He handed me one silently, without looking at my face. Or at least not noticing the damage.

I carried my cup back into my office while Eden began telling Paolo, with excitement and chagrin, about the wholesale destruction of Timberwolf Arts. I didn't want to hear it again.

The top message on my To Do pile was from Martin Ditolla. He had called three times. I had been avoiding him for the last week or two, since Paolo and I had had the talk. I still couldn't bring myself to tell Martin that we couldn't help him, couldn't buy his paintings. He was getting so good and was incredibly excited about this new venture, as well he should be.

Martin was badly injured in a snowmobile accident that changed his life. A skier, hunter, and fireman before, he had broken his back, then dissolved into self-pity and the bottle before finding a new life in art. He deserved my help and I gave it freely. One of the great satisfactions of being an art dealer was to bring talent to recognition, to nurture and celebrate it. But now I was going to have to go back on my word. We wouldn't be able to buy Martin's pieces. I had to face that.

The phone rang again. Paolo picked it up out in the gallery. In a moment he appeared in the doorway to give me the message.

"It's Frye," he said. I turned and saw the unsmiling look on the well-formed Latin face. Ten years older than when I first met him and getting a few lines around his eyes, Paolo was still heart-stopping handsome with dark golden skin and wavy black hair that curled over the collar of his white button-down shirt. "I thought you couldn't work for him anymore."

As police chief, Frye was out of the insurance business. Conflict of interest and all that.

Paolo was staring. "What happened to you? You try to ride that wild horse of yours?"

"I'm not that stupid." I touched my nose self-consciously, hoping it was true. "More like a wild paddle."

"Just so none of your boyfriends is beating you up," Paolo said, half serious. "You tell me and I send a couple of my goons over to rough him up."

"I'm flattered," I said, turning my chair to face him. "I didn't know you cared."

"You better wear those," he said, pointing to my Ray-Bans on the desk. "At least they make you look mysterious."

Paolo turned to go back into the gallery. In the last year his attitude toward life had lost its light frosting, as if our money troubles had darkened the whole world. Paolo loved the finer things in life and would do almost anything to make good fortune come to him and the gallery. No wonder his attitude was so bad, with our poor finances. Eden sat behind his desk, drinking coffee and munching muffins while she read the newspaper. Paolo got out window cleaner and paper towels, squirted the liquid on the new plate-glass window. I watched him as he moved gracefully in front of the window, rubbing the glass in circles. He could be a pain in the ass all right. But what an ass it was. Admiring it was one of the last perks as his partner.

I picked up the phone. Frye sounded impatient and irritated. "Goddamn Dalton is out of town. I'm supposed to be the silent partner in the insurance company now. This is sure putting me in a helluva spot," he grumbled.

"What can I do for you, Charlie?" He reminded me of a hard-edged Barney Fife, homey with a bitter undercurrent.

"It's the fire, that gallery. Your friend Chaffee. Dalton wrote a policy for the contents, a special one, just last, ah, let's see." He shuffled through papers. "Last June second. Covered this new show. And anything else she had in the way of fine art in there."

"You need some appraisal work done?"

"Yeah. That Tantro stuff. The guy we found. Christ, I hate to see somebody take their life like that. Against the Christian way, I say."

"I know what you mean." Charlie's mixture of epithets and piety had the effect of making me smile until I thought again about Ray. I doubted Ray Tantro was particularly religious. At least not yesterday afternoon.

"Anywaaaays," Charlie said, getting down to business, "I got to have an appraisal done for those paintings. Bonnie at the office said she called already this morning, all anxious. Ms. Chaffee, that is. I just want to get this over and done. No hassles. Monday, okay?"

I agreed and hung up. It was enough time, three days, to try to piece together what was in the gallery. It wasn't a big show, maybe twenty pieces, and I had seen it myself. Eden probably could remember most of it. I turned my chair around again to tell her, but she had disappeared. The two paper sacks were all that remained on Paolo's desk. Now where had she gone?

I peered into the gallery, not wanting to seem as if I was volunteering my sales services. Paolo was in the far front corner, gesturing and talking confidentially to a young couple with brand-new hiking boots and immaculate tans. No sign of Eden. I turned back to my handkerchief office and remembered suddenly what had come to me late last night.

Spirits lifting, I opened the door to the storeroom. Inside, old red-and-pink-flowered wallpaper hung limply on the walls. I flicked on the light switch that activated a single bare bulb. Simple wooden frames held paintings upright as they sat lined along the floor. Against the gaudy wallpaper from the frontier brothel that occupied this space a hundred years ago (I call it the House of the Grand Tetons) hung odd paintings that we didn't have room to display.

In the far corner, tucked away in the back, I found what I was looking for, my small, forgotten Tantro oil. In the days when I'd bought it I didn't have much money. (Some things change at glacial speed.) The hundred dollars I spent was an extravagance, but I'd just gotten my trust from my father and wanted something wonderful to remember him by. It had hung in every apartment I had until I moved to Jackson and somehow forgot to unpack it at all.

Kneeling on the dusty carpet, I slipped off the cardboard cover. It was a winter scene, a prairie in snow and pale light, framed in hunter green. I remembered the little shop where I'd bought it, in Livingston, Montana, a magical place that perhaps gave me the first inkling I might enjoy being an art dealer. I was still painting then. The small, eight-by-ten-inch oil painting had been dwarfed by the larger canvases Tantro had been selling like hotcakes. Lush, glorious landscapes in an impressionistic style. A penchant for white, for snow, a difficult artistic task that young Tantro handled with an unstudied genius.

Carrying the small painting into my office, I turned off the light and shut the door behind me. I set it at the back of my desk, against the wall, and admired it. It was still a beautiful piece, a little gem, a perfect composition. The gradations of purple and blue in the snow made the scene come alive with color. I pulled a soft rag from a drawer and lovingly wiped the dust from the canvas.

The bell on the front door clanged three times. The tourists are coming! The tourists are coming! Reluctantly I tore my eyes away from the Tantro painting and pushed back my chair. I took a deep breath and braced myself for the day.

THREE

TIMBERWOLF ARTS, once elegant space in a late Victorian storefront with two yellow awnings contrasting with the stained blue siding and ferns in the windows, now looked like a war zone. If only I could forget the way it looked before. I remembered too vividly the newly sanded hemlock floors, the quaint tin ceiling that Eden had spent hours detailing with gold paint, the open staircase with its delicate wrought iron-railing. The way the morning light made the room glow. The wine and cheese receptions, the laughter. All these images haunted me, echoes of the obliterated past.

I had worked the phones as much as I could between customers yesterday, trying to get some information on Ray Tantro. I had found an old listing through the local library of an article in an art magazine. The library in Cheyenne faxed it to me. Dated October 1974, it showed a young Tantro in a dark silhouette against a window in his Montana studio. Outside the mountains were graceful and commanding. The same could be said for young Tantro at the peak of his powers.

Eden had finally returned to the gallery after lunch, exhausted from trying to gather together her tenuous finances. She was too busy, she said, to talk to me about the appraisal. We would get to it tonight, I hoped. There wasn't much to it, but the lack of information on Tantro was disturbing. How much detail did Charlie Frye want? How little could I bear in good conscience?

I stood in the back doorway of Timberwolf Arts and wrinkled my sore nose. The smell of wet carbon, both acrid and sweet, was thick in the air. Rex Scanlon, Teton County fire investigator, slogged through the sticky, charred mess in pea green irrigation boots. Wearing jeans and a work shirt, Scanlon was well built like most firemen, but sagging a little. Despite the arsons over the years in Jackson, I'd never worked with him. He carried a clipboard and set a duffle bag next to the alley door.

"If you'll follow me," he said formally, then looked at my old, formerly white, leather athletic shoes. "Are those washable?" I nodded. I had washed them many times, being the type who gets attached to her clothes. My clothes and I need history together. Oh, the places we've been. I woke up this morning feeling better, still sore but rested and eager to dig into this assignment. My nose gave me the go-ahead. It now only resembled a battered banana. I followed Scanlon as he turned into the depths of the gallery.

The main room was the worst. I stood in the doorway from the back hall and stared. The floor was black with puddles of water standing in low spots on the warped wood boards. The walls, once pristine white, now were streaked with gray and black, Sheetrock sagged off them in slabs where the water from the fire hoses had hit hard. The pressed-tin ceiling was in decent shape, still showing a little of its green and gold color. The brass chandelier in the center of the old room lay smashed on the floor. Wires dangled from the spot where it hung. I wondered aloud if the building was safe.

Scanlon glanced back at me, then at the ceiling. "Safe enough. Power's shut off. I wouldn't go upstairs though." He stopped in the middle of the room near some unidentifiable debris. I tried to remember what had been in that spot. A chair, I thought, overstuffed variety. A floor lamp with a fringed shade and a small table. "You're just interested in the art? That's what Charlie said."

I nodded, venturing out into the room. The floor felt slick. The smell of wet ash and charred wood permeated everything. "I will need to go upstairs. Eden said she has a closet up there with some stuff in it."

Scanlon shook his head before turning his focus elsewhere. "Let us check it out first. Most of the art's down here, right?"

I agreed, taking out my notebook. I tried to count the canvases, most of which still showed a little pigment through burns, water damage, and smoky ash. All had fallen off the wall to the floor and been stomped on by firemen in their rush to put out the fire. I was relieved I disliked these paintings; seeing art destroyed did not make my day. It was sad what had happened to these paintings, but not mortally so. They could have been Picassos, although with Eden's luck, I doubted it.

Examining and measuring and counting and cataloguing, I made my way around the room, vaguely aware that Scanlon was concentrating on something else. The back room revealed a small stash of prints, most worth little to begin with. They had been ruined by water. I counted them, made notes of their sticker prices, and looked around for more. When I came back out into the main gallery, Scanlon was talking to a policeman. His brown shirt and pants blended into the shadows. They had their heads down, gesturing and looking at the floor. Their voices were low as they moved together and examined the floor again. They pointed at an odd marking on the wall, an arc of black ash.

The fire investigator had been in the news regularly whenever our local arsonist struck. In the paper he looked weary and disappointed. I had assumed it was because of the fires, but now I had the feeling that he always looked that way. Maybe it came from seeing so much. He had that hangdog look today.

Scanlon and the policeman walked toward me, deep in discussion.

"I think you're right, Scan," the cop said, clapping Scanlon on the back.

"We'll know more when we get the samples back," Scanlon said, looking startled as he saw me, as if he had forgotten I was there. "Ah, Alix Thorssen, this is Gary Hayden."

I shook the policeman's hand. It was a big hand. Better than average haircut for a cop but of the type.

"She's doing the insurance work for Charlie," Scanlon explained.

"Well, then," Hayden grinned, puffing out his chest, "you're probably wasting your time."

Scanlon frowned, flicking his eyes to the policeman. "I don't think we can make speculations to the public at this time, Gary."

"Oh, oh, sure," Hayden said, nudging Scanlon with his elbow. Rex looked at me, with *You see what I have to deal with?* in his eyes. "Sure, we'll keep it under our hats till the reports come back. Give it your best shot, Scan-man."

Rex and I watched Hayden go out the back door and spend a good minute wiping his boots on a piece of wet carpet in the alley. When he finally left I turned to Scanlon. But he had returned to the center of the room.

"What was that supposed to mean?" I asked, looking at the charred debris next to where Scanlon kneeled. It came to me then that this had to be the spot where the body had been. Where Tantro had burned to death.

"Hmmm?" The investigator was deep in thought. "Oh, Hayden? Pay him no mind. He's a—" He waved his hand to dismiss the policeman.

"Yeah. A moron. But what did he mean? I like to know if I'm wasting my time."

Scanlon didn't answer. He took out a pocketknife, made scrapings of the floorboards and put them into a plastic Baggie, and labeled it with a black felt-tip pen. He felt the floor in several places with his fingertips, then stood up.

"I've got a lot of work to do," he said. The tired look had deepened on his face. He was the kind of man some women want to take home and cook a good meal for. "If you're done here...?"

I glanced around the burned-out hulk, annoyed that he wouldn't answer. Eden wouldn't be happy when she saw this. I was glad I had talked her out of joining me today. "Yeah, I'm done for now." I stared at Scanlon. "Was this where he was?"

His eyes dropped to the spot. "What was left of him." He gathered up his samples and equipment and herded me to the door. We parted in the alley, both of us avoiding the slab of wet carpet where the policeman had left his mark.

I MADE MY WAY across the square, taking the long way instead of cutting through the grass. The weekend had brought a fresh onslaught of tourists to savor the day's shimmering sunshine and blue, blue sky. A line was forming for the stagecoach rides. I waved up at the stagecoach driver decked out in fringed leather chaps, muslin duster, and twenty-gallon white hat. His bushy red beard didn't obscure his grin as he jumped down, tipped his hat to me, and helped four boisterous kids with cotton candy into the stagecoach. I inched past, fighting for space on the boardwalk, and returned to the gallery.

Paolo was brewing coffee. He poured me some and I accepted. This seemed to be the limits of our courtesy these days. I pulled out a yellow legal pad at my desk to begin the listing of the artworks in Eden's gallery. I pawed through a file of gallery brochures and found hers for the Tantro show. Some of the works were pictured in the fancy, four-color brochure that must have set Eden back a bit of change. It was glossy and well designed by the best graphic artist in town. Unfortunately the bottom line was that it didn't improve her bottom line. I stared at the abstracts in the brochure and didn't like them any better than when I had seen them hanging. They were disjointed and jarring, neon green and dull brown with hard edges, almost cubist without any of the sardonic grace of cubism. So different from Tantro's early work that it boggled the mind.

I picked out the titles of the six works pictured in the brochure and matched them up with ones on my list. Eden had even included the prices in her brochure, something I had advised against, but now it was helpful and I plugged them into the list too. I wondered if she had a price list for the others somewhere in the gallery, and if it had survived. Probably not; she would have to rely on her memory.

I stood up to get my Rolodex down from the shelf and began finger-walking through it, looking for more contacts to call about Ray Tantro. Out in the gallery I heard the bell on the door ring several times and listened with half an ear to the conversations. Paolo was in his element, educating the public about the beauty of handcrafts and paints. He was in control, I told myself as I picked up the phone and called a friend who owned a gallery in Tucson.

A dead end. Not only did she not know where Ray Tantro had shown paintings in that area, she had never even heard of him. I sighed. This wasn't going to be easy. I tried someone else, in the East where Tantro went to art school briefly. I had met this gallery owner, Gordon Tell, at an auction in New York a few years ago. He lived in Boston.

"Ray Tantro? Sure, I remember him," Gordon said. "Sorry to hear he's passed on. Haven't seen any of his stuff in years. No, wait. A couple years ago somebody wanted me to buy one of his big landscapes, those Montana ones?"

"Did you?"

"Guy wanted an arm and a leg. What am I, a charity service? Seriously, Alix, I think he wanted fifty thousand. Ridiculous."

"Haven't his prices gone up on those old ones? What was the date on it?"

"I don't know, '74, '75. Yes, they have gone up. But what were they selling for then? A thousand, fifteen hundred. That's quite a leap."

"What would you have paid for one?"

"I don't know, possibly five. I could maybe get ten or twelve in the gallery. But I didn't even bother to talk to the seller. He wasn't rational."

"Ever see any new pieces of Tantro's? Or hear of any shows?"

"No, the latest thing I've seen is that '75," Gordon said. I thanked him and hung up.

Who else could I call? I tried two other galleries, but there was no answer at either. Then I looked at the fax machine.

I pulled out a sheet of paper and quickly wrote up a free-hand message to five art galleries: The J. Paul Getty Museum in Malibu, the Museum of Modern Art in New York, the Hirshhorn Museum at the Smithsonian in D.C., the Art Institute of Chicago, and the Yellowstone Art Center in Billings, Montana, since Tantro had once lived in Montana. I pleaded, in a lighthearted but urgent way, for information about Raymond Tantro paintings owned, bought, sold, or offered to them in the last twenty years. I sent out the fax, running the sheet through five times, sat back, and sighed. Their offices would probably be closed today, perhaps until Monday or even Tuesday. All I could do was wait.

Paolo stuck his head into my office and saw me sitting with my arms crossed, frowning. "I need you out here, Alix. Now."

He disappeared before I could reply. I stood up, stared at the fax machine one last time to will it to respond, and went off to do my duty to God and tourists.

IT WAS LATE at night—Saturday—when Eden finally showed up at the apartment. Business had picked up and I had no more time to make phone calls about Ray Tantro. Paolo brought us in lunch from the Cadillac Grill, an unexpected pleasure, and we ate and cajoled customers at the same time. Paolo sold a beautiful earth-colored weaving and I sold two clay pots and a watercolor. When the night girl, Megan, came in at seven, I dragged myself up the stairs, starving and feeling the return of the fatigue from my Snake River adventure. My lungs had taken on a low-grade ache. Just about every muscle in my body hurt, especially my arms. My shiners were now testing all the colors on paint chips at Coast-to-Coast Hardware. I realized on reaching the dark, empty apartment that I had been hoping my new roomie would have a big hot dinner on. Life was disappointing. I warmed up a couple of burritos and ate them smothered with hot sauce, then took a shower.

Eden arrived at ten-thirty, blowsy and giddy. The smell of her at first was of cigarettes, her personal perfume. I was wrapped in a plaid wool blanket, drinking a glass of wine, hoping to anesthetize my body for sleep. I wrinkled my nose at the smell of her.

A black beret was stuffed in the pocket of a thick Icelandic sweater I'd lent her. She wore baggy khaki pants, the same ones she'd worn the day of the fire—and every day since. The crying jag of the first night, the sorrow about Ray Tantro, all that side of Eden was not in evidence tonight. Her face was flushed and bright.

"Paolo took me out for a drink," she said. "Just to cheer me up." She looked at me squarely, in an uncomfortably intimate way, then walked over and squatted by my chair. She put her warm hand on mine. I could really smell her now, a mixture of barroom smoke and beer.

"You have to tell me, Alix. I mean it. Seriously. You and him . . . ? I know you had a big thing going. Does it bother you terribly, terribly if I go out with the gaucho?"

I squinted at her. "The gaucho?"

She smiled. "Paolo. I call him the gaucho. He is so sweet." She was lost in thought for a moment, then frowned at me. "So it's over between you two? You've been so good to me, letting me stay here."

The gaucho? Oh, please. I knew he cultivated the persona of the debonair swashbuckler with women but, honestly, I didn't want to know about it. I could imagine Paolo's smooth voice whispering in her ear, rubbing her back as she called him her gaucho.

Eden swayed, catching her footing as she stood up again. I set my wine down. It didn't matter what I said to her. She wouldn't grasp any meanings tonight. I wanted to work on the list of artworks for the appraisal due in less than forty-eight hours, but I'd get no work from Eden tonight.

"What you and Paolo do is none of my business," I said, getting up. I tried to mean it. Eden dropped into my chair. She rubbed her eyes and sighed deeply. The gaucho had made her forget fire, death, and broken dreams. He had that power.

Paolo. I walked to the window and wondered if he and I would ever be finished. Maybe there would always be that spark between us, struggling to light if we just gave it a chance. We hadn't given it a chance for some time. Was it possible I still carried a torch, still hoped it would work out? I had to admit to a twinge of jealousy at her blissful expression as she spoke of my partner. *My partner.* Once he had been so much more: my lover, my best friend. Was that all over? "We saw Martin what's-his-name in the restaurant tonight," Eden said behind me. "Paolo told me about your problem with him. What a mess. You gotta straighten that out, honey."

I turned back to her. She was rubbing her fingertips on her scalp, fluffing her short dark hair. "He told you?"

"I know you must feel sorry for him because he's in a wheelchair and everything. But you can't ruin your business because of that. I mean, Paolo said you guys are going to go broke if you buy Martin's stuff."

"Oh, he did, did he?" I struggled to control my hurt at Paolo confiding in Eden. I took a breath. He was not mine anymore. He'd been confiding in plenty of girls over the last couple years. "Well," I said, "those Latins, you know, they tend to exaggerate. Don't believe everything Paolo tells you."

"Oh, you've still got a little fire burning for him, don't you? Just tell me, Alix, just give me the word. I mean, it won't be easy. He is so hot! And that accent. Ooh!"

I bit my tongue. I didn't want to talk about Paolo. I didn't want to admit anything. So I did what my mother would have done. I changed the subject. "Listen, I wanted to work on the inventory of the Timberwolf tonight. So you can get your settlement."

"Mmmm." Eden's eyes were closed, her lips smiling. "Can we do it tomorrow? You want to drive out to the park and take some pictures with me?"

"It's my Sunday to work," I said. "Unless we go in the morning."

"Sure. Wake me up early."

I said good night. At my bedroom door I turned. Eden had turned on the television and was sitting in the light of the floor lamp, rummaging through her purse. I wondered if she was having trouble sleeping, if the death of Ray Tantro was sitting heavy on her mind.

As I crawled into bed, I tried to put aside my discomfort over her probing about Paolo. She was just being a good friend, seeing if the coast was clear. It was good she asked, I told myself. Even though it stirred up feelings that should have remained buried.

I stared at the ceiling in the moonlight, making myself think about Ray Tantro instead of Paolo. It was easier to deal with a dead man. But it would be even easier if he hadn't dropped out of sight for all those years. Tomorrow, I whispered, tomorrow Ray Tantro will reveal himself to me.

I watched the clock, and the square of moonlight that crawled across the floor. I got up and opened the window a crack, letting mountain-chilled air pour in. I made mental lists, of places to call about Ray's lost years: prisons, rehab clinics, art schools, art galleries, colleges. Could I do it by

Monday? How could I do it at all? I made myself think about the future, about Carl coming down to visit. About his big, warm body against me in this bed. Still, sleep did not come.

At two forty-five I got up and turned the television off. Eden was snoring again.

FOUR

THE JACKSON Town Hall is located in a modern wood-frame building with a big clock tower, a few blocks from the gallery. Unimposing, with no Roman columns, no corny western storefront, it reminded passersby of an overgrown chamber of commerce. Flowers cascaded from tubs on the decking that led through an arched walkway covered with moss rock. I pushed through the door and found the small, high-ceilinged lobby crammed with people, newsmen and -women from the looks of their spiral notebooks, sophisticated cameras, and huge video packs.

I was late. It was past eleven and I had intended to turn in this appraisal first thing this morning. But Eden had gone to dinner last night with Paolo again, after his polo match, and had come home late. The afternoon at the gallery had been busy but unproductive. Unable to rouse Eden in the morning, I drove my old Saab out to Wilson to feed my horse, Valkyrie. She is a spirited chestnut mare, very unpredictable. I have to bring her oats or she'll have nothing to do with me. She was friendly for a change and nuzzled me with her soft nose. Nothing like the love of a big, affectionate animal to bring you down to earth.

I did get an hour of information gathering out of Eden before she left for dinner. She knew a little about Ray, mostly from his early years, where he'd had shows back when he was young and famous. I spent the evening getting the bio together, what little there was to know. As I stood in the lobby outside the police department door, waiting for somebody to come up and escort me back to Charlie Frye's office, I read it again.

Raymond Wayne Tantro

Born: Torrington, Wyoming, 1950.

Died: Jackson, Wyoming, 1993.

Attended Rhode Island School of Design, 1968-70.

One-man show at RISD, 1969. Island Gallery, Providence, 1969. Cape Arts, Boston, 1970. Winston & Scharff, New York, 1970.

Moved to a ranch near Livingston, Montana, in the Paradise Valley, 1970. Shows at several galleries in the area, had one-man shows in Denver, Phoenix, Salt Lake City, and Billings. In 1975, he sold the ranch. Arrived in Jackson area approximately February this year.

The appraisal followed. A simple appraisal, based on the prices Eden told me they were asking, which were extremely overblown: $10,000, $12,000, $20,000 each for pieces that had no past and no future, that weren't of a style Tantro was remembered for, and weren't likely, had they survived, to be remembered themselves. I discounted the prices for such factors as quality, reputation, desirability, and availability, and put a price on them that was, like much in this business, the product of an educated gut reaction.

I looked at the facts on Tantro's life. They were pretty damn sparse. I had made calls to everyone on the bio—Cape Arts, Winston & Scharff, Rhode Island School of Design, all of them. They confirmed what I already knew and added nothing. Tantro had had no contact with any of these people since about 1979 when the last pieces in his ''Montana Cycle'' had sold. At that time he was living somewhere in Wyoming. There were people to call that I hadn't had time to call: gallery owners who may have shown Tantro's work during his ''dark'' years, unknown associates, drinking buddies and employers, relatives who could tell me where he'd been. The fax machine had gone off once this morn-

ing, with a reply from the Art Institute of Chicago that was
singularly unhelpful.

It was frustrating. I shouldn't have told Charlie I could
get this appraisal done in three days. Normally it wouldn't
be difficult. But with Ray Tantro we were dealing with thin
air. He had been so promising. What had gone wrong?
Where the hell had he been all those years? Nobody seemed
to know.

Tantro had a hole in his past big enough to drive a Mack
truck through. Consequently, so did the bio. I made up my
mind not to give the bio or appraisal to Frye, to work on it
some more. I would ask for time, a week, to do the job
right. Eden would just have to wait.

I closed the folder, slapping it against my hand in hopes
someone would hear. The man next to me jostled his camera bag as he checked the settings on his expensive black
lens. "Shit," he said to no one in particular. "I thought he
said ten-thirty."

The photographer was tall with a three-day growth on his
chin and a ball cap that read King Ropes. I wondered if he
worked for the *Jackson Hole News*. He bumped me again
with his voluminous bag.

"Excuse me," I said, pushing against the thing. The
photographer frowned at me. "What's the big deal this
morning?"

"Press conference." He looked away.

"With who?"

He frowned again, surprised I was still talking. He
thought he'd dismissed me from his presence. "Police
chief."

"Yeah? What about?"

As I asked, the sound of footsteps came toward us across
the dark slate floor. Frye led the way, in his gray suit and
string tie. Behind him came Rex Scanlon, the fire investigator, in the same jeans but wearing a navy sport coat, then
a woman I didn't recognize. They made their way through

the desks and glass door into the lobby where the newspeople waited. From the back of the crowd I had to stand on tiptoe to see around the photographers.

Frye took out a pair of reading glasses and hooked them over his beak. Looking at a sheet of paper in his hands, he cleared his throat, then looked up as the strobes blinded him. He winced, his bone-hard face creased in a frown.

"Good morning. We have a short statement to make, then we'll take questions." He cleared his throat again. "Last Thursday, the Timberwolf Arts gallery at 142 East Cache was burned. Inside the building the body of a man was found. This man has been identified as one Raymond Tantro, a self-employed artist who lived in the Jackson area. The fire is now believed to have been arson. Investigation into the fire is ongoing. The death of Raymond Tantro has been judged a suicide."

Charlie stopped abruptly, pressing his lips together, removing his glasses from his nose. He looked like he wanted to say more but thought better of it. Immediately the questions began from the reporters.

"How was the fire started?" someone up in front asked. I craned my neck; I knew that voice.

Frye turned the question over to Rex Scanlon. He looked as tired as ever. "A final determination hasn't been made, as Chief Frye stated. But..." He brightened. "But we believe the fire was begun with a balloon full of gasoline and a candle. The balloon was placed near the burning candle. As the candle burns down, it gets closer to the balloon until it melts through the plastic. At that time the gasoline lights on fire."

"Where was this in the building?" Now I recognized the voice of Danny B.

"On the main floor," Scanlon said.

"Near the victim?"

"Yes."

"Was that the only point of origin?" someone asked.

Scanlon's eyebrows went up, with effort. "Actually no. There was another fire in the attic area."

"Is that what happened to the roof?"

"Yes."

"*What* happened to the roof?" another voice wanted to know.

Scanlon paused and looked at his feet. When he scanned the crowd, acknowledging me briefly, his voice held a mild excitement. "An interesting technique. Another candle, or at least the waxy remains of one, was found on the attic floor. The roof of the building was literally blown away. We believe this may have been caused by vaporized gas that was ignited by the candle as it settled around the flame."

"Say *what?*"

"Do you have a suspect? Or is this Tantro the one?" An impatient voice.

Frye took over. "We don't think Mr. Tantro would have been capable of the arson at this time."

"Why not?"

"Margaret?" Frye held out his hand for the woman behind them to step forward. "This is Margaret Elliot, county coroner."

Margaret was a fiftyish woman with steel gray hair in tight permed curls around her pale face. Her air was one of officiousness, propriety, right down to her thick ankles. Her lips were colored a hideous peach, an impertinent slash across her iron countenance.

"The victim had a high blood level of barbiturates, pentobarbital, to be exact."

"How high?"

Margaret blinked at the interruption. "About two grams. High enough to cause respiratory failure, circulatory collapse, and coma. Even if he hadn't had a blood-alcohol level of point one-oh."

Charlie interrupted Margaret, who clamped her mouth shut irritably. "We found liquor bottles and a syringe at the scene, consistent with the coroner's findings. Excuse me, Margaret.'' He smiled at her, waving gallantly for her to continue.

She nodded her reluctant acceptance. "As I was saying, we suspect the victim plotted to take his own life by injecting a lethal dose of barbiturates and drinking alcohol. A common and fatal combination.''

"Did you do the autopsy, Ms. Elliot?" a reporter said.

"No, that would be Dr. Miller," she said.

"Will there be an inquest?"

"Yes," Frye said. "Tomorrow. But we expect no further evidence to surface. It will be ruled a suicide.''

As Frye and entourage disappeared back into the building and the reporters filed out the door, I had a few more questions. Who had set the fires? Wasn't the motive for the fire as important as the motive for Tantro's suicide? And what was that? There were so many things left hanging. I waited as the newspeople packed up, muttering.

Ten more minutes passed before I could get one of the secretaries to take me back to see Charlie about the appraisal. When I arrived in what passed for the squad room—a dirty white coffee room with a metal desk shared by the two policemen—the police chief was talking to Scanlon over a cup of coffee. I waited at the door, trying to eavesdrop nonchalantly. At last, Scanlon looked up.

"Hi, Rex," I said, trying to be pleasant. "Charlie, can I talk to you for a minute? I've got this appraisal.''

Rex excused himself as Charlie sat on the edge of the desk, pushing aside a dying plant and a framed picture of towheaded kids.

"I can't be doing this insurance crap," Charlie sighed, setting down his coffee cup to rub his face. "I got all I can do here with fires and people dying. And all these dickheads that work for me can think about is jaywalking and loose horses.''

He wouldn't have enjoyed that press conference. Unpleasant death was never fun. He should have stayed in insurance. But fires and dying were part of that too.

"Will Dalton be back soon? Maybe I should just wait and talk to him," I offered, seeing a way out of my own problem of the inadequate appraisal.

"Who the fuck knows?" Charlie took a sip of coffee. "His mama got sick in Gillette. Supposed to be dying. I can't very well tell him to get his rear end back here till she buys the ranch." He looked at me for the first time. "What the hell happened to you?"

My hand flew to my undereye decor. "Oh. A little mishap with the business end of a paddle."

"Jesus, looks like the way I feel," he said, frowning. "Anyway, I wish I knew when Dalton was getting back. When his mama dies, I suppose."

More people dying. It must be getting to Charlie. "Bad weekend?"

He sighed, the bags under his eyes slightly violet, a nice complement to my own hues. He stared at the file in my hands. "Let me see it."

I pulled it to my chest. "I was thinking of working on it some more. Scanlon wouldn't let me go upstairs. I couldn't get any comparisons for the art. That Tantro..." I shook my head. "Did you find out anything about him?"

"Not much. His mother came up and identified him, but she wouldn't say much."

"Came up from where?"

"South. Star Valley, I think. She was pretty broke up."

"Is she going to bury him down there?"

"Cremation, I think she said. Makes sense." He raised his furry eyebrows to make the point. I got it.

"Maybe I could talk to her for the appraisal. If I could find out what some of his recent stuff has been going for it would be better. You know, the prices he and Eden put on that stuff were pretty far-fetched."

Charlie was barely listening. He nodded and sipped, somewhere else.

"Doesn't really matter now, Alix." He paused and looked up. "The A word—arson."

"So somebody torched the place. You mean the insurance is no good if someone burns you out?" The thought gave me a serious chill. "What about Jack Dennis?" When Jack's sporting goods shop had burned a few years ago, he relocated across the square and was back in business within months. "I always thought, I mean, didn't his insurance pay?"

Charlie shrugged. "Not mine, but from what I hear that one was the pyro. But listen, hon. There is one main reason for arson. That is for the owner to collect. You may not want to think that about your friend, but open those big blue eyes and smell the coffee."

I squinted instead. Smell coffee with my eyes? "You don't seriously think Eden burned down her own gallery?"

"Don't know. She's a suspect. Being the owner, she's at the top of the list."

"But that gallery meant the world to her." I thought of her sobbing in my arms. "Anyway, she was with me, down in the canyon."

"Nobody was nearby by the time the place went up. Didn't you hear Scanlon?"

"Yeah, but..."

"Somebody planned their alibi. It was very slick." He ran his hand over the brush of gray on his scalp, sighing again.

"If it was so slick, how come Ray Tantro was found burned to a crisp inside?"

"Okay, listen, Miss Alix Thorssen. You keep working on the appraisal. It may come out like Jack's place, the happy pyro. Who knows? But tell Ms. Chaffee to start counting her pennies and getting her lawyer lined up.'' He slurped his coffee and looked at me over the rim of the plastic cup. ''Now get out of here.''

FIVE

SINCE WE BROKE UP I often think about how Paolo Segundo and I ever got together. We were both living in New York, which is a prescription for never meeting anyone attractive who isn't married or gay. Maybe it was just the shock of finding someone handsome and available that threw me over. I used to come into the gallery where he worked in the Village, and we'd talk about the paintings, what we liked, what we were doing ourselves. Both of us still dabbled then. I was slaving at the Met, taking tickets and seeing all the installations for free, and in my spare time trying to get the colors mixed right on my own palette.

Paolo's paintings were terrible. Violent like something he had to get out of his system. In person he was gentle, very sweet. But he had a tumultuous history. His family in Argentina was powerful and wealthy. They owned a huge ranch, kept a string of polo ponies, were active in politics. Paolo went to an expensive prep school until he was sixteen and his father was murdered in a coup led by the army. His mother, sister, and he fled to Costa Rica. They sent him to the U.S. for college. He went to Columbia for a year, until the money ran out. The art gallery was his sixth or seventh job but one that he succeeded the best in because of the absolute inability of rich women to withstand the onslaught of his charm.

Okay, the same could be said for me. I fell for him like a ton of bricks, madly. He moved into my apartment within two hours. All right, two weeks. When we decided to move to Jackson, it was as if we had embarked on our personal mission of the soul, our life journey. We would travel in each other's shoes. This was it.

Of course, we never legalized it. It never occurred to either of us. But the point came when I couldn't tolerate the other women. I suppose they had always been there. I must have refused to see them, but all at once that was the only thing I could see.

We still worked well together, victims of habit, of knowing each other's strengths. But it wasn't what it had been, and there was no denying that.

In the afternoon, Paolo asked me to come over to his place for a drink that evening. I thought he wanted to talk about the Ditolla prints and what I'd done about them. We were in the gallery, enjoying a lull in the afternoon traffic.

"We have to talk," he said, grabbing my arm while a couple in matching Eddie Bauer outfits, duck boots to camouflage hats, debated the merits of a group of hand-colored intaglios by a Native American artist from Montana. She thought the green one would go better in the bathroom. He liked the power in the orange one.

Paolo and I stood in the doorway to my office. I felt the heat of his hand on my arm unexpectedly and jerked it away. I don't like people touching me unaware, even Paolo. To let him touch me would be to admit a lot of things I wasn't ready for.

"Why do you do that?" Paolo frowned.

"Do what?"

"Pull away like I got cooties or somezing." His accent hardened when he was angry.

I turned from my desk, sighing. "What is it you want?"

"Just to have a drink and talk. Is that so much?" He glanced out at the Eddie Bauers, smiling at them in his sweet, phony way, and turned back to me. "We are partners. We need to talk."

"Isn't this talking?"

"You are so busy, in and out, in and out. Talk, talk, talk on the phone. What are you working on?"

"The Ray Tantro appraisal. For Eden's settlement. Did you see my little Tantro?" I pointed to it propped up on my desk. Paolo leaned over to look at it.

"Nice. I remember it from your apartment in New York. That one time you let me stay over." He straightened, heat in his eyes.

"It was more than once, I seem to recall."

"Do you, now?" His smirk was self-satisfied. I was sure he would have continued, his machismo heating up notch by notch, but just then the Eddie Bauers picked the green bathroom print and wanted it wrapped.

PAOLO LIVED IN a house he'd bought after moving out of my apartment a couple of years ago. The small, creamy white bungalow with a rose-colored door sat at the base of Snow King Mountain, in an area of town where you were just as likely to see a guy living in a camper up on blocks as a family living in a renovated, gingerbread Victorian with a white picket fence. When Paolo bought the house, it had been a rental for twenty years and showed every year of wear and tear. Holes in the walls, ancient, food-encrusted range, no refrigerator, leaking toilets, and bad plumbing.

But it had charm. I remember the day he took me to see it, about a week after he'd bought it. Even through the mess and stench of the four ski bums who were camped out in it, the charm was real. Carved woodwork, a real wood banister curving up to dormered bedrooms upstairs, wood floors, all the nuts and bolts for a great place. Not big, just three rooms down and two up, but perfect for a single guy. Hell, I'd even helped paint the walls three shades of peach, I'd been so eager to prove that we could be friends after the romance was over.

I sunk into the mauve leather sofa that felt like butter in a bed of feathers, a gin and tonic in my hand. The kitchen

door was open to the backyard, a handkerchief lawn with
wonderful flower beds Paolo had been working on little by
little, getting them into shape like an athlete readying for a
marathon. Minutes before I had walked around in them in
the soft evening light, admiring the white phlox, the orange-
faced pansies, the astilbe, tall and proud under the aspen by
the back fence. This was the kind of solitude I needed. I
imagined the backyard of my own dream cabin, filled with
flowers and birds and scents hanging on the breeze like sugar
candy.

The gin and tonic stung my tongue, not unpleasantly.
Paolo sat down on the edge of an antique oval-backed chair
covered in exquisite needlepoint. He looked at me in-
tensely, and I squirmed a little under his stare.

"Alix." He ran his hand through his black hair. He wore
jeans and an orange silk shirt, as casual as he ever got. I had
wondered about the clothes when I came in. He used to
dress that way years ago, for me.

"You're scaring me, kid," I said, trying to tease him and
convince myself it wasn't true.

He leaned back and crossed his legs. "Sorry. This is just
hard for me to say."

"You've got a disease." I smiled to show him it was just
a joke. "I warned you about that."

"This is serious, Alix." He took a sip of his drink. "Okay,
here it is. I've been thinking of selling my share of the gallery."

He gave his sweet smile, covered with apologetic dark
eyes. He was serious. I couldn't believe it. I could imagine
him telling me he was getting married, or buying a new car,
or wanting a month off to visit his mother, or climbing
Mount Everest. But not this.

"Say something," he said, looking sheepish.

"Okay. You can't. I won't let you. You have to sell to me
or nobody. That was our agreement."

"Okay, I sell to you."

I blinked. "I don't have the money, Paolo. You know that." I stared at the lime in my drink. "You don't need the money, do you? I thought your relatives sent you that pile when your grandmother died."

"You're looking at it." He waved his hand to indicate the bungalow he loved so much.

"All of it's gone?"

He nodded, glum.

"But what would you do?"

"Go back to the city. To New York. You know I miss it. This place is too... you know, too rustic for me."

I felt empty, the gin now churning in my stomach. I shut my eyes and tried to imagine my life without Paolo. I was proud of my independence, and fiercely protective. Still my mind resisted the notion of being free of him.

"Listen," I said, "if this is about Martin's paintings, and all that, I'm working on it. I'm speaking to him tomorrow about it. I'll explain and—"

"Have you set up an appointment with him?"

"Well, no, but I plan to. I couldn't take it on my conscience, knowing and not telling him. I've just been so busy with the Tantro appraisal."

Paolo sighed, his shoulders sagging. "This is part of it. We don't have the same focus anymore. Remember when we worked together, when everything we did was for *us*, for the gallery?" I was stunned by his emotion, his dismissal. He held his fist half clenched as if clutching at something just out of reach. "Now you do your thing, your appraisals and stolen art and all that. That's fine. But I want to do my thing too. I remember that, Alix. And I need that kind of commitment again. No, no, not from you." He must have seen my eyes bug out. "Commitment to my work, to my art, to nurturing artists. I need that."

"And you're not getting that here?" I said quietly.

He went to the back window, then turned back. "I've tried, Alix. It has been grand, good, whatever you call it.

But my heart isn't in it anymore." He walked out the kitchen door into the garden and sat on a wrought-iron bench in the grass next to stately blue delphiniums. I followed, sitting beside him.

"Remember the time we hung all those abstracts, the ones by that weirdo from Idaho—what was his name?" I smiled.

"Vincent?"

"Yeah. With the Van Gogh complex." I laughed, remembering. "We hung them all upside down by mistake and when Vincent came in for the reception he was half crocked. Remember? He didn't even notice for about an hour."

Paolo smiled. "Then he exploded. The prima donna."

"Threw his drink against the wall. We had to repaint. And you were so worried he was going to cut off his ear." I laughed too hard, too long. Then it was silent again, with the gulf of years shared and not shared. "Maybe we just need to regroup, Paolo," I said softly. He looked at the flowers mournfully. The night air was heavy and still. "I want to nurture artists too. We want the same things."

He shook his head. "This thing has been inside me for months. The time has come."

He had made up his mind. What could I say to change a stubborn Argentine's decision? I felt hollow and tried to take a deep breath of the cool mountain air. I hated change. I felt sick.

Paolo turned to me, examining my face as he held my shoulders in his hands. "You don't need me. You know that. We have..." He paused and frowned. "Oh, stop with those sad eyes." He pulled me toward him and tenderly kissed my eyes. "There, now. Better?"

I pulled away and stood up. I would be fine without Paolo. It was just such a shock. We had been operating independently for some time. I would survive. "Don't start—it'll be all right, Paolo. I understand. I really do. I just need to know your plans. What you want to do." I heard myself talk, talk, to calm the hurricane blowing inside me.

He stood up and we walked together back toward the kitchen door. The lines on his face deepened as he took my arm. "I know somebody who might be interested in my half. Someone you know, you get along with. I think it would work. Of course, you have to agree."

We stepped into the kitchen. I turned to him in the harsh light, frowning. "I don't know if I could have another partner. You've spoiled me, Pao—" A lump formed in my throat. As I swallowed hard, trying to maintain composure, the doorbell saved me. There on the threshold was Eden Chaffee dressed in something new, a black, floaty number with skintight legs and chiffon over. She swept into the room, bubbling about the beautiful evening, then saw us staring morosely at the floor.

"Well, Alix, I didn't expect to find you here," she said, a touch of jealousy in her voice. Paolo caught it too, looking quickly at me, then smiling wanly at Eden.

"Are you ready for dinner?" Paolo said to her without enthusiasm. He rattled the ice in his glass.

"How about a drink first? A little social hour," she said, sitting at the far end of the sofa and crossing her shapely gams at Paolo.

"I was just leaving," I said. "Thanks for the drink."

"Oh, stay, Alix. Finish your drink," Paolo said, now annoyed at me.

I turned to Eden. "I spoke to Charlie Frye about your insurance today."

Eden brightened. "When do we settle?"

"He wasn't optimistic, I have to tell you."

"What does that mean?" She frowned.

"Because of the arson, there are problems." I glanced at Paolo. This wasn't the time to get into all this. I would tell her later. "I'm still working on the appraisal. It may take some time."

"But I thought we finished that, Alix." Now Eden was pouting. I moved toward the door.

"We have reservations for eight, Eden," Paolo said, looking at his watch. "Five minutes."

"Have a good time, you two," I said cheerfully, closing the rose-colored door behind me. My head was pounding and no amount of fresh Teton air was going to help that. The most I could hope for was a taco and a Dos Equis and a little peace and quiet to try to sort out my future.

I CLIMBED INTO my old car, the Saab Sister, in the alley behind The Merry Piglets. Spicy fumes warmed the air behind the building. My headache had relaxed over the beer and good food, although like many nights, I ate alone. The Saab, a '67, was running well tonight for a change. The Wyoming license plates—handsome blue mountains with the bucking horse and SIS in red—made the old beater look even shabbier. I had managed to get new tires, after a raft of bad tire karma. But Sis ran when you pulled the choke out just right.

I drove out of town, toward Wilson and the Fish Creek pasture where Valkyrie roamed. She was nowhere to be seen and I didn't have oats. I drove down the road and parked outside the Stagecoach Bar, a local hangout. I could hear billiard balls clacking and the sound of laughter through the open door. Backpackers, musicians, waitresses, and drunks went in, came out, smoked joints, drank beer. I sat there for half an hour, trying to process Paolo's announcement. Would I have to change the name of the gallery, a reflection of our common vision, our partnership: Second for Segundo, Sun as part of Thorssen?

I stuck my elbow out the open window, slumping down in the seat. The night sky was a violent purple, the mountainsides thickening with evening. On the breeze the smell of fish and moss and water floated up from the creek.

"Hey, kayak queen. We on for Wednesday?"

Startled, I bumped my knee on the underside of the dash. Pete Rotondi had his hand on my elbow, a big hand with long fingers. He squinted down at me. "We're on, right?"

I swallowed and tried not to look like the mess I felt like. "What're you doing here?"

He dropped his hand and gave me his toothy, confident smile. The breeze blowing into the car carried the piny smell of him, in jeans and a flannel shirt smudged with dabs of something white. "I could say the same for you. You want me to buy you a beer? Or are you waiting for somebody?"

"No. I mean, yes." He was just being polite. Music started up, an amateur cacophony of guitar and harmonica. "I was just heading home."

"How's the nose?" He leaned over again, cocking his head to get a look in the open window.

I touched my nose. "It's okay. I guess."

Pete nodded. "Good. See you Wednesday, then." He waved as he turned away, his long stride taking him just a few steps into the saloon. I couldn't think about kayaking. I had too much to do to take another day off. Carl would be disappointed when he got here if I wasn't up to snuff. Well, business comes first. I still had remarkable color from last week, for God's sake. Not to mention my partner turning his back on me and a crisp with a mystery life.

As the stars popped out, I spun my new tires on the gravel and headed back into town. To my smoky apartment where I would sleep alone. I tried not to think about Carl or kayaks. I had bigger problems. Like why was my former best friend abandoning me to the four winds?

I cleared my mind, letting the sage-filled meadow air rushing in the window cleanse me. But as I crossed the Snake River with the moon a silver slash across its gravelly flats, a new, disturbing thought hit me. I knew whom Paolo had in mind for my new partner.

Eden Chaffee.

SIX

THE INQUEST AT the county courthouse Tuesday morning was as unsurprising as Chief Frye had promised. After brief testimony by the powers that be, the death of Ray Tantro was ruled suicide. Margaret Elliot, the coroner, had in my opinion run a pretty fine line between death by burning and death by drug overdose and booze. But she appeared efficient and thorough, and sure of her findings. Although she admitted a small amount of soot was found in the victim's bronchial tubes, a sign of smoke inhalation, she was sure he had died before the smoke or flames got him. Dr. Miller, the pathologist, took the stand and concurred. Ray Tantro wanted to die, they seemed to say. No one injected several ampules of Nembutal into their veins without a pretty distinct plan. Plus drank a bottle of Wild Turkey to get up the nerve.

Okay, but what about the fires? Frye worked hard during the hearing to keep the death of Ray Tantro and the fire itself separate. Frye was sitting on the arson evidence. Or hiding the lack of it. Arson was hard to prove under the best of circumstances, despite his threat about Eden. He might never have enough evidence to go to court. Was linking Tantro's suicide to the arson of the Timberwolf too big a leap for Frye? Was he too hung up on his insurance business to care? Too focused on putting the clamps on the arsonist to give a rip about Tantro? Maybe whoever torched the Timberwolf Gallery, and consequently Ray Tantro, would never be brought to justice. As I stood up in the courtroom, I told myself that wouldn't be true. I had promised Eden I would find out what happened to Ray. This inquest was only a beginning, not a finale.

I ran into Danny Bartholomew on the way out of the courtroom. His black beard was stuck in a reporter's notebook while he scribbled away. We literally bumped into each other. It took only minor arm-twisting to get him to agree to a cup of coffee before he went back to his desk at the *Jackson Hole News*. We sat at the bar at the Bunnery, smelling ethereal bakery smells, and sipped a cuppa.

"You kayak, don't you?" I asked Danny. He grunted, preoccupied. "You've done the Canyon, then."

"Sure, a few times. My wife doesn't like me doing it much anymore, with the kids and all," Danny said, his head down over his coffee cup.

In the warm cocoon of the café, sitting at the counter on stools, gave me a comforting feeling. A mess of morning papers toppled at the end of the counter.

"Plus I haven't got the time anymore." Although not tall, Danny fit easily into the lean-bodied Jackson male image, wearing well-worn hiking boots and carrying an intense look on his patrician but hairy face. "They've got me working all the damn beats at once. Too cheap to hire anybody. Only me dumb enough to work for peanuts anyway."

This lament was sung on a regular basis by most of my Jackson friends. It was tough to live on sardine wages in a caviar town. Housing was out of sight, and the biggest joy for locals was the opening of K mart, where at least one could afford to buy underwear. Having time to enjoy the natural wonders of the place—the reason most of us lived here—meant not working.

"So what do you think?"

"About what?" His eyes were bloodshot and had dark circles under them. I was surprised to see him looking so unhealthy.

"This fire. Tantro."

He slumped again. Back to business. "I don't know. Just some dumb schmuck abusing his body who got caught in the wrong place at the wrong time." He drank some coffee. I said nothing. Something about that picture of Ray Tantro, the artist who had captured the early-morning light of the foothills in snow, was wrong. Maybe he'd been a mess for years. But was that the end of it? I drank coffee. Finally he said, "What? You know something else?"

I shrugged. "Seems kind of weird, doesn't it?" He lowered his dark eyebrows in question. "A guy wants to kill himself. Shoots up barbiturates, drinks a bottle of bourbon. Okay, you want to die, that's one way. But why do it in the gallery?"

"His paintings were there. He wanted to see his beloved art on his way out."

"Maybe. But why does the place explode into flame while he happens to be there?"

"The sixty-four-million-dollar question." Danny B. turned on his stool to lean his elbows on the counter, staring out over the cozy restaurant and the diners sitting at picnic tables on the sunny patio. His eyes seemed to clear slightly, squinting at the windows. "The wily pyro again?"

I pushed my coffee away. "What do you know about this pyro guy?"

"The cops did a psychological profile on him a couple of years back. The usual stuff, a male probably, gets sexual kicks watching a place burn down. A power trip, I guess."

"They like to watch, don't they?"

"Yeah, voyeurs." Danny turned back as the waitress refilled our cups on the counter.

"So why would a person go to all the trouble to set up these fires so that he—or she—would be somewhere else when the fun begins? Just to establish an alibi? I don't know. These things were pretty elaborate, weren't they?" I didn't really get the gist of the attic blast and was hoping Danny would explain it.

"The first-floor one was basic. Gasoline in a balloon sitting next to a candle. The one that blew the roof off was different." He shook his head. "That one kinda scares me."

"How so?"

"Did you see the building? It took the whole damn roof off."

"And it was vaporized gas?"

"White gas, like in a camp stove." Danny warmed to the subject. He drew me a picture on his napkin, showing a small hole in the attic door through which the pyro sprayed a gas-and-water mixture into the enclosed space. "He lights the candle. As the airborne gas cools, it settles on the floor, near the candle. Then...ka-blooey." He threw his hands up in the air. "An inventive way to blow, you gotta admit."

I imagined the blast for a moment. Its force must have been incredible. Why two fires, one in the attic and one next to Ray? "Why didn't Frye make an issue of the fire at the inquest?"

"I asked him about it. He thinks the guy, Tantro, just happened to be there. Thinks they're unrelated. The guy would have offed himself one way or the other. The booze and drugs did him in, so the fire was irrelevant."

"Is that what you think?"

Danny's caffeine fix perked him up, and he gave me a sharp look. "Makes sense."

"You don't think there's anything strange about Frye? I get the feeling he's glossing over this somehow."

Danny squinted his eyes, inquiring-mind-like. "What's your interest?"

"Frye asked me to appraise Tantro's art for the insurance."

"You don't have to know what killed him for that. The guy's dead. That's the bottom line."

As we left the Bunnery and went our separate ways, I wondered about that bottom line. Raymond Wayne Tantro was dead. Was that all that mattered? It should matter to

Frye who started those fires. It mattered to me what happened to Ray Tantro. He was on the way back from the wasteland. He had a new show of his artwork. Why kill yourself when things are finally looking up?

DR. LYLE MILLER was on his way out of the pathology lab in the basement of St. John's Hospital when I got to the door. The afternoon at the gallery had ripped by, filled with Paolo's obvious solicitude and people who consider art galleries places to look at art for free. The door to the lab opened before me, revealing the tall, pleasant-faced doctor in bifocals. His hair was graying and receding, his nose sunburned with evidence of small scars like skin cancer excisions. He seemed surprised but flattered by my request to discuss his work on the Tantro case, but then I laid it on rather thickly. Oh, those feminine wiles.

He turned the fluorescent lights back on in the small outer room. The secretary's tidy desk and the two vinyl-covered green chairs had the look of clinical death to them. The only lively piece in the stark room was a photograph of a skier in midair, careening down a steep snowpacked chute in a tuck position.

"Is this you?" I asked, examining the photo. "Is this at the Village?" Teton Village is Jackson's main ski area, about ten miles out of town.

"In Corbet's Couloir." Dr. Miller smiled as if remembering the thrill of skiing down the nearly vertical chute, cradled in hard, glittering granite on each side. It was a double-black-diamond run that I considered a death wish. In the photograph Miller looked strong, in control, arms wide but legs bent and ready for the landing somewhere down below.

"Wow. You must be good."

"Younger mostly. That was ten or twelve years ago. I've had to give up extreme skiing. Two knee operations." Miller was a trim man with a touch of sadness around his eyes when he spoke. He wore his white lab coat with an open-necked green shirt and blue jeans.

"You still ski though, don't you?" Everyone in Jackson skied. If not downhill, then cross-country. It was impossible to survive the winter without it. The cabin fever was lethal.

He gave a weary nod. "Not like the old days." He blinked out of his reverie, looking at his watch. "Now, the Tantro case?"

"The insurance. Charlie Frye is the agent." I dropped Charlie's name easily. "You did the autopsy?"

"Hmm. Tragic case. Between the drugs and the burns there was plenty to see, though."

"What do you mean?"

"Not *see* in the visual sense of the word. When a body burns that badly often there is little to examine. But the forensic signposts are there. And the eyeball almost always survives."

I blinked. "Pardon?"

Miller sat on the edge of the secretary's desk, getting comfortable. "The eyeball. It usually doesn't burn. So we get blood samples from there, tissue samples."

I felt a shiver up my spine in the cool basement lab. All that was left was the eyeball? I was grateful once again for not seeing the body.

"How did his mother identify him if he was burned so badly?"

"From his effects. Scraps of clothes, wallet. She was quite positive. I was here with her at the time. A strong woman."

"Not the hysterical type, huh?"

Miller sighed. "It's difficult sometimes. You forget if you work with the dead how it affects other people. But Mrs. Tantro handled it well. A shock, no doubt."

No doubt. Jesus, what an understatement. My overactive imagination already had a clear view of the corpse of

Ray Tantro, and it wasn't pretty. Flesh gone, blackened char where the skin was—I had to stop.

"No fingerprints, then?"

Dr. Miller shook his head. "His hands were badly burned. As was his face. His teeth were fairly intact. But the mother said she didn't think he'd had any dental work done for years. Didn't know if he ever had."

"And he had taken drugs?"

"That's right. Barbiturates, a sedative called pentobarbital or the brand name, Nembutal. Where he got the dosage, I'd like to know. Very tightly controlled since it's habit-forming. Of course, like everything there is a black market on it."

"He injected it?"

"Right. Probably had just the one syringe and kept refilling it till he had enough."

"How much is enough?"

"To kill a person? Depends on the person. He was drinking alcohol too, so the lethal dose was less. He had about two grams on board, about ten times the usual dose."

"What would that do to a person? You know, physiologically?"

If Dr. Miller thought my questions were off base, he didn't let on. He rubbed his knee, which stuck out from his lab coat. "Causes a comalike condition, then the respiratory system fails, circulatory fails, everything shuts down. Of course, in a guy with liver damage the barbiturates work pretty darn quick."

"He had liver damage?"

"From what we could find of his liver, it looked like it. I questioned the mother too. She said he had been an alcoholic for years." Miller shook his head. "The barbiturates and alcohol knocked him cold before the fire could kill him. He definitely died before the fire." Dr. Miller looked up from his roughened white hands. "I hope we don't see another one like that."

I glanced through the opaque glass in the doors to the back, where the real work was done.

"The body. Is it still here?"

"Released to the funeral home early this afternoon."

I thanked the pathologist and walked out of the hospital basement, up the stairs with him, into the social milieu of the carpeted hospital corridors with fresh-faced nurses and emergency room jocks, and finally into the evening air. It smelled sweet and alive, without a trace of smoke or death.

As I drove back to the gallery along Broadway, the sun was disappearing behind the black hulks to the west, our guardian mountains, sheltering us from the outside world of big-city torments. Or the mountains held us here, shackled and crazed, against our wills. There were at least two truths, two ways to look at small-town life and our glorious Rockies.

I slammed on my brakes to keep from hitting the group of people who suddenly swelled out into the street. A peaceful group, they were laughing and carrying signs. I inched the Saab closer and tried to read them. "We Back Buck," said one. Darlene, my decorator and purveyor of wrinkled linen, turned to me, laughing, her red hair aglow in the twilight. I waved at her, and she skipped over.

"What's happening?" I asked.

Darlene bent down, laying her freckled arms on the window. "Buck's announcing his candidacy for mayor. Of course, we all knew he'd run again. Just an excuse for a party. Park your car and come with us."

I looked at the crowd. *Republicans.* Happy, jeering Republicans. Buck Boyle was the biggest, most obnoxious Republican of all, though his support ran across party lines to include a majority of true Jacksonians, that is, anybody who'd lived here longer than six months.

The truth was I had nothing against Republicans in general, as a group. I even voted for a few. It was the individuals I couldn't stomach, and Buck Boyle was their king. He was cowboy through and through, from the shit on his boots to his old-time saloon complete with scantily clad dancing girls, around the corner from the Second Sun.

I was shaking my head at Darlene when I spotted Boyle, towering in white straw hat and bulging pearl-button shirt on the steps of a pea green Victorian office building, looking down on his disciples, so beneficent. A man stepped up next to him. I craned my neck to see but knew that profile, that anvil shape of the head. Charlie Frye clapped his arm around Buck's shoulders, they grinned at each other, and the crowd went wild.

Darlene waved me around the edge of the people. As the Saab inched away, down the street, a piece of the puzzle clicked into place. Charlie Frye was smoothing over the investigation of Ray Tantro's death because Buck Boyle was running for reelection. They were old cronies. Probably bowled on the same team. Belonged to Rotary, Masons, Elks. That was how Frye got appointed in the first place, a non-law-enforcement type heading the police department.

It would look bad for an unexplained death to take place in our little burg right before the election. An arson investigation could take months, no one would blame Frye for that. But a homicide declared, then not solved? A black eye for Buck's gang. With Frye at the helm, that possibility was brilliantly imminent. So call it suicide and bury it.

For once, something made sense.

SEVEN

WEDNESDAY MORNING had a little trouble getting started. A low cloud cover filled the valley, promising a chill and showers. Eden looked so forlorn I invited her along with me to Star Valley. I could use the company, and besides, I wanted to check her out as a potential partner. I was trying to think positively about the whole thing. If Eden's insurance came through, she could pay off at least part of what Paolo had invested in his half of the gallery.

Last night Eden had seemed down. Evenings out with Paolo had made her forget her problems for a while, but my partner's ardor had cooled. (Now that he'd broken his news to me?) The last two evenings he had found a rich client to entertain, one of the last merger-and-acquisition bankers on Wall Street and his glamorously thin wife.

Now Eden slumped against the window of the car, staring silently at the limestone cliffs along the river as we wound south toward the Mormon town of Star Valley. I had spoiled our pleasant drive by asking her not to smoke in the car. She hadn't spoken to me since. When I stopped at a gas station to ask directions to Esther Tantro's house, she ran in and bought a can of root beer. She was slurping noisily on it as we wound up the dirt road east of town, into the rolling foothills where the sage grew tall and the grass had burned to golden straw next to the road.

"Can I come in? Is it all right with *you*?" Eden whined as I stopped the Saab Sister in an overgrown driveway in front of the farmhouse. A decayed look permeated the place, the white paint cracked and dirty, a porch step broken, barbed-wire fence sagging and piled with tumbleweed.

No animals grazed the dry pastures unless you counted prairie dogs.

I sighed. "Do what you want, Eden. I asked you to come because I wanted you along. If you'd rather do something else"—I paused, trying to keep my tongue in check—"feel free."

I slammed the door of the car and examined the house. The heat rose from the pale dirt. The air was still, dead calm. Even the hardy Russian olive trees were twisted with sharp thorns where leaves should be. No clouds blanketed the wide-open sky here. I squinted up at the white-hot dome and remembered how dry and desolate Wyoming could be when you got out of the mountains.

When I called Mrs. Tantro this morning she sounded weak and I worried about overtaxing her with questions. Yet Dr. Miller said she was a strong woman, and she had agreed to my visit when I complimented Ray's work. I told her I was interested in seeing some of his paintings for the gallery. Strangely enough, this was true. I had three calls yesterday about Tantro paintings, all from people jolted by his death into finally taking an interest in the guy. Art ghouls, I called them. The human psyche is sometimes a strange, dark maze.

Eden ran around the front of the car and grabbed my hand. "I'm sorry, Alix." I thought she was going to cry as I pulled my hand away. "You've been so good to me. Forgive me?"

"It's been a rough week." I headed toward the house. "Just let me do the talking, okay?"

Eden skipped to keep up. "I won't say a thing. It's so good to get out of town for a few hours. I was feeling so cramped up in your apartment. I don't know how you stand it. There's no sunlight in there. It's so dark. Oh, I don't mean I don't appreciate staying there and everything, it's just my place was bigger and it made all the difference with the south windows."

Eden had to stop for a breath. Fortunately we reached the door then and I knocked. The door, like the rest of the house, was painted gray or faded to that color, with dirt and black boot scuffs of years' duration. It opened, creaking, and Esther Tantro stood squinting at us. She was a big woman, with long gray hair that she wore loose, giving her a wild look. Her face was mottled with age spots, but her eyes were clear and dark as night.

"Alix Thorssen from Second Sun Gallery in Jackson. Mrs. Tantro?"

She smiled without moving her lips and stepped back to let us in. I introduced Eden, watching for a reaction to Eden's name from the woman, but there was none. Ray must not have mentioned the name of the owner of the gallery where his new pieces hung. Eden shook Mrs. Tantro's hand, something I had forgotten to do, and the old woman seemed to warm.

"Would you like coffee? I made some biscuits yesterday I could warm up. Put a little honey on them. Be no trouble?" Her voice was pitifully urgent, and we felt obliged to accept. "Sit down, please. I'll be right back."

Eden obeyed, choosing an overstuffed chair covered with flowered velvet cushions that emitted clouds of dust in the morning sun streaming through the east windows. The parlor, this room would be called, with fussy, uncomfortable furniture dating from the thirties, knickknack shelves, and lace doilies. Wallpaper graced the walls, an extravagance no self-respecting parlor could do without, although in this case it would have been an improvement.

Over the small, cold fireplace with wooden mantel and shallow brick hearth hung a large oil painting. As I stepped up to it I knew immediately it was one of Ray's. The colors in it were magnificently imaginative, similar to my small winter scene. His prairie, glowing with autumn-ripe wheat and a rainstorm threatening in the purple sky, evoked a sense of the wonder of the land. He had a sure hand, a confident stroke, sometimes precise and other times bold and loose. The date in the corner read "72. 0;

"Did you see this one, Alix?" Eden whispered from across the room. Esther Tantro rattled pans in the kitchen. I turned and saw the painting Eden stood in front of, a small piece sitting on an easel on a tabletop in the corner. I crossed the faded oriental rug.

"Why didn't he do some like these for me? I could have sold these in a wink." Eden folded her arms, a cross look on her face again, and turned to the big painting.

I bent down to look at the little piece; it was equally gorgeous, a tiny still life of mossy rocks in a stream. I gave a low whistle and whispered to myself: "No shit, Sherlock."

Mrs. Tantro came in with a tray of coffee and warm biscuits. We sat and did polite, even though the biscuits were hard as hockey pucks. After chewing and smiling for a seemly time, I set down my coffee cup and wiped my mouth.

"I'm sorry to bother you so soon after...all your trouble. We have had a number of requests for Ray's work this week. This often happens when an artist dies. People get interested."

Esther nodded, smoothing back her gray hair that had tumbled into her coffee. "I understand. You know, Ray and me wasn't too close these last years." She stopped suddenly, a distance in her eyes that could have been sorrow or just regret.

"It must be awful to lose your son," Eden piped up. I glared at her. I didn't want Mrs. Tantro to find out it was Eden's gallery where Ray had died. Eden gave me a contrite look and folded her hands.

"Do you know of any galleries that might have sold Ray's work in the last ten years or even fifteen years, Mrs. Tantro?" I said. "So that I might locate some of his work?"

Esther frowned into her lap. "Just that one where...in Jackson. He hadn't had a show in, oh, I don't remember the last one before that."

"He hadn't been painting?"

She shook her head. "He had, kind of, some problems. He couldn't paint." That would be booze and drugs. She went on, perking up in memory, eyes on the window. "He was so excited about the new show, his new paintings. I couldn't believe he was painting again. But he did it."

Her voice didn't sound proud, like a mother's. Only the pain of his loss came through, in flat tones.

"Do you have a picture of him, Mrs. Tantro?" The only picture I'd seen was the murky shot in the library's faxed article.

Mrs. Tantro was sitting in a straight chair, her head turned toward the window. The sun dusted her wrinkled features, sharpening the lines of sorrow. She turned to me, suddenly, as if from another world.

"Why, yes. Of course." She rose, moving not as wearily as before, and disappeared into another room. In a moment she was back with a large black-and-white photograph in a frame. She handed it to me.

"He was seventeen then," she said. "A long time ago."

The photograph was a group shot of the Star Valley basketball squad, circa 1966. They wore big canvas high-tops and loose sleeveless jerseys and grins as wide as childhood.

"State champions that year. That's Ray, there." An arthritic finger pointed at the tallest boy in the center of the photograph. Eden came over to the sofa and sat beside me.

Ray had a crew cut and a square jaw with small, wide-set eyes. I looked at Eden, who raised her eyebrows and frowned. Mrs. Tantro took the framed picture into her hands, smiled at it, and flattened it against her flowered housecoat.

We stood. I took a last, covetous look at the piece over the mantel. I lingered, knowing the visit was over but hoping she would offer something, hoping she would remember where Ray sold his paintings, where he hoarded them, who had bought them, anything. I didn't have the heart to ply her for information, the grief on her face as she stared at her long-ago teenage son still fresh in my mind. I couldn't help but feel the awful shock it must have been to find him burned beyond recognition, a blackened, charred life-form that had once been a tall, proud basketball player, a successful artist, a son.

"Will you have a service, Mrs. Tantro?" Eden said behind me.

"Last night. We had it in the moonlight." She walked to the window again, the photograph still against her breast. "We scattered his ashes there, on the hill."

Eden stepped next to her, gazing at the burned brown hills behind the house, the twisted apple trees with drooping leaves and deformed fruit.

"Will you stay here?" Eden asked quietly.

"This is my home," the old woman said. "Ray is here."

Eden looked grief-stricken as she turned to me, her eyes filling. She dropped her head and started for the door. I turned to go too, when Mrs. Tantro spoke.

"My nephew has some paintings. He helped Ray out during some bad spells."

"Your nephew?" I said after a pause, wanting to hear more.

She set the photograph on the doily-covered table. "Wally. Wally Fortney. My sister's boy. He works at the cheese factory."

AT THE CAFÉ in town, drinking weak iced tea and staring at Eden devouring a mound of grease-laden hash browns, I mulled the prospect of tracking down Wally Fortney. It was the middle of the day, twelve-thirty, and he would probably be working. The prospect of a cache of Ray Tantro paintings pulled at me like a drug. I shut my eyes for a moment and saw a room full of dusty canvases, all wondrous and full of light and color and feeling.

I paid the bill and waited for Eden in the overheated car. The Saab had no air-conditioning. It was a rare day that I missed it, but this was one. I rolled down the windows, feeling the sweat begin to roll down my back. Eden emerged, red-eyed. Heading north into the Snake River Canyon again, I realized it was the day for my kayak lesson. I hadn't called Pete to cancel. It had been in the back of my mind yesterday, nagging at me. I had put my wet suit and helmet in the trunk in case I changed my mind. But I was too busy, too preoccupied.

The air cooled. The deep shade of the pine forest gave way to the narrow canyon with steep cliffs to the west. I was resigned to skipping my lesson, although I didn't feel good about it. My nose was still sore though, and my eyes had faded to a pumpkin yellow. I concentrated on the road, winding along above the river, looking for Pete, wondering if he had called the gallery for me.

Eden squealed, pointing out a deer along the riverbank. I glanced to try to see it and had to jerk the car back onto the road.

"What's that sound?" Eden asked.

I listened. A faint bumping, an irregular sound, came and went. "Probably a rock in the hubcap."

I maneuvered the Saab Sister around a rock slide that littered the road with square chunks of debris. Last fall I got a flat tire in just such a slide, the sharp edges of a rock piercing a sidewall. I wanted no further bad tire karma with my new set of rubber.

But after the rock slide the sound came back. Louder. *Ka-thump, ka-thump,* then *rat-a-tat-a-tat,* like a machine gun. It varied, got worse, then better, then terrible.

"God, Alix, what is that?" Eden grabbed the dash. "Don't you want to stop and check it out?"

The shoulder on the right side of the highway was nonexistent. The rocky bank plunged thirty feet down to the river, broken only by a few pine trees and clumps of willows. The road curved and I drove on, listening to the rattle get worse and worse. I slowed the car, but it didn't improve. If anything the sound got louder.

At last a turnout ahead. The line of cars and pickups behind me would be happy. I slowed to pull over. As I did, the car suddenly felt wobbly.

"Oh, God, another flat." The car swerved and jerked as it dropped off the pavement onto the gravel. The steering wheel jumped out of my hands.

Eden was out of the car before I killed the engine, as if it was going to explode. Her hands deep in the pockets of her shorts, she stepped back from the car, frowning at the front right tire.

"There's nothing wrong with it." Eden frowned, baffled.

I knelt next to the wheel. She was right. I felt the treads for nails. The tire was firm, completely inflated. I got the tire iron from the trunk and pried off the hubcap. As it fell forward into my hand, six nuts came with it, rattling against the metal cap.

"Christ. They didn't put it on tight." Even as I said it, though, I knew they had. The boys at the Conoco station where I bought my tires wouldn't have left the lug nuts this loose. If anything they would have put them on so tight that I couldn't change the tire.

I felt the remaining two nuts. One fell off into my hand, leaving one, also loose, holding the wheel on the car. My mind reeled. The desperately steep riverbank, hugging the highway, was a terrible panorama in my mind. I pictured the wheel rolling off, tumbling ahead of the car. Then the Saab crashing onto the axle, sparks flying and turning, turning onto its side and over and over down the bank.

"Look at this." Eden was standing by the rear tire, the hubcap in her hands. She knelt by the wheel and counted. "One, two, three, four gone." She touched the remaining ones as if they were contaminated. "And the rest loose. What tire place did you say it was?"

"It wasn't them." I slapped the tire iron against my palm, its weight reassuring, like Thor's magic hammer.

"What do you mean?"

"Somebody loosened them."

Eden squinted at me, then at the wheel. "But why?"

I knelt by the front tire and began replacing the nuts. My hand trembled. Why had someone tried to kill me? That was the question Eden hadn't finished. Articulating it in my mind made it more real suddenly. My stomach tightened, and I sat hard on the gravel and tried to concentrate.

I moved to the rear wheel, taking two of the front lug nuts to hold it on until we got to town. What was I doing that would make someone try to kill me? I racked my brain for my faults, my curiosities, my deviant behaviors, and came up with a fairly substantial list. But only one thing made sense. Over the last week it had become my obsession, my morbid infatuation. And this attempt on my life made it all the clearer, my purpose sharpened and refined until it sparkled in the high mountain sun.

Ray Tantro. His life and death had come to define, for me, the hazards of a life in art, a life devoted to beauty but doomed to personal tragedy. The contradictions and foibles of the sensitive soul. Was it possible to contribute to the greater glory of mankind through art and still be a whole human being? I had to know. This was Ray Tantro's secret. A secret someone didn't want me to find out.

EIGHT

UNDER THE steady gaze of the rocky crags of Teewinot and the frying-pan glacier of Mount Owen, back from the dirt road, behind a grove of aspens and over a small bridge sat the small log cabin. The sky glowed with summer heat, a red-tailed hawk circling on the thermals. In the yard, grown long with blue harebells and white yarrow, granite boulders and barn-siding birdhouses faded in the dappled sunlight.

Down the dirt road the almost nonexistent community of Moose, Wyoming, just inside Grand Teton National Park, hummed with summer traffic. A restaurant, a climbing-gear shop, a general store, and king-sized parking lot surrounding tepees where tourists ate barbecue sandwiches—this was Moose. Above the Douglas firs and lodgepole pines you could see the tops of the mountains, scraped by recalcitrant snow and glittering gray against the cloudless sky. They looked distant today, unfriendly. As many times as I saw the Tetons, they never looked the same. The weather, or the glaciers, or the light was different, transforming the elegant upthrusts of granite from moment to moment like natural magicians.

The cabin belonged to Ray Tantro, at least until last week. As I parked the car and walked up the drive under the cooling shade of the aspens, the scene made me stop. This was the cabin of my dreams. Secluded, private, shaded but sunny, hell, it even had a creek, something my fantasy hadn't conjured but that fit right in. It looked like my uncle Lars's cabin in the Crazy Mountains, where as a child I went every summer with my cousins and played dominoes and crazy eights and made pearly everlastings into necklaces. Ray, wherever he was, must be missing this cabin, these flowers, the breeze, the smell of sage. Not to mention his mother's kiss, good sex, and eggs over easy.

I stood still, trying to feel Ray's spirit. Would he remain here, was there unfinished business that caused his creative energy to hover, dissatisfied, unable to rest? I strained to feel him, to use my instincts, but again they failed me.

The air rippled with heat. The yard around the log cabin was dry and lifeless, the grass burned yellow and flowers dead. Ray hadn't been much of a yardman. The house, made from peeled pine logs, was small, twenty feet wide and fifteen deep, with a green metal roof glinting with sun. The window trim had once been green too but had disintegrated in the intense mountain sun.

After getting extra lug nuts from the Conoco guys (who were appalled at my story and scurried about guiltily) and dropping off Eden at the gallery, it was close to three before I was out of Jackson again. The traffic was getting worse as the weather got warmer. It was approaching what I considered the best week of the summer—weatherwise if not stresswise. The first week of August, a time when you didn't have to put on your down parka in the evening. Somehow the tourists had heard about my weather prediction and come in droves.

I hadn't expected to find that the police had sealed off the cabin for evidence, since the death was officially a suicide. Besides, it hadn't taken place here. I was right. The cabin looked as if Ray had gone into town for a six-pack and was expected back shortly. I circled the house, looking for anything that might tell me something about Ray. In the back a long metal chain was wrapped around a tree and stretched straight into the matted grass. A large plastic bowl sat under the tree and evidence of the canine variety was everywhere. It was all I could do to avoid stepping in the dog shit.

Where was Ray's dog? I turned toward the house, hoping the animal hadn't been left inside. The back door was scratched and chipped by what looked like clawing. A well-used red woven leash hung from the knob. A ratty curtain covered the door's window on the inside. I tried the knob and the door swung open.

In rural America people still don't lock their doors. Especially if they're not home and there's not a rapist or axe murderer on the loose. Ray had no reason to fear burglars. He probably owned nothing of value. As I stepped inside and looked around the dim, dirty interior of the cabin, that much was obvious.

Idyllic setting aside, this place was a dump. The cracked linoleum on the kitchen floor was covered with muddy tracks. A small sink overflowed with dirty dishes, and the cupboard doors hung open, revealing blackened fruit and empty cereal boxes. Junk mail and advertising flyers, a couple of last week's newspapers, and a postcard post-marked Las Vegas lay scattered on the kitchen table. I read the card quickly:

Hi. Laid up here with nothing but TV. Don't know no-body. Nurses are cute—esp. Tonya! WOW! Feel like shit. Coming this way? G.

I tucked the postcard into my pants and tiptoed out of the kitchen that smelled like onions, fungus, and beer.

The living room was furnished in early Salvation Army. An old burnt orange sofa was covered with yellow dog hairs and fronted by a wobbly metal TV tray on which sat three Pabst Blue Ribbon beer bottles and an empty bag of Chee-tos. On the floor more dead soldiers lay on dirt-colored shag carpeting. An old television set with a rabbit-ear antenna was propped up on a fruit crate on the other side of the room.

No paintings graced the log walls. They were bare but for an auto-shop calendar in the kitchen. The place had an ex-pectant staleness. It waited for the master to return, to come back with another six-pack, to clear his mind, to find a meaning in the chaos.

A strong Scandinavian urge to hose down the place grabbed me. I fought it off and moved on. A door led to two small bedrooms and a bath. I went into the bathroom first, looking for anything that looked personal. Instead I found Ray had run out of toilet paper and Comet. His medicine cabinet was cleaned out. Not even a toothbrush remained.

In the back bedroom a single mattress on a Hollywood frame was covered with two old wool blankets, a rumpled white sheet, and a bare pillow. The dresser was wood-grain vinyl. I pulled open the drawers carefully and looked under a couple of pairs of jeans, a mangle of T-shirts and socks, and worn boxer shorts. More of the same sat in a pile in the corner, waiting for laundry day. The closet held cowboy boots, Ray's most extensive wardrobe item, some eight pairs in various states of disrepair. A jean jacket, a couple hats on the shelf. A spare life, depressing in its dullness.

The front bedroom was Ray's studio. North and west light streamed in through the windows, making it bright and giving the artist a view of the Tetons proud in the distance. On the floor Ray had thrown a huge olive tarp held down at the corners with bowling-ball-size rocks. In the middle was a heavy wood easel, a card table on which paints and brushes sat in an untidy heap, and a small wooden stool. On the easel a heavy green drape covered a canvas.

I stood in the doorway, my heart pounding. This was the artist's sanctum, his place of imagination, the heart of his soul. Here Ray exercised his talent, searched his subconscious. I had been inside dozens of artists' studios, including Martin Ditolla's, and never gotten the charge I felt at the door to Ray's studio. He was alive in here yet. He would be alive in his paintings forever.

I stepped inside the room. The tarp crunched, an awkward arrangement over the carpeting. It was matted down in the center and in a path to the door. The folding card table full of supplies caught my eye, the mashed tubes of paint, the smeary palette still full of puddles of tints. I picked up a big brush, over an inch across with a long, batonlike handle. It had a hefty feel to it, substantial. I waved it around experimentally and set it down. I stared harder at the table. All the brushes had color on them, paint dried on the bristles. Most artists are compulsive about cleaning their brushes, caressing them with paint thinner until the bristles are spotless. There were close to twenty brushes of all sizes, all ruined with hardened oil paint. Ray was awfully careless with his supplies. But then, he wouldn't be using these brushes again.

I lifted the drape off the easel carefully. The hope of finding a masterpiece in an unlikely place was the curse of the art dealer; a surge of anticipation charged through me. This could be it, the moment that changed my life, that made my reputation, that set me for life. As I threw the heavy cloth back to reveal the canvas, my heart sunk. Blank, completely empty, untouched by the hand of the artist.

Blank as Ray Tantro's last twenty years.

I MADE two phone calls at Dornan's before checking my lug nuts and heading back into town. With the best hamburger in a basket and best view in America, Dornan's is Moose's restaurant, an unimposing ranch-style place attached to the wineshop and general store. An old-fashioned back bar is its main attraction—that and the incomparable view of the incomparable Tetons. I didn't come out here enough, I thought, walking through the airy dining room to the pay phone in the back. A couple of cowboy types sat at the bar, sipping beer.

High Mountain Veterinary served as the county animal shelter on the side. The woman who answered had the warm voice of an animal lover.

"I'm curious about a dog that may be up for adoption. It belonged to Ray Tantro, the man who died in the fire last week," I said.

"Oh, yes, how sad that was," the woman replied. "He brought the dog in early in the week. Monday, I think. I guess he planned to do it then." She gave a shuddering noise. "The poor thing acts like it knows. Always whining. Such a sweet dog."

"Has anyone been in to claim him?"

"Not a soul. We talked to Chief Frye about it and he didn't really know what to do."

"Can I put my name in, then? I can't get him—oh, what's his name?"

"She's a she. Saffron. 'Cause she's a yellow lab, I guess. He called her Ronnie. God, I'm getting all choked up now."

I let her blow her nose, then continued. "I can't pick her up right away. And there's still a possibility somebody might claim her." I gave her my name and phone number and told her to call me if anybody came in to claim Saffron.

My next call was to Margaret Elliot, the county coroner. She was reluctant to speak to me, but finally, with effort, I made an appointment to see her at home that evening.

Out in the parking lot the sun seared the dull eggplant paint on the Saab Sister. A swarm of biting flies hovered over two kids drawing with a stick in the dirt. The air smelled of pine and clover and sage. I tipped my face to the sun and made a promise to myself to enjoy summer. It wouldn't last forever. It would disappear, replaced by a familiar chill that colored the aspens golden and brought a violent end to the burst of flowers with a hammer of frost. I opened the door of the Saab and got in. Summer would have to wait.

EVEN THE FACT that someone had illegally parked in my private alley parking spot, causing me to drive around for fifteen minutes to find somewhere reasonably close to the

gallery and triggering a summer-afternoon craving for a gin
and tonic—even all that couldn't quash the feeling, the
hunch that had formed in my mind on my drive back from
Moose. All I had to do was prove it.

I bounded up the four worn wooden steps into the Second Sun. Preoccupied, I hadn't looked in the windows or I
might have circled the block and gone up the back stairs as
usual. Inside the air was warm with laughter and salsa. Two
groups of tourists roamed the left side of the gallery, their
heads together. On the other side Paolo was dumping a huge
bag of tortilla chips into a wooden bowl next to Eden.
Wearing a blue work shirt that belonged to me, she drank
something cool and talked to a dark-haired man with his
back to me. Looking at the art on the walls was Martin Ditolla in his wheelchair chatting with another local artist,
Jacob Laughlin.

My running shoes made my approach next to silent; I was
grateful. Maybe I could escape this impromptu party and
collapse upstairs by myself. I had to think, my mind seemed
to be exploding with half-formed ideas. I patted Martin on
the arm as I passed. He smiled up to me.

"There she is! Alix is here, everybody." Martin's voice
boomed around the hard surfaces of the gallery. Even the
tourists turned for an instant to recognize my arrival. Martin's sandy-gone-gray hair was pulled into a ponytail above
his blond beard. He looked healthy and tanned. Jacob sa-
luted me with his drink.

I stopped midstep. Maybe a drink wouldn't hurt. I was so
jacked up from this day. From out of nowhere I could hear
the lug nuts again, falling into the hubcap. With the perspective of a half-dozen hours the incident seemed clearer,
the intent obvious and menacing. The scene on the road
changed in my head. The Saab teetered on the edge of the
asphalt, then plunged off, tumbling, crashing toward the
Snake River below. Inside I was a Ping-Pong ball. A cold
sweat climbed up my back.

"Alix, my dear," Jacob said. "How is the tourist trade treating you?"

Like a dead skunk in the middle of the road. I smiled at Laughlin. "Peachy, Jake. And you?"

The man talking to Eden was now looking at me. All right, a drink, a few chips. It wouldn't kill me. My throat was on fire anyway. Martin had a club soda in his hand, balancing it on his knee.

"How about a drink, Alix?"

I jerked my head. The voice, God! It was Carl. His clipped, police-duty haircut was grown out and he'd grown a mustache, a rather nice one. His tanned face crinkled into a smile. "You look surprised."

Eden and Paolo had smirks on their faces. "I—I'd love a drink," I said, hoping to regain my composure. "What are you having?"

"Gin, vodka, tonic, soda, limes, or any combination," Paolo said, glancing at his desk, which had been transformed into Party Central. He looked over his shoulder at the customers. "Carl, can you do it? I've got some work to do." He stepped away. We could hear his broad conversation with a couple admiring a print of the Tetons.

"Um. Gin and tonic, okay?" I ran my hand through my hair, suddenly aware of the grease still on my fingers from the tire work and the rank smell wafting from my armpits. "I've got to put my backpack down. I'll be back in a second."

In the tiny bathroom I dug out a brush and tried to do something with my hair. Pushing it behind my ears and trimming my bangs once a month was the extent of its pampering. At least I had a little color in my cheeks. Probably from blushing at the sight of Carl. Had I forgotten he was arriving today? Had I missed a message? I tried to remember when I'd looked at notes on my desk. I found an old peach lipstick in the bottom of my backpack and tried to apply it to my cracked lips. I got most of the grease off my hands after three washings. Dirt and grease clung to my jeans, and ugly sweat stains darkened my short-sleeved plaid shirt. I splashed water on my chest, feeling it run down my invisible cleavage. No wonder old lady Tantro hadn't opened up to me; I looked like a bum.

Eden, Martin, and Jacob had moved to the front of the gallery, where two of Martin's pieces were prominently displayed. I still hadn't talked to Martin about the prints. He was probably under the assumption we were still dance partners in the great ballroom of fame and fortune. I hated the thought of telling him the whole thing was off. Well, I'd been doing a great job avoiding it so far. I didn't know what Jacob Laughlin thought he was doing here. He came around now and again to try to get us to show his elk-bugling stuff, but we always told him no. He looked sunburned today, his round jowls soft as he downed his drink.

Carl handed me the drink, the glass sweating and bobbing with a lime. He pulled me closer, giving me a small kiss on the lips. "It's good to see you. I wish I could say you look the same."

I took a sip. The gin charged through me. "I'm sorry, I... Did you call?"

"Three days ago. Didn't you get the message?"

I shook my head. "I mean, I knew you were coming. I've just been busy."

"Did you have your lesson today?"

"Lesson?" *Yes, by God, I learned a lesson today. Check your lug nuts before driving.*

"Kayaking." Carl examined my face, his eyebrows together. "Last week didn't scare you off, did it?"

"No, no. I've just been too busy. I had planned on going today, but Eden was with me then..." I stopped, toying with the idea of telling him about the near-disaster and wondering how much I would have to explain. "Have you ever heard of lug nuts spontaneously loosening themselves?"

Carl frowned, deeper than before but not enough to mar the golden tan of his face. He was wearing exceptionally far-out clothes for him, baggy, knee-length shorts and rafting sandals and a T-shirt that read "A River Runs Through Me." He looked—dare I say it? He looked kind of groovy—for a cop.

"You're looking healthy," I said, giving him an approving smile.

He reached out and took my chin in his hand, tipping it up toward the lights. "You didn't tell me about this."

I pulled away. "What? You can hardly tell anymore." I touched my eyes self-consciously. The yellow and green had almost faded. Or I was just getting used to it.

"Looks pretty crooked to me. When are you getting it fixed?"

My hand flew to my nose. "Fixed?"

"The zigzag. I had one like that once. A drug bust that didn't go quite the way it was planned. It hurt like hell."

"Is it that bad?"

Carl shrugged. "Didn't you notice?"

I opened my mouth to explain my mirror time has been pretty limited when Eden grabbed my elbow, bumping me so that I almost splashed my drink down my shirt. "She has been soooo wonderful to me. I bet she didn't tell you that, did she? Well, she has." She gave Carl a drunken grin and slipped her arm through mine. "We have some kind of weird cosmic destiny, us two. Don't we, Alix? Like those Norse gods, we're headed across the rainbow bridge on a grand adventure together."

Carl and I stared at her, swaying with her drink held high in a one-woman toast.

"You've been reading too many 'Mighty Thors,' Eden," I mumbled. What the hell was she talking about? I forgot all about my nose. Eden had that effect on me. I forgot about everything else but her problems. Weird cosmic what? Oh, shit. Where was Paolo?

I saw my partner talking to another couple with surfer hair and Day-Glo hiking boots about some local pottery. Californicators, no doubt. For a moment I had an urge to march over there, take Paolo by the ear, and tell him what I thought of his mouth. He must have told Eden about selling his share of the gallery. He had told her she could be my partner. Then Eden pried her hand off my arm and staggered away. Carl was looking at my nose again, and my lips. I felt my anger dampened by gin and fatigue and the immediate presence of Carl Mendez.

"Listen, can we get out of here?" Carl finished off his drink and looked at mine like he wished it were empty. "You want to get something to eat?"

CARL WAITED for me while I showered, blew-dry my hair, and changed into clean pants and a low-necked silk blouse that I had been saving for him. I even put on mascara to take his eyes off my schnoz. I stuck Ray's postcard on my dresser mirror before throwing the jeans into the laundry basket. By that time it was seven o'clock. Carl helped me on with my dad's old hunting jacket, my favorite comfort. He seized the opportunity to nuzzle my neck, then turned me around for a real kiss.

"God, I missed you," he said. He touched his nose to mine, rabbitlike, which caused me to jump back in pain.

"Ow! Shit." I held my nose, feeling the crook at the bridge and surveying the damage.

"You've got to get that fixed," he said. "I bet you can't even breathe out of that one side."

"I have developed quite a snore." I grinned, the pain receding. "You may want to sleep in another room."

He pulled my hand. "I can stand a little snore."

I looked at my watch, then the door. "Can we eat kind of fast? I have..." He frowned. "I'm sorry. I made this appointment for eight."

He walked abruptly to the window. "We don't have to do this."

I watched his tense back, silhouetted against the glass. "Dinner, you mean?"

He sighed and turned around. "This visit, vacation. I can tell you weren't expecting me." He glanced at the pile of blankets on the couch.

"Eden is staying here, but it's temporary. She had nowhere else to go." The double bed in my room was the only place for him. I guess I had made up my mind on Carl for the evening. It would be nice to lie next to his warm body again. But somehow the fatigue and anxiety in my brain wouldn't let me grasp the anticipation. Where was the electricity of last summer? My mind reeled with the events of the last week that I hadn't told him. Where would I start? The prospect of it tired me more. "The appointment shouldn't last too long. I have a lot of things to tell you."

He came toward me, moving slowly in his own fluid way. "I have a few things to tell you too."

I held out my hand. "Come on, I'm starving."

BY NINE O'CLOCK the streets of Jackson crawled with tourists, streaming into and out of bars and restaurants, shopping bags on their wrists, sandals and hiking boots and cowboy boots on their feet. The glitter on their new shirts caught the streetlights as the sky turned purple. Carl and I fell into step silently, dodging shoulders and children lost in the murky shadows of the crowds. We walked with hands in pockets, heads down, thoughts of the coroner's meeting pounding against our skulls.

Carl had read the autopsy report four or five times, memorizing it while I questioned Margaret Elliot. She lived in a small upstairs apartment in an old house near the playground, an apartment filled with old-lady things like her spoon collection and china poodles from all over the world. Margaret didn't seem old, but her collections dated her. I made small talk about poodles and spoons, telling her I was a collector too. There is a bond, an understanding of the irrationality of possession, between collectors.

As we talked, not necessarily about Ray Tantro, I watched Margaret. She had been pretty once and still took care of herself, even though she had the blocky backside of a desk dweller. Tonight she wore a silver nylon jogging suit that looked brand-new. It matched her hair in an uncanny way that made you thankful for that slash of pink lipstick on her mouth. Her bridge glasses, tinted lavender, added color.

She was opening a case to show me a china dog when I noticed we were the same height. I guess it wouldn't have been unusual, but it struck me like a blow to the back of the head that we were not that different. Single, living alone, professional women. My first reaction was to reject that. I was not like Margaret Elliot. I would not grow old alone. I would not wear bridge glasses. I would not crochet.

But stoics are strong believers in fate. The trade winds took the Vikings wherever they blew. I could learn to collect spoons. I could start perming my hair and go on bus trips to Las Vegas. Yeah, right. And pigs could fly.

All these thoughts, and the lack of a breakthrough from the autopsy report, led to a mild depression as Carl and I walked through the crowds back to my apartment. He told me he thought the autopsy results were conclusive, from a law enforcement point of view. Tantro had died from his drug and alcohol binge. The fires were just a coincidence.

"Do you want to go get a drink or something?" I said, pausing at the corner of the square. The night sky was a melted velvet color, soft and high. Wood smoke hung tangy and motionless in the air. A rangy cowboy with his tiny girlfriend wrapped under his arm laughed as he fell off the boardwalk into the street. She reached down, took off her high heels, and he swept her up into his arms.

"I gotcha, darlin'!" he said as her hair fell in a curly blond waterfall. Her laugh filled the air. "I won't let the crocodiles bite yer ankles!"

Carl took my hand. His was warm, despite the chill in the air. He backed me against the pillar of the overhang next to a sportswear store on the corner, pressing close. I felt my breath catch in my throat. "I'd rather go back to your place," he said.

He smelled like aftershave and wine. With a fingertip I touched his short, dark mustache that hid flavors of oregano and pepper. He was a handsome man, there was no denying that. But he'd changed since last summer, and there was a year under my belt as well. I couldn't say, if anyone asked, how badly I needed him. How badly I wanted him.

Over Carl's shoulder I watched the cowboy weave his way through the crowd and under the antler arch on the corner of the square. The girl kicked her bare feet, her tight dress inching toward her crotch as passing tourists' eyes bulged and they whispered behind their hands.

"Tell me again," I said.

"What?"

"The basic stuff about him. From the report."

Carl sighed and stepped away. "Okay. Male, Caucasian, between thirty and fifty years old, weight approximately one fifty, height five foot eight, old fractures in right femur, left tibia, clavicle, and left thumb, enlarged liver, poor dental health . . ."

"Wait. How tall are you?"

"Five eleven. Why?"

I grabbed his hand. "Come on."

I unlocked the gallery and picked up the phone at my desk, rifling through the phone book. I found Esther Tantro's number, looked at my watch, and dialed. After four rings she answered, a wary voice.

"Mrs. Tantro, this is Alix Thorssen. I talked to you this morning about Ray's paintings." She murmured. "I was thinking about that picture of Ray you showed me. The basketball squad? What position did Ray play? I'm just curious.''

"Position? I—I..."

"Like forward, guard, center? Was he the center, Mrs. Tantro?''

"Let me think. I believe so. Isn't that where the tallest boy plays? He was tall by then. Some of the other boys passed him by later. But then he was the tallest.''

"I remember that in the picture. How tall was he?'' I held my breath.

She sighed. "I'll never forget the day he passed six feet. He was fifteen. Couldn't even drive yet and don't think he didn't point that out. Used to be the best apple picker we had. So tall, with those long arms.''

She rambled but I only half listened. Six feet tall. Ray was six feet tall, or more. Not five eight like the burned corpse. I tried to sound sorry about his death again and hung up. Carl stood in the doorway to my office, arms folded.

"He was six foot. At least.'' I spun, grinning.

Carl frowned. "So. It wasn't him. Who's the crisp?''

My heart was pounding, and I had a strong urge to put my arms around Carl to celebrate. I gave in, pulling him close. I squeezed his chest and let out a little squeal of delight. Ray Tantro was still alive! He hadn't died in the fire at Timberwolf Arts. He could still talk and paint and tell me the secrets of the magic profession of light and illusion.

Carl kissed me. I remembered last summer, when his lips tasted like honey. For a moment Ray Tantro receded as Carl's mustache tickled my upper lip. Then I pushed out of his arms and spun around. Grinning, I turned back and held out my hands. Carl took them and pulled me in. "The question is . . . Where is Ray Tantro?''

NINE

CHARLIE FRYE, in all honesty, was not a bad person. A Republican with a crew cut is not necessarily bad. Not at all. Frye had grown up on a ranch in Idaho, just over the Tetons, grew potatoes with his father and grandfather, then spent his entire adult life selling auto, home, and life insurance to good old boys like himself here in Jackson Hole.

He and his friends were the hidden people of Jackson. They sold feed, fixed axles, wired family rooms, wrangled a horse of two, and generally stayed out of the tourist business. They were normal, everyday people, hardworking and not particularly ambitious. They weren't interested in skiing or eating gourmet food. They wanted a good life and believed they had found a piece of it here in paradise. They put up with the rest of us because they had to.

Frye's office in the town hall faced north. The room was grim and stale with the venetian blinds half closed. Someone had run their fingers across the slats, emphasizing the filth. The morning was dull and cold, not like August is supposed to be. I tried not to smell the banana peel in the wastebasket. It was too early in the day to gag.

I stood in front of Charlie's desk and crossed my arms. "Ray Tantro is still alive."

Charlie sipped his coffee, amused. "You see him, did you?"

"The man in the fire was five eight," I said, laying my hands on the piles on his desk. The police chief responded by grabbing his plastic coffee mug and sitting back in his chair. "Tantro was—*is*—at least six feet tall. His mother confirmed that."

Charlie Frye smiled, slyly. "She just offered that up, huh? Little Ray was six feet tall?"

"I asked her."

Charlie was casual today in a frayed, blue-and-white plaid cotton western shirt with pearl buttons, turquoise string tie, and polyester jeans. "Isn't this a little out of your line?" he said between gulps of coffee.

"You hired me to appraise his paintings," I said. "That involves doing a bio on the artist. I spoke to his mother to try to get more information."

"And she spontaneously offered that her son was six feet tall? What, pray tell, does that have to do with his paintings?"

"Did you ask her?"

Frye slammed his mug down on the desk, sloshing the last drops onto a sheaf of forms. "Don't push me, girl. We got trained detectives on this case—"

"Like Gary Hayden? What's he trained in? Shoe shining? You said yourself your men were more interested in jaywalking. Come on, Charlie."

Frye was standing behind the desk, turning purple.

"Charlie, please. Look at the autopsy," I pleaded. "The man in the Timberwolf was only five eight."

His brush of gray hair had been recently mowed, revealing a white scar near his left temple that had begun to glow like a headlight. The pulse in his temple throbbed, nearly audible. With concerted effort, mostly in his neck, his violet shade receded, ending at his fingertips with a quiver.

He took a shallow breath. "So you said. And the so-called *real* Ray Tantro was a fucking skyscraper." He leaned forward menacingly. I stepped back before we could crack heads. "Now. You got the appraisal finished?"

Jesus God, the man was impossible. With his tantrum checked, I felt my temperature rising. I clenched my fists and made myself look through the venetian blinds at the bicycles and tubs of flowers and grayness that had cloaked the town in the night. The first day of August and the weather should be great. The bleakness wasn't much better looking than Charlie Frye.

My hands shook. I stuffed them in my pockets. "I'm working on it. That's how I found this out. Talk to Mrs. Tantro."

"I have. She identified him. She had him goddamned cremated. You want me to tell her that, maybe, just maybe, they shake-and-baked the wrong guy? That some artsy-fartsy says, Oops, you fried the wrong guy? *Wait a sec,* your loving son may still be walking and talking?"

He stepped out from behind his desk, staring at a group of certificates on the wall proclaiming him president of Kiwanis 1985, Good Citizen of the Year 1989, Rotarian Extraordinaire.

He turned to me with a Father Knows Best look. "Let the guy go, Alix. He's dead."

I stared at him, unwilling to engage in the comment *artsy-fartsy.* I thought I knew Charlie Frye. When I'd worked for him at the insurance agency he'd never been more than a redneck good ol' boy, greasing the way for the flow of money, or, if he smelled a rat, turning off the spigots. But this was different. "He's not dead. Don't you see, Charlie? He's alive. Somebody else died in that fire."

Frye squinted, his bushy eyebrows wiggling. He crossed his arms and squinted at me. "You want to know what I see? I see a private citizen with a bee in her little bonnet, trying to stir up the hive. Go back to your artsy friends, your little art gallery, those rich fags and hippies." He walked back behind his desk and sat down, swiveling royally. "This is big-league stuff. Let the boys handle it."

I felt my color rising. My throat swelled with emotion. *"The boys?"*

Frye reached over and patted my hand. "And brush your hair while you're at it. You're much prettier when you brush your hair." He picked up a form from a pile on his desk and began to read.

My breath was shallow and tight. My ears pounded. I shut my eyes tight for a second, trying to stay in control. Think, girl, think. His words swirled in my head instead: *You're prettier... brush your hair.* I'd owned my own business so long that this kind of dismissive chauvinism hit me like a bitter wind in August.

"Charlie Frye, I'm going to say it one more time," I said just above a whisper, the only way I could talk at all. My shoulders were hunched, tight, and I felt like I could explode. "The man in the fire was not Ray Tantro. You made a mistake. Ray Tantro is still alive. If you choose not to acknowledge that mistake, it'll be on your head."

Frye folded his hands together. His supercilious calm repulsed me. "His relatives identified him. We had an inquest. It's over. Everyone is satisfied."

"Everyone but me." My voice was low, and if it hadn't been wavering it would have been hard. It rose suddenly as I spit out my last bullet: "Is it because of Buck Boyle? The election? Is that why you won't investigate?"

Charlie's left eye twitched. A snarl entered his voice, something far from Good Citizen of the Year. His eyes burned at me. "I'm going to forget you said that. And you can forget the fucking appraisal. I got work to do."

IT WASN'T YET eight-thirty in the morning when I left the town hall. To control my anger I had to do *something,* so I drank a double espresso straight up at the coffee bar down the block. When I stepped back outside into the mist that *obscured the mountains, I felt like a rocket ready to take off.*

I hadn't slept much last night. Eden and Paolo invited themselves upstairs to continue the gallery party in my apartment. In my excitement, I didn't care. I sat in a corner, wrestling with theories. The others treated me like a potted plant. Even Carl gave up on me and got happy on the chardonnay, falling dead asleep on my bed at eleven. When I finally collapsed onto the bed, I felt nothing but a warm presence. My mind reeled and spun all night.

In the apartment now Carl had made coffee and looked mildly hungover. Glasses, wine bottles, and pizza boxes littered the coffee table and counter while Eden snored, face-down on the sofa. Her blankets had slid to the floor, revealing short sun-tanned legs and cotton underwear with holes. Carl was getting a good look at her left cheek. I covered her up.

"Where'd you go?" Carl poured himself coffee.

"Police chief. The asshole." I flopped down in a chair. "He won't investigate. Says I should let the boys handle it."

"Ooh, bad move, chiefie." Carl grinned at my scowl. His black hair was wild this morning. He wore my old yellow chenille robe. As he turned to look in the refrigerator for milk for his coffee, the fabric split up the back in a loud crack. I laid my head down on my arms at the table, trying to think.

"Hardly likely, eh?" Carl said, setting a coffee mug in front of me. It was the last thing I needed after the espresso, but I wrapped my hands around it anyway, the warmth reassuring.

"Hmm?"

"I said," Carl repeated, sitting at the round oak table, "it's hardly likely you'll let it go."

"Would you?"

Carl shook his head. "I just take orders. Either I'm on the case or I forget about it."

I straightened up. "Well, I can't forget about it. Somebody died in that fire. I want to know who. You asked the question last night yourself—who's the crisp? It was made to look like Ray Tantro, which leads me to the conclusion that the man didn't die willingly. You know he didn't drink and shoot up downers on his own accord. But even more, I have to know what happened to Ray Tantro. It's like I know him somehow. Like I am him.''

Carl frowned and excused himself to the bathroom. I guess I was a little too much to take this early in the morning. The sun worked its way through the fog, a traveling rectangle of blue light from the east window. It hit Eden's bare foot sticking out the end of the blankets.

Carl didn't understand. What was Ray Tantro to me? I felt so strongly about him, but why? I had tried to become an artist. From being the best artist in my high school class I had studied under a strict, belittling taskmaster at St. Olaf's. That art professor hadn't seen in me whatever it was the high school teacher had. He rode me constantly, criticizing everything, praising nothing. When I decided not to go back to St. Olaf's it was the biggest relief of my life. Also, I thought later, the biggest failure. Maybe I should have stuck with it. Maybe that professor was some kind of test I had failed.

I was never the equal of the early Ray Tantro, but still I felt communion with him in the force of our mutual failures. I had moved on, successfully I'd like to think—although lately, with the gallery problems that's a question. Tantro had crashed and burned, unable to repeat the genius, unable to handle the pressure of fame, unable to remake his life into whatever he wanted it to be.

Last night I had stared at my little painting by Tantro, looking for answers in the magenta patches of snow and in the sagebrush shadows. There was a violent beauty in Ray Tantro's painting, a lushness that threatened to explode. The edginess of his painting gave it its power. Now, in the blinding glare of hindsight, it also predicted his demise.

What had happened to him? Where was he? The words Charlie Frye had dismissed me with only hardened my resolve. I would not quit. I would not fail.

I would find Ray Tantro.

I LEFT CARL to his own devices. He wanted me to beg off work today, but I was too charged up to relax. Besides, I had promised Paolo I would talk to Martin Ditolla about the paintings and hadn't yet. So I gave Carl a street map, a Grand Teton National Park map, and directions to the canyon if he wanted to watch the kayakers do the white water. He was on his way to the shower when I made my way down the back stairs to the gallery.

I put in a call to Rex Scanlon first. The fire investigator sounded tired again.

"Rex, I'm not sure why I'm asking you this, but have you done an insurance check on the beneficiaries of Ray Tantro?" I asked, fiddling with a pencil.

Rex sighed. "We put all that to bed. You have to know?"

"If it's not too much trouble." I waited while he went through files and returned.

"Yeah, it was done. Let's see," he said. "He had a life insurance policy. Beneficiary was the mother, Esther. Just the one."

"Did it pay?"

"Hard to say. That's not my bailiwick. Sometimes they don't pay for suicide. But it had been more than six months since the policy was taken out. That's usually the cutoff, if there is one."

"Was it a local insurer?"

"Umm, let's see. Looks like it was taken out in Cheyenne at the headquarters of Financial Life Insurance."

"Any other policies?"

"Well, the two the gallery owner took. One on the building itself, and that special one on the art show."

"Those haven't paid."

"From the looks of it, they probably won't."

I paused, thinking of Eden upstairs. "So it definitely was arson."

"Incendiary liquids everywhere."

"Yeah. Thanks, Rex."

I hung up the phone. There was nothing unusual about Ray taking out a life insurance policy. I put in a call to Financial Life Insurance anyway and reached an agent named Kathy. I introduced myself as a creditor who was checking out Esther's finances.

"I understand Mrs. Tantro received a sizable payout on her son's insurance policy after his death," I said.

Kathy was friendly but not forthcoming. She refused to discuss it. A few other angles failed miserably and I hung up. Then I called my friend Maggie Barlow, who owned a small insurance agency here in Jackson. I explained the situation and she said she'd see what she could find out.

Next I began the herculean task of working through the messages that Paolo had scribbled on a pad of paper. His messages were notoriously cryptic, often requiring a Spanish translation. Phone numbers were the worst. I found the one from Carl, dated four days ago and barely legible, and tossed it. The rest went into two piles: readable, and Call Army Intelligence.

The phone rang. I picked it up, its cackling jangling my caffeinated nerves.

"Miss Thorssen, this is Sandy at High Country Vet. We talked about the yellow lab. Saffron?"

I held my breath. "Yes?"

"I'm sorry. She was picked up last night."

"She was? By who?" I heard the pointedness in my voice and coughed to cover it. "Ah... One of the relatives got her, then?"

"What a sweet dog. We have some other ones down here, available for adoption. Do you want me to get the list?" Sandy said. A bell jangled in the vet's busy office. A Wyomingite without a dog? Shoot him at sunrise.

"Oh, I guess not. You don't know who adopted her, do you? I might know them. Maybe I could, um, visit her sometime?"

"It was just before closing last night. I guess I could find out from the kennel attendant."

"Would you?"

Sandy set down the phone. A long minute later she was back. "Sorry, the girl's new here. This is so embarrassing." She laughed nervously, lowering her voice. "I hope she didn't do the wrong thing. She said Mr. Tantro picked up the dog."

"Ray Tantro?" I held my breath.

"That's right. She must have gotten the name wrong. He's dead, right? But the dog knew him, she said, licked him all over the face."

"Of course she did." Ray Tantro was alive. He was here in Jackson. I stood up at my desk, my head light. I heard Carl talking to Paolo in the gallery behind me, far away. I knew it, I knew it. *Ray is alive.*

"She's new. She probably got the name wrong. Maybe it was his father or something? Gosh, I hope this doesn't cause any trouble. People are so, you know, possessive about their pets."

"It's all right, Sandy. Hey, thanks." I hung up and spun around. I made myself walk slowly into the gallery. Carl and Paolo were drinking coffee and waiting for the late-morning lookie-loos to start nosing around. "Carl." I motioned him over to the doorway. "I have to go out to the park. Did you call Pete?"

"Yeah, we've got a date at the river at twelve-thirty," Carl said. "I hope the fog burns off."

"Do you want to come with me? I—" My hands were shaking again, making my voice quiver. Calm down, girl. I took a breath, trying to relax. Damn caffeine.

"What is it?" Carl frowned at me.

"Ray Tantro is back," I said. I felt foolish for an instant. Nobody cared about Tantro the way I did. But Paolo heard the name as he walked to his desk.

"Tantro, you say?" Paolo sat down and put his boots on the desk, leaning back in the chair, lord-of-the-manor style. "What's the story on that guy? First everybody wants to buy his stuff now that he's dead. Then yesterday we got a whole big bunch of calls from people who are being offered paintings by Tantro. Some of our biggest customers, too."

I spun to face him. "Who? Who is being offered paintings?"

Paolo glanced at Carl, hesitating.

"It's all right," I said. "Carl's not in the business. He doesn't care who our customers are."

Paolo continued looking suspiciously at Carl, as if he were to blame for the turmoil around Ray Tantro. As if he would steal our customers and sell them paintings. Carl frowned at me, confused and a little hurt.

Finally Paolo nodded, satisfied Carl wasn't a spy. "Yeah, well, Janet Weinstein called from the City, Junior Orms in Milwaukee, Fred and Gayle from Palm Springs, Patsy Silvers. Even the Metropolitan Museum of Fucking Art!"

"Wait a minute. The Met was offered Tantros? When was this?"

"Yesterday. Day before. Something like that."

"Did they say who was offering them? Was it one gallery?"

Paolo shook his head. "Not a gallery. A relative. Some guy named . . . let me see, I got it." He put his feet down, shuffling scraps of paper on his desk. "Wallace Fortney. That's it. In fact the Met wants you to go take a look at them, see if they're for real. Did you see that message on your desk?" He threw up his hands. "Jeez, all a guy has to do is commit suicide to be popular."

My eyes met Carl's. *Exactly.*

THE LOW CLOUDS over town broke up as we drove to Moose, giving the sky the look of spangled pearls. Puddles of rain-water dotted the dirt road leading to the cabin, past a couple of pseudomansions made of logs that belonged to the president of a sportswear company and a television news personality. The caffeine had worn off, but a tight knot in my gut took its place.

I parked the Saab Sister across the road from Tantro's cabin, half in the ditch. A big white pickup truck, early seventies vintage, dented and rusty, was parked in the driveway. It had 22-county plates, Teton County. Carl gave me a warning look as we approached it. His questioning on the way out still rang in my ears.

"The guy could be a relative, cleaning up Tantro's stuff. Or a friend. Probably Tantro asked the guy to take care of his dog if anything happened to him. Either way they're just doing what has to be done."

"Or it could be Ray Tantro. Come into town to pick up his dog and a few things and disappear," I said.

"Then he's real stupid. Or real desperate." Carl had turned in his seat to watch a herd of antelope in the foothills east of the road. "Either way he's dangerous."

We paused now, near the front fender of the pickup, listening. Birds flocked high in the aspens, out of sight but noisy. Bees hummed in the sweet clover grown tall in the shade. The smell of damp earth and sage was on the breeze. The cabin was still half hidden around the bend in the drive, obscured by trees and the tall grasses. Carl reached through the open window and checked the visor. He pulled out a plastic registration case and examined it.

"What is it?" I whispered. He handed it to me. *Raymond Wayne Tantro, Little Snake Road, Moose, Wyoming,* it said. Issued December, last year. My heart was in my throat. He was here. He'd come back.

Cart put the registration back. As we walked toward the cabin, he kicked a few rocks, making noises to announce us. On cue, a dog began to bark. When Saffron didn't make an appearance, I waved Carl on. At the front door I knocked loudly.

The dog continued its yapping from the back of the house. I knocked again. Carl went to the window and cupped his hands around his eyes. I knocked with my whole fist.

"Tantro? Ray?!" I hollered.

Carl looked up. "I don't think he's home. Come on." He went around the cabin to the kitchen window. "Nope. Gone."

"Maybe something happened to him. His dog's here. And his truck." I looked in the bedroom window with the dog stretched long on the chain behind me, barking to wake the dead. The room looked as lifeless as it had before. The bathroom and studio were also empty.

We walked back down the driveway. I paused, looking back at the cabin. It looked softer now in the filtered light through the high clouds than yesterday in the heat. I tried to imagine green grass and zinnias and sunflowers, but all I could feel was a beaten-down spirit, an emptiness.

The truck was a Chevy with wide, flat fenders. I opened the door on the passenger side. A loud metallic creak sounded. Carl put his hand on my arm. "Not a good idea."

"I just want to look," I told him. "I'm not going to take anything." Carl scowled at me, the dutiful policeman.

"I've got an hour to be down at the river."

"Your stuff's in the car. You'll get there." I turned away, staring greedily at the glove box. For Carl's sake I didn't actually get in, just leaned over the seat and opened the compartment.

A tumble of papers fell out, littering the floor. Carl bent to rescue a couple that made it to the ground.

"What's that?" I asked, pawing through gas receipts and worn-out road maps.

"A rodeo program and a coupon for Wendy's." He handed them to me.

"Eden told me she saw him at the rodeo," I said. The program wasn't for a Jackson rodeo but for Frontier Days in Cheyenne. July 22 through 27.

"This is from last week." I showed Carl the dates. "Do you think Ray went to Cheyenne?"

In the distance the whine of an engine broke the stillness. The dog had stopped barking, finally. Carl frowned at the house, then at the dirt road. "Put that stuff away. Let's get out of here."

A FEATHER BOA of vapor wrapped along the Snake River Canyon. We'd driven the Saab Sister through the McDonald's drive-thru window, something I swore on the honor of Thor I would never do but managed at least once a month. Satiated with grease we found the turnoff to the river full of buses, trailers, and vans. People were everywhere, chattering in the wet chill as they readied their life jackets for the white water.

With his arms outstretched over his head, Pete Rotondi was carrying one of the purple kayaks to the river. His red wet suit, all six foot four of it, with paddle jacket and peeling Roman nose, had turned the heads of forty tourists waiting for a raft. Here was how it was really done, their slack jaws seemed to say. They stopped talking as he dropped the boat on the cement ramp next to an identical kayak.

Pete saw me. "Alix, you coming too?"

Carl was changing into his wet suit in the car. I shivered, glad I had worn jeans today instead of shorts. The river looked gray and fast. I wasn't sure if it was the weather or my memories of my last run causing me to shiver.

I rubbed my bare arms. "I'm sorry I stood you up."

He was putting on his helmet. "It was a great run. Lunch Counter was maxed out."

"No kidding." Now I was sure the shiver was relief. "I've been busy with that artist who died in the fire. Ray Tantro." *Or whoever he was.*

Pete nodded. "Eden must be crazed about all that."

"Yeah, you should call her. She could use a shoulder right now. She's staying with me."

Pete looked down the river, his face tanned and flat. "That fire was massive, all right." He brightened and turned to me. "Say, my brother called from New York, said there was a mention about that artist in *The Wall Street Journal.* He said to try to find a painting for him." He laughed derisively. "He doesn't care what it looks like. He's just into investment value."

The Wall Street Journal? No wonder we had all the calls.

Pete pulled on his spray skirt, a rubber circle that fit around his waist and the kayak's opening, unaware of the giggles it provoked in the crowd of onlookers. "I might be interested too. Got any?"

I was startled for a moment, thinking about spray skirts. Pete buying art? He never had before. But he had money, it was just that I thought of him as a local, a ski bum. He never acted like a trust-funder. The word was he got a huge payout when he turned twenty-one, as a tobacco heir or something. Hadn't worked a lick since, unless you count being a ski and kayak instructor when he was in the mood.

"I'll keep an eye out," I said.

Pete nodded, already into the gear at his feet. Carl arrived in a sleeveless, form-fitting black wet suit, his well-toned shoulders bulging like sausage from a casing. I couldn't help smiling, seeing him for the first time in costume. He squinted at me self-consciously.

"What?" He looked down at himself encased in neoprene.

"Nothing." I couldn't stop smiling. I put my arms around his waist and kissed him lightly. "I've got to go."

Carl glanced at Pete, then whispered, "So that means I can't throw you down on the gravel and ravish you?"

"Afraid not." I let him go. "Pete can give you a ride back. Maybe we can have a drink later or something," I offered, then gave him a fanny pat, backed out the Saab Sister, and sprayed gravel.

ON THE DRIVE south to Star Valley the fog made the going slow. An Airstream trailer pulled by a Suburban wound around the tight turns. The canyon was mystical in its shroud, the tops of lodgepole pines disappeared, cloaked in vapor. Wildflowers came and went mysteriously. I tried to put myself inside the mind of Ray Tantro. What would I do if I found out everyone thought I was dead? Would I make a big deal out of announcing that I was still alive? Or would I sneak off into the night?

By Star Valley the ceiling lifted, creating a soft canopy of blue-purple stripes above the tiny collection of buildings. I followed the smell that permeated the town toward the square gray hulk of the cheese factory where Wallace Fortney worked. If Ray was dead, his paintings would be worth more. A lot more. If it was possible to be dead to the world and not in reality dead, an artist could have the best of both worlds.

As I pulled into the gravel parking lot next to the cheese factory, I let a glimmer of hope shoot through me. Joe Crisp had died in Tantro's place. Ray would keep painting, his prices would go through the roof, and he would be a wealthy man. He could start over with a new identity and paint whatever he wanted.

I looked for flaws in the theory while crossing the parking lot to the small entrance in the concrete block wall marked in red letters. The gravel was coarse and sharp. The lot was full of pickup trucks not much different from Ray's.

There had to be flaws. Why would Ray show up at his own house after he was dead? Or had he? His truck and his dog had, but I still had yet to get a gander of Ray. And what part, if any, did Wallace Fortney have in the plan?

TEN

WITH A CLOUD of suspicion on her haggard but dutiful face, the receptionist in the factory front office went looking for Wally Fortney on the floor. To ease matters I had brought along The Suit, my official companion, a blue gabardine blazer and skirt that made me look like a Fed; it had never let me down. I straightened the white T-shirt under the jacket while I waited. Changing in the gas station had been hurried. I wanted to catch Fortney before the end of his shift.

It took ten minutes for him to arrive. The receptionist came back, took up her station at a gray metal desk, and began typing. I sat in a black vinyl chair, staring at a calendar hung as sole decoration on the cement-block walls. In honor of cheese, a thin layer of green mold crept up from the floor. The smell of overgrown bacteria and sour milk hung in the air.

Fortney came through the door, curious and cautious. A once-white uniform smeared with various liquids in shades of yellow and brown hung on this shoulders. A sinewy neck held up a large, bony head with a thin layer of auburn hair. His face was pale, freckled, and rather dull. I stood and put on a professional smile.

"Mr. Fortney," I said, introducing myself. "The Metropolitan Museum of Art has asked me to evaluate the paintings you are offering them. The Tantros?"

The receptionist stopped typing and was doing a bad job of covering her eavesdropping. Fortney blinked three times and nodded. "Ah, sure. I . . . let's see." He twirled to survey the clock on the wall above the door he'd just come through. "I don't get off till three, but the wife's there."

As I hoped. "I could have access to the paintings now?"

"Sure, no problem." Fortney began to rub his hands together. "I'll call her, then as soon as I get off we can . . . ah, talk."

The receptionist was now staring at Fortney, her mouth agape. He turned to her and she started. "Can I use the phone, Beth?" He spoke tensely to his wife and hung up.

"She'll be expecting you. The paintings are out in the garage. Just have her take the tarp off 'em." He rubbed his forehead with long, thin fingers. "I forgot to tell her that."

"I understand the Museum has its pick of the paintings," I said. I wanted to look at them all.

"Well," Fortney sputtered. He was out of his league and knew it. "I offered them three. I think they're the best three. Ray gave 'em to me, you know. He gave me all of 'em. We took care of him lots of times when he was sick, you know." He frowned at Beth, who spun to face the typewriter. "But if you want to have some of the others, I guess it's okay."

I picked up my briefcase and patted him on the arm as I left. "We'll discuss it when you get there."

As I opened the door, desperate for air that didn't smell of cheddar or vinegary mold, he shouted out directions: "Just go down the highway to Cedar, take the first right, we're down one block on the corner. White house."

By some quirk of fate, every house in Star Valley was white. Snow white, dirty white, mozzarella white, Mormon underwear white. There were a few, brave souls who dared paint their siding pink or green, or build a house of brick. But on the corner of First West and Brigham no one was brave enough to buck convention. Four white houses, four corners. I sat in my car for a minute, deliberating. Then I chose the house with the swing set in the front yard clogged with children's toys, reined in by a peeling picket fence.

The brown-haired woman who came to the door looked
expectant in more ways than one. Her tired face had been
recently sparked with fresh lipstick. The thin cotton housedress did not conceal her swollen belly. She introduced herself as Wally's wife, then as Dixie, as she let me into the
house. Three children, stair-steps from about two to five,
stared from a doorway.

"Wally said you're from New York?" Dixie had a breathy
voice that peaked at high octaves.

"Not exactly. I have a gallery in Jackson," I said. "The
Museum sent me down." I smiled at the kids, the warm odor
of freshly baked cookies coming off them. They were
dressed in faded but clean shorts and T-shirts.

"You kids go outside now," Dixie said, shooing them out
the front door barefoot.

"I wanna drink," said the smallest one, a girl.

"Use the faucet. Jimmy, help Rose use the faucet for a
drink." She shut the door and sighed. "Now we'll have a
few minutes of peace before the older ones get outta
school."

Dixie led me through the kitchen and out the back door.
The house was thirties-era, with deep eaves and a small front
porch. Inside the walls were plain and in need of new paint,
the floors worn wood. Dixie stooped multiple times on the
way to the back door to pick up toys and shoes and way-
ward cookies. Despite her condition she didn't complain
beyond an occasional sigh.

The detached garage was a two-car version with one side
empty, waiting for an automobile, and the other filled with
boxes, a washing machine, a huge chest freezer, shelves lined
with canning jars sporting tomatoes, corn, beans, peaches,
applesauce, and unidentified meats. Behind the workaday
portion of the storage side, protected by a tall stack of
cardboard boxes, a huge army green tarp covered the back
fourth of the garage.

Dixie grabbed a corner of the tarp and began to struggle with it. I took another corner. Together we pulled the heavy tarp back, revealing the canvases, stacked on end, frameless. They sat directly on the concrete floor of the garage. The first thing I would have to check for was their condition.

"How do you want to do this?" Dixie said, putting her hands on her hips. She pursed her lips, as beads of sweat popped out on her forehead. She had been pretty once; I doubted she was older than I was, but we had taken different paths; all of hers showed on her face. "Do you want me to hand them out to you?"

The closed-up heat of the garage worked its way through me. I set my briefcase down and took off my jacket, folding it carefully and laying it on a box. Dixie wiped her face with a handkerchief.

"I work better alone," I said. "If you don't mind."

"Oh. Well." She looked offended. Then the cries of the children in the front yard reached us, and she turned back into the dutiful mother. "Wally will be home soon anyway. I'll bring you out some ice water in a minute, okay?"

In the hour before Fortney arrived I counted, spot-checked for water damage, and did a quick catalogue of each Tantro canvas. They were dirty, as I suspected, and some had stuck together in the heat, but there was little moisture damage. I figured they hadn't spent long on the cement floor of Wally Fortney's garage, or he kept it uncommonly dry.

There were thirty-nine canvases here all dated from 1969 to 1975. These were the kind of pieces I'd seen in the Livingston gallery back in '74, when I'd bought my own small Tantro. Some were prairie scenes, rain driving at an angle on the flat plain, some farm scenes with horses or bales of hay, forests, snow scenes, and even a few with human figures, rare in a Tantro. The collection was, I thought as I hyperventilated, a fucking gold mine. My palms began to sweat.

This collection was the biggest thing I had ever come across. The biggest I would probably ever come across. It would be spectacular news in the art world. I would be the one and only Tantro expert. If only... I immediately started calculating how I could take it off poor, dear Wally Fortney's hands.

AT FIVE O'CLOCK we sat in the front room of the Fortney's house, drinking ice water and eating Dixie's cookies. Wally had changed out of his work clothes but still carried the curdled smell of the cheese factory on his gray dress pants and short-sleeved white shirt. His knees poked up from the sprung seat of the old chair where he sat, giving him a cartoon-character look. I sat in a straight-back chair at a higher level, my legs crossed and my notebook on my knees.

Negotiations for a collection, any collection, are a delicate thing, full of nuance and emotion. When a family member is involved the ante is upped, even with a cold-fish cousin like Wally Fortney. I waited, gave him time to trust me, to like me, even as I was supposed to be just appraising for the Met. This collection was too rare, too fabulous to let get away. I felt my heart pounding against my chest as I tried to relax, to be rational, to make my palms quit perspiring.

"In my letter," Fortney said, balancing his water glass on a knee, "I offered them those three. *Field at Noon, Winter Glass,* and *Gloria.* Do you think those are the ones they'll like?"

"Possibly." Wally was unsure of his assessment skills when it came to art, and I wanted to keep it that way. He needed *me,* he had to have *me* to represent him. Even if he was right: The three he'd picked were probably the best of the lot. "It's hard to say what they want. Those three are good. They're fine."

"But you think some other ones are better?"

I cocked my head. "Back in those years, Wally, Ray had the gift."

Wally relaxed back in his chair, smiling. "They're all great, huh? I knew it, I knew it."

"Assuming you sell those three to the Museum, what will you do with the rest?"

"I want to keep 'em, you know, but I can't. I got eight kids and one on the way. I got to sell them."

"Have you offered them to anyone?"

Wally's eyebrows twitched. *God, I'm pushing him. Back off, Alix, back off.* "What I mean is, I might have some buyers for you. Some people who are interested." I paused, wondering if he knew Ray's prices were likely to go through the roof now. It would be good to control the flow of these new pieces out into the marketplace so the prices stayed high. But then, the best I could do is represent Wally on commission. My finances didn't offer pockets deep enough to purchase them all, much as I salivated at the thought.

"I heard about some people," Wally said cautiously.

"Wally," I said, leaning forward toward him. Then I remembered my manners and smiled at his wife. "Dixie." I leaned back and took a shallow breath, the best I could do. "I know a lot of art buyers. People all over the United States. Some in Europe and Canada. Rich people who think nothing of dropping, say, a hundred thousand on a painting." His eyes widened, point taken. "Now, I'm not saying I could get you that for a single piece. I couldn't guarantee that." I sat back and sipped water to cool both of us off.

"What do you think they're worth? How much?"

I shrugged. "I can't tell you right now. Since Ray died, everybody's been waiting to see what will happen to his prices. But I guarantee you they will not go down. Not for the good ones."

"And these, these ones." Wally gestured toward the garage with a cookie. "These ones are good ones, right?"

"They're good, Wally."

He grinned and took a long drink of water, his Adam's apple bobbing. Dixie smiled nervously and wiped her hands on her dress. I stood up with my briefcase and put on my jacket. Maybe it was the jacket. The Suit had brought me to my senses before. Whatever it was, my elation at finding the collection sunk like lead. Ray Tantro wasn't dead. What had I just said? If he was dead these paintings would be worth five, maybe ten times as much. I closed my eyes and swallowed.

"Wally," I said. He stood up, looking at me curiously, as if he could see my mood had shifted. "What if Ray's not dead?"

He glanced at his wife and squinted. "Wh-whadda you mean?"

"Did he give you permission to sell these paintings?"

Wally's face loosened. "Oh, sure. They was presents from Ray. He don't care if I sell 'em or not."

"You mean he wouldn't care even if he was still alive?"

"Right. He gave 'em to me because we took him in." Wally scratched the reddish stubble on his chin. "What do you mean if he's not dead?"

I shrugged. "It's just that with Ray passed away the collection has a different price. There will be no more Ray Tantro paintings." I looked at Dixie, who was frowning into her water glass. "If he isn't dead, well, it's a whole new ballgame. You understand, don't you?"

Wally stood with his hands in his pockets, shoulders hunched around his ears. His face was flushed with the heat. I noticed for the first time the sprouts of gray hair over his temples.

"But he is dead, Miss Thorssen," he said, almost pleading.

I looked at the paintings on his walls. One was a small Tantro not unlike my small piece. Winter landscape, close by a river, sky shimmering with crystals. Close by cheap posters were tacked on the wall with tape or thumbtacks, or children's drawings. I turned back to Wally Fortney. "It's important," I said. "I have to be sure."

Dixie looked up, face placid and smiling, as I turned for the door. It would be tricky business pursuing this collection when I wasn't sure Ray Tantro was dead. It wouldn't be right to offer the works as those of a dead artist unless he was absolutely, without a doubt, dead as a doornail, having bought the entire, complete, and final ranch. It would be unethical, immoral, but very, very lucrative. Thoughts of buying off Paolo, of keeping Paolo in town, of buying Martin's paintings, of buying a cabin in the woods, of getting out of the small time into the big time, all swirled inside my head, making me giddy and nauseous.

On the way to the car the words sang in my ears, as surely as my heels tapped the cracked cement sidewalk: *But he isn't dead, Alix. And you know it.*

WALLY INSISTED ON my taking the three pieces he was offering the Metropolitan back to Jackson with me. Maybe my sudden hesitation scared him, but he fell all over himself twisting my arm to take them. It wasn't necessary; I was glad to have a chance to examine them. Just having them hanging in the gallery would be a coup.

But on the way home, glancing over my shoulder to look at them in the back seat, I felt strange, like the dead were watching. This was Ray's dirty lucre. We—Wally and me and who knows who—might get rich off Ray's art. I guess I could deal with that. But what about Ray? Would he get rich too? The smell of his ambition filled the car. The scent of beauty, of the illusive dream of the perfect painting, of success and financial stability, all of them filled my nostrils and bloated my brain.

ELEVEN

I PROPPED THE three Tantros against the wall on the floor in the gallery. They were big—three feet by four—and brash and fabulous. Megan, our evening help, gasped at their beauty. I felt like a proud mother. I spent another few minutes staring at them; they remained as lush and luscious as they had in Wally's garage. I cleaned them carefully with a damp rag. But something held me back from all-out adoration. Not something—some*one*. I had to know Ray's situation before I could unconditionally covet his paintings. *Situation*—an odd word for being dead.

Upstairs I changed back into real clothes while I tried to talk to Eden. She was in a bad mood, smoking and moping. She told me Carl had called to tell me to meet him at the Rancher, a saloon on the square. With a little effort I talked Eden into accompanying me. She needed to get out of the apartment.

Carl and Pete were upstairs in the bar playing pool, a flock of empties crowded on a nearby chair. The room was a yuppie billiard hall, stained-glass lights hanging over the tables, mirrors on the paneled walls. At the sight of Pete Eden immediately perked up, smoothing back her black curls and sticking out her chest, giving him a shy smile. Pete beamed down at her. He looked tanned, a little sloshed, and washed like a river rock.

Deep in an immediate and boozy discussion with Eden about clear-cutting and spotted owls, Pete relinquished his pool cue and I finished his game with Carl. Carl moaned when I cleared the table on my second turn.

"Remind me to have you on my team next time," he said, taking my arm as we headed down the winding stairs to the bar proper. The Rancher had been remodeled into an oak-lined saloon a few years back, with green wallpaper, a small stage, and a dance floor. The tables crowded together in the open room, complete with a carved wooden back bar and swinging saloon doors. We found a table in the half-empty room and sat down.

Eden and Pete came down the stairs after us, arm in arm. I gave Carl a nudge. "How's that for matchmaking?"

He watched them, smiling. "Mutt and Jeff fall in love."

"So how was the river?" I asked.

"That Kahuna is a rush."

"It went all right for you?"

"It was great." Then his face clouded and he frowned into his beer.

I sipped my own, waiting. "What is it?"

"I was thinking about reflexes. It's something that goes with police work." He leaned back, drained his beer, and looked me in the eye. "Last week I had to draw my gun. Sometimes it's months, even three years once, that I don't get the thirty-eight out of the holster except to clean and check it and practice with it."

"What happened?"

"Robbery at a 7-Eleven. When we got there the guy had two customers and the cashier down on the floor inside. Jesus, I hate hostage situations." He frowned at the foam in the bottom of his glass. "Anyway I had the gun out for about two hours before we talked the guy out."

"Anybody hurt?"

"Not a bullet fired. One of the good ones. But the point was that I didn't want to get it out. I hesitated, you know? Like I didn't want to deal with the power, with the problems caused just by drawing your gun. I froze up for a few seconds."

"But you did it. There weren't any problems."

"No. No problems." Carl looked at Eden and Pete sitting cozily on barstools.

"Did you hesitate today?" I remembered my own fleeting feeling that I shouldn't be on the river, that it was the wrong day, that I should turn back. I hadn't, but for a long moment I wanted to.

Carl shook his head. "I was watching myself, you know? Like a test. That's what I like about white water. You get the same rush as police work, that breakneck instant when you must act."

"Why were you testing yourself?" I asked, sipping.

He frowned and didn't answer for a while. When he did, his voice was low, his eyes away. "It's a long story." Then he turned to me, smiling to cover his mood. "You don't want to hear it now. I can tell. You've got that look about you."

"What look?"

"That hungry look."

WE RETURNED TO my apartment after red meat, red potatoes, and red wine. The food helped the fatigue, but still my legs were sluggish on the stairs. I flopped onto the armchair, exhausted. Carl stood for a moment and turned around in the living room, head cocked.

"I don't believe it," he said. "It's actually quiet."

I lifted my chin from my chest and murmured. "Nice."

Carl slipped a record from my meager collection. The room rippled with Marshall Tucker's "Fire on the Mountain." The rhythm perked me up a little. Carl held out a hand, his feet sliding on the old wood floors.

"I can't dance," I moaned. "My feet feel like lead."

I watched him dance by himself, not an unpleasant sight. He dipped and spun, his eyes closed. He had good moves, easy feet. I remembered watching Paolo dance once in New York. At a Spanish dance festival he and a partner did the tango. He wore a scarlet silk blouse with balloon sleeves that floated and skin-tight black pants. Oh, his hips, I could never forget those hips. Paolo who would soon be gone from my life. Paolo who once had held me close in this very room while the moonlight tripped across our shoulders.

Carl stopped dancing and sat on the couch. He put his chin in his hand, studying me. "What are you thinking about?"

I straightened a little, tucking my legs under me. "My partner actually. My short-time partner."

Carl frowned. "Paolo?"

"He's leaving. Did he mention it?" Carl shook his head. "He doesn't want anyone to know yet. But he's selling his share of the gallery and bugging out."

"And that isn't what you want?" Carl asked.

"What I want hasn't got anything to do with it."

"That isn't what I asked."

"Well, I'm disappointed. We had a lot of good years together. I'll miss him," I said.

"Just as a business partner," Carl said.

"And as a friend."

"You two lived together, didn't you?" he asked. I looked away, silent. "You still got a thing for him."

I cleared my throat. "I don't know, Carl. It's been over for a long time. But if it's honesty you want, I have to say it's possible a part of me still cares." I heard him get up and move to the window. I was examining the paddling calluses on my hands. "You must have girlfriends you still care about."

In the window the reflection of his face on the glass was unreadable. Outside, the night faded into purples and midnight blues. An alpenglow from the Tetons rose in the north, challenging the stars.

"She was on the force," he said. "When I was a rookie. I was just out of the navy and full of it. She was a couple years older than me. She taught me a lot. We were partners for a while, until the lieutenant found out about us."

"That you were lovers?"

"She was married. We weren't lovers. Not the way you mean. But I loved her."

"What happened?"

"Somebody started sending her flowers and candy. At first it was secret, then somebody found out and made a big joke about it at the station."

"It was you?"

He nodded. "I couldn't help it, I guess. I was young, and stupid."

"And you loved her. I think it's sweet," I said.

"She didn't. Neither did her husband, who was a sheriff's deputy." Carl came back to the couch and plumped a pillow. His face held resignation and sadness.

"Is she still married?" I asked softly.

He shook his head. "She died. Last year." I waited while he regained control. "Just before Christmas. She wasn't even on duty, just helping break up a domestic dispute."

"She was shot?"

"She lived about forty-eight hours," he said. He swallowed and looked me in the eye. "So that's my sad story."

"It's awful. Especially the part about her not loving you back."

His black eyes flashed. "I didn't say that," he said angrily.

"Oh." I rubbed my forehead. How had we gotten started on this, anyway? I was sorry Carl's love had died, sorry that it had never worked out, sorry that Paolo was leaving me. But what good did it do to reexamine old loves, to pine for what had passed and would never be again? I felt my heart swell for a moment for the crossed signals and lost opportunities of love. For the unrequited, the untouched, the hopeless. Why was I moping about Paolo? Did I still love him?

Carl got up to flip the record. I slouched in the chair, a headache forming between my eyes, radiating up from my cracked septum. The silence, until the music started, was deafening.

CARL LEFT EARLY the next morning to meet Pete at the Snake River again. We had slept side by side in my bed, afraid to touch each other, treating the other like a fragile piece of glass likely to shatter if moved. We didn't want to be moved. We had been moved by previous lovers and look where it got us. So we lay still, staring at the old plaster ceiling until the sheer weight of our eyelids dragged us down into sleep.

The new Tantros were the buzz of the morning. Paolo could hardly quit talking about them. He called up several clients he knew were interested, even though I told him they were not for sale.

"Never mind, never mind," he said, the consummate salesman. "We'll just wet their whistles."

"You mean make them drool," I said.

"All over themselves." He grinned.

Eden finally got up about ten and stumbled down to see the new paintings. She had been out late, with Pete, I assumed.

Her hair was wet, dripping on her shirt. "Jesus, Alix. Man, oh man." She stood in front of the paintings, sweeping a bothersome customer out of her way with a hand. "Do you mind? Oh, this one. It's my favorite. What's it called?"

"*Winter Glass,*" I told her. "It's something, all right."

Winter Glass exhibited all of Ray Tantro's extraordinary talents. There was snow, ice, sky, river, and prairie, all swirled into a mirage of light and color that gave the feeling of both intense passion and frozen death. It was a curious piece that drew you in to examine tiny fragments of color, delicate lavenders and dots of cerise and built-up reds and browns in the barren trees. Then it pushed you out again to revel in the joy of its composition.

"These are even better than the ones the old lady had," Eden said. "Way better."

I couldn't agree with her. They were similar, done at nearly the same time with the same verve and intensity. But Esther's were just as wonderful.

"Where did they come from?"

"The cousin, Wally Fortney. Did you ever meet him?" I asked.

She shook her head. "I never met anybody in Ray's family. Until we went down to his mother's." She bent closer to *Gloria*. "What are you going to do with these?"

"They're to go to the Met in New York. It's a fitting tribute to Ray, don't you think?"

"He would have liked that." She couldn't take her eyes off the paintings.

"And of course now that he's dead, the prices will shoot up," I said, watching her.

"Yeah. These are probably worth—what? Fifty, sixty thou?"

"I don't know," I said. "Everybody's kind of waiting to see what's going to happen with his prices." I paused, examining *Field at Noon* with its golden hay and cloudless sky. "Of course, if he's not dead, Wally's collection won't be worth as much."

Eden frowned at me. "But he is dead."

I shrugged. "What if it wasn't him?"

She shivered. "Shit, Alix, you're crazy. Of course it was him."

"You're sure?"

"Sure, I'm sure," she said, crossing her arms, her brown eyes clouding.

"How tall was he, Eden? You knew him."

"How tall? I don't know. Everybody's taller than me." She closed her eyes, remembering. "Five ten, eleven."

I stared at her. "How tall do you think I am?"

She looked at a spot even with my bangs. "Five ten, I guess. Why?"

"Nothing." She obviously was no judge of height. I was five ten in high heels. "I've got to make some calls," I said, backing away. "You going out for coffee?"

"You want some?"

I told her to bring me a latte and headed toward my office. Today was the day I told Martin Ditolla the bad news. But when I dialed his number I got his answering machine. I left a message that we needed to talk and hung up, relieved but also guilty that I once again managed to avoid the inevitable.

IN THE EVENING, before we ate, Carl lifted my mountain bike from its dusty closet and down the stairs. We rode double, he pedalling, standing, me on the seat with legs splayed, to Danny Bartholomew's and borrowed his bicycle. Then we rode through town, past the new hospital toward the Elk Refuge. The dirt road was deserted except for the occasional hikers enjoying the evening air.

We didn't talk. We watched the bluebirds dance in the tall grass, darting and catching the night's insects, their azure feathers like indigo ink against the yellowing grass. Down in the marsh a great blue heron stood like a statue, one leg bent. An owl hooted high in the rocky hills and a hawk circled. A ground squirrel sat up and watched us pass in the gravel and dust. The light faded in the west. The mountains turned into mysteries of darkness, tombs of color. My legs felt useful and strong, and I stood up high on the pedals to catch the scents rolling down from the evergreen- and sage-covered foothills before we stopped and turned back toward civilization.

AT TEN O'CLOCK that night the charred alley door of Timberwolf Arts was creased by icy moonlight. Illegally parked cars lined the alley, with parking a scarce commodity at high summer. Moving around a Subaru with two bikes on its roof, I turned the knob on the once-blue door. It was locked, dead-bolted.

"What did you expect?" Carl said, arms crossed. He didn't like this, had said so emphatically at our late dinner. We were not treating each other so carefully anymore. Since his day on the river and our bike ride, we had mellowed. At least Carl had forgotten about our mutual pains enough to tell me exactly what he thought of my nosing around in other people's business. "This is not the same as rifling a glove box."

"Eden has permission to enter, doesn't she? She's the owner. I'm her friend, mentor, and all-around do-gooder." I rattled the knob and gave the door a little shoulder action. "You can stay outside if it bothers you."

"You don't even have a damn flashlight, Alix."

"Yes, I do." I fished in my backpack for a moment and held up the penlight. "You coming?"

He frowned, the blue moonlight giving his face a fierce look. "It would be nice if you had a key."

"Keys are for the uncreative. Besides this door is old, half burned, and about to fall off its hinges." On cue we both checked the hinges. The door had warped away from the frame to the point that the hinges were visible through a large crack.

"You hold the light," Carl said, extracting a Swiss army knife from his pocket. In a moment he had loosened the hinge pins. I found two scraps of wood to use to knock them out. I told him he would make a good second-story man and he smiled, a little. We were inside, propping the door back up, in five minutes.

"Now what, Sherlock?" Carl whispered, standing behind me, his hands on my shoulders. "This place stinks like rotten drywall."

"Yeah, I know. Upstairs, Watson." I moved toward the stairs, bouncing the tiny beam of light off the charred floors, the stack of damaged Tantro canvases still piled in the corner where I'd left them beside the sagging plasterboard and dirty piles of trash, twisted lamps, and soggy debris. From the quick look of the first floor it looked like nothing had been touched since Scanlon and I were here the day after the fire.

"Are the stairs safe?" Carl asked, stomping down hard on the step behind me. Scanlon, the fire inspector, had told me the second floor could be unsound. We were about to find out.

"I'll let you know," I said, pointing the flashlight at each riser and tread. They were covered with a tight, gray carpeting that looked water damaged but intact. The stairs rose from the middle of the room, a straight open staircase with a wrought-iron banister, the kind used on porches. As my head rose above the ceiling level of the first floor, the gloom thickened. A heavy smoky smell hung in the air.

As Eden had so tactfully pointed out, her apartment was bigger than mine. It had south windows too, three of them across the length of the main room. All three stood empty of their glazing, naked to the night, with a view of the flat tar roof of the building next door, which was littered with broken glass, shingles, and trash. Unlike my apartment, the stairwell led directly into her living room with no door closing off the private quarters from the gallery below. Probably against fire code, this omission had no doubt fanned the fire, creating a funnel of oxygen up the stairs.

An eerie purple glow hung over the upturned wooden chairs, the wrecked sofa, and dishes piled on the counter and broken on the floor. An ethereal white dust covered the floor with chunks of plaster everywhere. It took a minute to realize the glow was the result of cracks in the exposed lath ceiling letting in moonlight. The roof—and the attic—were gone.

Carl stared at the ceiling. "Holy Mary. What happened up there?"

"Explosion. Vaporized gas." I took a step into the apartment, but Carl held me back.

"Better look around first with the light. You don't want to step into any holes."

I checked the floor rapidly with the light, thinking about the tin ceiling on the floor below. As far as I could remember it was intact. A rug lay in a twisted heap under the coffee table. An ashtray filled with cigarette butts had been beautified by the plaster snow. I headed for the bedroom. "You look around out here, there's more light."

"Wait a minute. What the hell are we looking for?"

"A closet with some paintings. Something about Ray Tantro. Anything about the fire."

Carl grunted his displeasure as I stepped into the bedroom. Eden had furnished it with a twenties bedroom set, curving headboard, dresser, and bedside tables, inlaid with wood, veneered in a fashion that hadn't endured. The fire had been minimal in here, yet the windows facing the square had been blown out. Someone had stapled clear plastic over them. Through the plastic the moonlight was watery and weak.

The bedcovers lay in a heap, the pillow still indented with Eden's head. The other pillow on the double bed also had an indentation. The dresser was a small three-drawer unit with a mirror attached. I opened the jewelry box on the top. Inside three pairs of earrings and a cheap beaded bracelet lay in two compartments. The rest was empty.

The dresser drawers showed Eden wasn't much into clothes. Six pairs of worn-out underwear, two white shirts, an orange and a black one, a couple pairs of shorts, a pair of faded jeans. I zipped open my backpack and stuffed them all in. At least she'd have some clothes that fit.

The girl really needed shoes. I opened the closet, a walk-in with parallel racks, very roomy for an apartment. The beam of the flashlight shone off the empty hangers. No art in here. Down on the end hung a dirty trench coat and a long evening dress made of velvet with lace at the bodice. I'd never seen Eden wear it and wouldn't have been caught dead in it myself. On the floor sat a pair of Birkenstocks that predated the sexual revolution; I put them in my backpack. A last look at the floor revealed matching heels for the evening dress. I abandoned them with the gown.

The shelves of the closet were stacked with boxes. I pulled one down and found a jumble of old clothes in it. Another held a stack of photographs that Eden must have developed herself, if fuzzy focus and chemical spots were any clue. The last box was heavy, long, and skinny and held, of all things, a croquet set.

After a final peek under the bed I found Carl in the kitchen, his hand on the refrigerator handle.

"Find anything?"

"Darkroom." He pointed at a door near the bedroom. "Lots of chemicals, I'd guess. It burned pretty bad in there. There might have been some paintings."

"Things are pretty scorched out here." The sofa cushions revealed springs and blackened stuffing. "The bedroom's all there. Just the windows blown."

"I was going to check the fridge," he said, hesitating.

"Don't."

"Why not?" He had his policeman look on again even though he wore baggy jeans, Patagonia T-shirt, and cowboy boots. I was finally getting used to that mustache.

"It'll be rank. They turned off the power a week ago." I had smelled that left-the-fridge-unplugged odor before. Once was enough. "Did you look around in here?"

"Not yet."

We started opening cupboards. "Just dishes. Cereal boxes. Regular shit," Carl said.

"What's not here?"

"Huh?"

"What's missing?"

"Oh." He looked around the kitchen, taking the penlight from me, searching the countertops. "No coffeemaker, no toaster, no electric can opener, no dirty rag in the sink, no Cuisinart, no garbage can, no microwave. Is that what you mean?"

"Yes, Watson. That's what I mean."

WE WALKED ACROSS the square in the moonlight, dragging our shoes through the grass to clean the plaster dust and ashes off the soles. I had the backpack slung on my back and my eyebrows knit together. What we'd found, or hadn't found, in Eden's apartment was on my mind.

I always prided myself on my judgment of people's characters, like a colored aura around them. I could sometimes smell the foul odor of deceit, although this wasn't very accurate. But at least I should have seen, should have known that Eden hadn't been straight with me.

The moon was just past full, waning into the starlit sky. A cool breeze rattled through the elms as we reached the other side of the square and paused to let the stagecoach cowboys spray down the horse manure in the street. The odor was fragrant and alive with hay. Carl wrinkled his nose as I unlocked the front door of the gallery.

Just inside the front door of my apartment, we stopped and listened. Now an old Emmylou Harris album was on the turntable, turned down low. A single candle burned on the coffee table, its vanilla fragrance cloying. The kitchen clock ticked. But the most conspicuous noise was from my bedroom. The door was closed but the sound of springs squeaking in a suspiciously rhythmic manner, as if keeping time with Emmylou, was unmistakable.

"I feel like Goldilocks," I said. "Somebody's screwing in my bed."

"You mean the three bears. Goldilocks is beating the mattress and I'd lay money her name starts with an E. At least she didn't break any chairs." He sat down on the couch and propped his feet on the coffee table next to the candle. "Sounds like ol' Pete got lucky. This is better than renting a video." He grinned.

A wail rose from behind the door. "Jesus Christ." My whisper wasn't as soft as Carl's, and he hushed me. "This is my apartment, for God's sake. If I want to curse, I'll curse."

Not that my cursing made any difference. The bedsprings continued their lament, Eden sang along, Pete began to grunt. It *was* better than renting a video. All the sound effects were in place.

I opened my backpack and dumped Eden's clothes and shoes into an unceremonious heap on the floor by the kitchen counter. It wasn't a big heap, I noticed again. I hung up the pack in the closet and poured myself a glass of wine. The smell of soot clung to my fingers as I sipped, leaning against the counter, waiting for the climax of the bedroom movie.

Eden and Pete went together, in loud, exultant doggie yelps, straight out of a *Joy of Sex* exercise. I felt like having a cigarette. Carl gave me an I-know-what-you're-thinking look.

We didn't wait long before one of them came out. I had my money on Eden, naked, prancing to the bathroom, maybe singing a Beach Boys ditty like "I Get Around." But Pete came first, strutting across the short hall, bare-assed, into the john. Eden emerged a minute later, in my split yellow chenille bathrobe. She had her head down, belting it, as she stepped into the light.

With a long sigh of contentment she lifted her head. The pile of clothes caught her eye first, then she saw me by the kitchen counter and Carl on the couch.

"Hi, guys. You're back." She made a beeline for the fridge and took out a bottle of Evian, gulping it. When she turned again, her ruffled edges were smoothed over. "I hope you don't mind about the bed, Alix." She smiled, her lips curling as if savoring the memory. "To tell you the truth I don't even remember how we got in there."

"Kind of a rush?" Carl said.

Eden laughed. "Good things come to those who don't wait."

"Operative word *come?*" I said. The sharpness of my tone surprised me.

"Alix." Eden turned to me and crossed her arms. "You sound jealous, honey." She glanced at Carl. "Don't tell me you had your eye on my Pete too? First Paolo, now Pete. What about ol' Carl? You going to share him with me too?"

Carl was staring at me, a question on his face he wanted me to answer. I clenched my teeth. How did I let her get me into this? I took a slug of wine.

"Eden. Darling. We were up in your apartment tonight." I walked around to see the pile of clothes, the worn-out sandals lying on top. Eden looked at them too, her expression unreadable. "Picked up a few things for you. Not much left up there."

"You went up there?" she said.

"I tried to talk her out of it," Carl said. I gave him a look.

Pete emerged from the bathroom, a towel around his waist. "Hi, y'all." His tan began at his collar and went up. The whiteness of his hairless chest was stunning. "Ready for a party?"

What a pair. I tried to focus on Eden, now circling Pete's waist with her arm. He nuzzled her hair with his chin.

"Eden, we have to talk."

Her eyes were slow but wary. "About what?"

"Your apartment. Its magnificent emptiness."

"Wait a minute, Alix," Carl said, stepping up to the counter. I felt him scrutinizing the set of my chin. "It wasn't empty. You found her clothes. Her dishes and stuff were in the kitchen."

"A few things were left to make an impression. If the whole building had burned no one would have been the wiser." I watched Eden, her eyes darting to the clothes and to Carl.

"What are you say—" Carl began.

"Let her explain," I interrupted.

"I don't know what you're talking about," Eden said, dropping her hand from Pete's waist. "Are you accusing me of something? I thought we were friends."

"This is serious, Eden. We're talking about an arson conviction. Jail. Did you know your building was going to burn? Did you move your valuables somewhere? Your television, your kitchen appliances, your jewelry, your clothes?"

Eden looked shocked. "Where would I have moved anything? And why?"

"Why would she burn down her own gallery?" Carl asked.

"Come on, Carl, you can't be serious. Tell us, Eden," I said. "Tell us why you would want to burn down your gallery."

Eden tensed, wringing her hands. "I don't know what you're talking about. My insurance covered all that. You have no right to *interrogate* me like this." Her eyes filled.

"We're not accusing you of anything," Carl said. "We're just saying it looks suspicious. If it looks suspicious to us, then it looks that way to the police."

"They know it's arson. The first person they suspect is the owner. Chief Frye already told me he suspects you," I said. "You took out all that extra insurance on the new show. I didn't believe him. Not Eden, I said. She loved that gallery, I told him. She put her heart and soul into it. But now—"

Eden put her face in her hands, tears flowing. Pete put his arms around her and pulled her into his chest. He looked helplessly at Carl. We let her sob noisily, not ready to give up on the discussion. If you could call it that.

Finally she took a gulp of air and sobbed, "I did love it, Alix. You know that. But everything was getting so terrible, just awful.'' She cried some more and Pete patted her back.

''Shhh, now. Shhh. You don't have to say any more.'' He shepherded her into the bedroom and closed the door.

I finished my wine. My stomach hurt. I was upset. I turned to Carl. ''What should we do?''

''You're the one who beat the confession out of her.'' He walked back to the couch and sat down. Outside the moon had set and the Milky Way shone bright and creamy.

''What's that supposed to mean? You saw the apartment. It was stripped of everything of value. She may not have lit the match herself, but she arranged that arson job. You know it, Carl.''

''I know no such thing.''

''You just said she made a confession.''

''Not a legal one. She only admitted the gallery wasn't doing so hot. That's not a crime.''

''Carl!''

He looked out the window for a few minutes, silent. The laughter of passing pedestrians walking down the alley floated up. In the bedroom we could hear the low voices of Pete and Eden, her crying, him cooing. The candle flickered and I reached over and blew it out, sending hot wax flying across the table onto a stack of plastic-sheathed Mighty Thor comics. I cleaned the splattered wax with my shirttail.

Finally Carl said, ''All right. We should go talk to the police. Whoever is handling the arson case.''

''That'd be Scanlon, the fire inspector,'' I said. Was Frye in charge too? I looked at my watch; it was 11:30. ''We'll go first thing in the morning.''

TWELVE

I PULLED THE wool blanket over my head as the birds sang outside the window. What was Valkyrie, my horse, doing this fine summer morning? Munching grass, contented? Smelling the mountain air for stallion blood? Pawing the fresh earth in search of adventure? I didn't picture Valkyrie as ever contented; she was always looking for trouble. I felt a yearning for her suddenly. I needed to stroke her soft brown neck, feed her an apple.

It was too early to get up even though my neck had a permanent crick in it. I was curled into my not-so-overstuffed armchair. Carl stretched out luxuriously on the couch, his feet still in cotton socks sticking out the end of the quilt. Under the blanket I could smell the smoke from Eden's apartment on my clothes.

The phone on the counter behind my head rang, loud and obnoxious, as if trying to compete with the birds. My watch said 6:15. Normally I would ignore such an early call. Even my mother would wait until eight for an emergency. But since sleep was elusive, my butt numb and my back twisted into a question mark, I got up.

"Alix." Danny Bartholomew whispered into the phone, his voice hushed and anxious. "I got a weird call."

I blinked, trying to concentrate on the phone call and not on the note on the counter from Eden. "Danny?"

"Guy said he was Ray Tantro."

I was awake. "When?"

"Minute ago. He said to meet him at his house in Moose."

"Okay," I agreed for some reason.

"At eight o'clock. Said he had some information about the fire at Timberwolf Arts. About the guy who died in the fire."

My mind processed all this, the pieces falling into place. A small measure of satisfaction glinted in my fingertips. "Are you going?"

"It's probably a prank. I have to call Frye."

"Sure," I muttered, thinking hard. "It's Saturday. He won't be in his office."

"I'll go when I get ahold of him. I really don't like getting summoned at dawn anyway. It reminds me of the army. Besides, why does this joker call me?"

"You did the story on the fire, Danny. You gave it a more objective slant than the cops did." I looked at my watch again. "Thanks for the call."

"Wait, Alix. What are you going to do? Do you want to come out with us? Frye may balk, but if I'm going..."

"No. But let me know what happens at your meeting." I hung up the phone and watched Carl's chest rise and fall. He lay on his back, his mouth slightly open. He wouldn't like the idea I had. He would try to talk me out of it.

Before I stepped into the bathroom to brush my teeth and find my shoes, I read Eden's note. She and Pete had gone to his place. Thanks but no thanks. Some friend you turned out to be, it read between the lines. A copy of this month's Mighty Thor comic book lay under it, corners bent viciously. How could someone who loved Thor as much as I did do this to me? She had used me, claiming innocence as I helped her bilk the insurance company of thousands of dollars. I shook my head, trying to rid it of thoughts of Eden's treachery, and grabbed my clogs.

ON THE DRIVE to Moose the guilt for the botched relationship with Eden seeped through me, something I rarely allow. Guilt is better left to the Catholics, who understand these things from the get-go. For a Norwegian, guilt is a luxury. Life goes on, sin or no sin, mistake or no mistake. No sense wallowing, there's cleaning to be done. But this morning I wallowed, trying to figure out how I could have misread Eden, how I could have trusted her, how I could have been a better friend. Conflicting regrets, these. How I could have kept her from being who she was. How I could have, through a higher form of kindness, stopped her.

The fire still baffled me. I had no doubt now that Eden was in some way responsible. She didn't seem like the type to plan an arson fire, despite her upped insurance and the emptiness of the apartment. She was too emotional, too disorganized. Imagining her planning the blast in the roof, lighting candles by gas-filled balloons—no, it didn't figure. She must have contracted it. But that meant finding an arsonist. A trustworthy arsonist isn't anybody a middle-class Lackawanna girl would know. But Eden had surprised me before with her choices of friends and acquaintances. Last night with Pete was only a recent example of her excellent judgment. Three months ago she had the hots for a rodeo cowboy; last winter she let a truck-driving couple stay with her for four days when they got snowed in. I guess I should have wondered about our own friendship. But my vanity, that I was teaching her the trade, educating her, grooming her, didn't allow me to see her true nature.

That's not completely true. She had good qualities. In many ways Eden reminded me of Paolo in his early gallery days. Bringing home strays, feeding hitchhikers, opening his heart and home to everyone. I had been one of Paolo's strays in New York, friendless and lonely, nearly broke. He had made me bean soup and flat bread and stroked my neck until I almost cried. Those days seemed so far away now. Soon Paolo would be gone for good.

Eden had that same gregarious nature. All good salesmen did. They liked people, and wanted people to like them. What's that lounge anthem about people who need other people being lucky? I didn't believe that. People who need people are lonely. People who can rely on themselves are lucky.

Did I count myself among the lucky? As I turned off the highway into Moose, the Grand Teton and Teewinot twinkling in the red glow of the rising sun, I wasn't sure. Maybe I thought I was, maybe I just wanted to be.

Ray Tantro's pickup truck still sat in the shade of the aspens in his dirt drive. I turned in, killing the engine on the Saab Sister as I rolled it to a stop behind the truck. My heart began to pound in my ears again. Was this The Moment I am right? When I meet the dead Ray Tantro and shake his hand? I shivered as I walked up the drive.

The air in the bottomland along the creek held the night's damp chill. The grass outside the shade of the trees was dry and brittle, with drooping seed heads; it crunched under my feet as I approached the cabin.

The morning sun hit the tops of the trees, big blue spruces thirty feet tall shadowing the tiny cabin in its dark hole. As I got closer I stopped, listening for the dog.

"Saffron," I sang out quietly, my voice shaking a little. All around me forest sounds were muffled, scampering, chattering, birdsong. "Ronnie?"

There was no answer. I glanced at the cabin, then veered around to the back corner to look for the dog. I could see the food dish and water bowl at the edge of the lawn. "Ronnie," I called halfheartedly again. "Here, girl."

I stepped closer. The weeds were matted down under the tree where she had been tied. The end of the chain was empty. I went to the back door and knocked loudly, wondering if Tantro would be presentable. My watch said 7:10.

A mountain blue bird landed on a stump in the lawn and began to peck at something in the wood. A goldfinch flashed its gay colors at wild sunflowers growing on a pile of dirt.

No answer. I went to the front, knocked again, waited. I walked around to the back again and put my nose up to the

door. Did I smell coffee? The slight pressure of my hand
pushed the door ajar. Another, different odor hung in the
air, acrid and bitter.

I pushed the door wide, my ears pounding again. The
kitchen was dirty, and empty. Not even coffee.

"Ray! Ray Tantro?!" I called from the stoop, softly at
first, then louder. "Mr. Tantro! Are you there?"

When there was no answer, I stepped through the kitchen
into the living room. It was empty, the ugly carpeting and
ancient sofa still covered with dog hairs. His bedroom was
dark, shades drawn. I squinted into the gloom, looked behind the bed. Nothing. The bathroom was empty.

The door to the studio was half open. I pushed against it,
a feeling of dread upon me. This was not the fear of the
river, this was an evil dread, a certainty as clear as morning. The door hit something and stopped. I could see the
north window bare of curtains. Where was the easel? I
looked harder and began to turn to sidle through the door
when I saw the easel lying on the floor, on top of the canvas and drape.

And a body. The feet stuck out, holding the door. Cowboy booted feet, Levi's, then a pile of art debris. I stared at
all of it for a minute, paralyzed, then pulled off the heavy
easel, a professional model that was built for years of use. I
stood it up automatically, taking my time to get the angle of
the legs correct, then made myself stop, hands shaking.

I grabbed the stretched canvas and set it on the easel. It
was still blank, a rectangle of nothing. The man lay there,
half covered with the dark green drape like an army surplus
blanket made of stiff cotton.

The blood stopped rushing into my ears. I could feel it
drop back into my neck, my chest, the calm of death settling in. For a moment the room's air was still and I held my
breath. This stillness was death, this moment irretrievable.
I wanted to talk to Ray, to find out what happened in the
fire, what happened to *his* fire. To find out where his talent

had gone. To feel the glow, however tarnished, of his genius.

But now he was only a body, his creative life drained away like so much fish guts. To everyone else he was already dead. I felt a brief bittersweet rush that I had been right, that he was alive, then caught myself staring at the drape, wondering about his face, his eyes. Although his second death would create problems for the law, one thing would not change: Ray Tantro was legally dead.

THIRTEEN

My HAND TREMBLED. My breath stuck in my throat. The room was warm and rancid with the smell of oil paints and human sweat and something else, a sharp odor. The green cloth drape lay heavily on the body. Several folds covered the face as he lay on his back on the dark tarp so thoughtfully laid down in his art studio. The tarp that now kept his blood from staining the dirty brown carpet. As I stepped close to the body, indenting the olive green tarp with a crunching sound, a trickle of blood ran to the toe of my clog.

I pulled tentatively at the drape. Did I really want to see his eyes, the eyes of a dead magician who transformed lumps of gooey pigment into pictures that tore at your heart? Tantro clutched the cloth in his left hand, fingers curled around. He was missing his ring and pinkie fingers. I pushed the cloth aside. He wore a blue flannel shirt with his jeans and boots and had somehow kept his strained gray cowboy hat on his head while taking three shots to the chest. The holes were dark, clotted—and very final. His face, rough with several days' growth of beard and now an icy blue, showed surprise.

The eyes of artists have always fascinated me. They have special powers to see things that the average person cannot. X-ray eyes, supernatural eyes, the eyes of God. An artist is someone who conjures the invisible for the blind.

Ray's eyes were a dark, ocean blue. Now they stared, dead. I closed them like I had seen hundreds of TV cowboys do to their fallen loved ones. The skin was stiff and clammy and I wished I hadn't done it.

How long did I kneel there? I remember the color of the blood on his chest, maroon, dark and lifeless. Inside that chest was a heart that no longer beat, no longer loved. It never would break again. But there was little comfort in that.

I held his right hand for a moment and thought I should say something to comfort his soul, wandering the cabin or maybe just hovering, wondering what to do next. What would Thor say to soothe the way to the spirit world? Ray had large, muscular hands, callused. I looked at the brushes on the card table. Some had fallen to the floor like Tinkertoys, their dried paint dusty with age. I frowned. This wasn't your studio, Ray. Why did you come back?

The sirens began. I could hear them far off, echoing off the mountains like the howl of coyotes. Before they got close I heard the footsteps, then voices behind me.

"Alix, we saw your car, you didn't come by yourself, did—?" Danny B. stopped in the doorway, looking down on Tantro. Frye pushed him out of the way.

I stood up. There was nothing to say.

"Jesus Mary Mother of God," Frye grunted, grabbing my arm. "You didn't touch anything, did you?" He looked at my hands. I spread my fingers and saw the blood there. "Christ. Just stand there, will ya? Don't move." Frye turned to Danny, whose face was stuck in shock as his eyes shifted from me to Tantro and back.

"Don't let her move. Can you fucking do that?" Frye let go of my arm. Pushing Danny aside again, Frye gave him a shake on the way by. "Can you, boy? Don't move, neither of yous."

I felt numb. I stared at the body and the red seams on my palms. I heard Charlie Frye running back to the cruiser. Danny held his notebook limp at his side, immobile. Finally, as we heard Frye coming back, Danny spoke.

"Wh-why'd you come out, Alix? You could've come with me and Frye and you wouldn't have seen all this by yourself. Why'd you come out by yourself?'' He paused, looking at Tantro. ''Is that him?''

I nodded, following his stare. ''The real one.''

THE NEXT FOUR hours were a blur of policemen, detectives, park rangers, blue-suited FBI men who drove in from Riverton to take over the investigation because it took place inside a national park, questions, questions, and more questions. For a couple hours they set me up outside under a tree, assigned a Deputy Michaels to me, and kept a rotating crew of cops asking the same questions over and over. After that, Michaels drove me back to Jackson to the police station in the back of city hall, where he fed me stale turkey sandwiches and burned coffee. I told them everything.

I SAT ON the linen-covered sofa, head in my hands. Fatigue and bad coffee had my head buzzing. Carl had picked me up at city hall about two and something was bugging me. It nestled deep in my psyche, a buzz that I was both trying to ignore and trying to recognize.

The toilet flushed and Carl emerged from the bathroom. He had been quiet, moody, since picking me up. I knew he was pissed I had gone out to Tantro's alone. I didn't want to talk about it. There was no other way.

''Alix, have you seen a biker around? All dressed in black?''

I tried to remember. ''I don't know.''

''Well, he's parked out front, sitting on his Harley. Come take a look.''

We went to the bedroom window. Across from the gallery a big motorcycle was parked at a slant. The rider was dressed in biking leathers with studs down the legs of the chaps. He faced away from us, toward the empty square, his black helmet still on.

''Do you recognize him?'' I asked.

"Hard to tell. But I know this is the third time I've seen him." Carl squinted as if trying to read the tiny license plate.

He went into the kitchen and looked in the refrigerator, pulling out a beer. He grabbed a box of saltines and stuffed several in his mouth, washing them down with beer. If there was a message he was trying to send me, I wasn't getting it. My head pounded. Every time I closed my eyes I saw Ray, lying in his own blood. A biker didn't even register. The vision bounced off my brain that was too full of other shit. The stinking mess of the human race that produced people who killed each other.

"So," Carl said. Disgust in his voice, irritation.

A pack of Eden's cigarettes, crushed, lay on the coffee table. I picked it up, sitting back on the sofa. It was empty. My hand opened slowly, letting the package fall to the floor. Carl's word lingered in the air.

"You have something to say?"

Carl frowned. "Yeah. This is turning out to be some great vacation."

"Am I responsible for your vacation pleasure?"

Carl laughed harshly. "I'd be in deep trouble then." He stuffed a couple more saltines in his mouth.

"You want some cheese for those? It's in the fridge." I was getting the feeling he wanted me to make him something to eat. I had no energy to even lift my hand to flick away a fly buzzing around my ear.

"I don't want any damn cheese," he grumbled, swigging his beer.

"Well, what do you want? What can *I* do for *you?*"

"Goddamn it, Alix." He sighed, putting his hands on the counter and staring hard at me. "You don't get it, do you? This is serious shit. You just can't keep your nose out of things, can you?"

I stared back at him, meeting his challenge. "So go home, then. I didn't ask you to come. Go back to work. Go kayaking, spin around in the waves. Do whatever you damn well please. Nobody's stopping you. Just don't tell me how to live my life.'' How had I ever thought him sensitive? He was no different from any of them, just another big, dumb cop. I had my fill today. I went to the window, suddenly trembling. I felt hollow. I wanted him to leave. Carl Mendez was another person in my life I had let down. There was Paolo, and Martin. I thought of Eden again, how miserably I had performed as a friend, how she had fooled me. How would she react to Tantro's second death?

Carl moved behind me. Out of the corner of my eye I could see him picking up his clothes, putting them in the duffle. Good, he was leaving.

''Where will you go?'' I swallowed hard.

''Got a week left of vacation. No reason to go back anyway.''

''Meaning?'' I faced him now as he put his jacket over his shoulder. He was wearing baggy shorts again, and sandals, his face clouded.

''Meaning I quit the department.''

I stared at him. ''You quit? Why didn't you tell me?''

He looked away. ''Doesn't matter.''

''What do you mean?''

''Why I quit—it doesn't matter. I just got tired of it. Burned out on hippie crime. The pettiness, the endlessness. We never make a dent.'' He shifted his bag. ''Well, it's been real.'' He opened the apartment door, pausing as if I might stop him. Then he was gone.

THE APARTMENT WAS quiet. Also a disaster area. It was the first time in over a week I had it to myself, and I couldn't stand it. Without the energy to clean it up the way my Norwegian grandma Olava would have, I did what any self-respecting single girl would do. Took a shower, washed my hair, put on a yellow linen shirt and blue slacks, shut the door, and went to work.

Paolo had hung the three Tantro paintings on the main gallery wall so that they could be seen from the sidewalk. He had even made gallery cards with their titles and "NFS": Not For Sale. The kind of thing that drove passionate collectors mad. A group of tourists twelve strong was flocked in front of them when I came down.

"Fancy meeting you here," Paolo said, the words more acid than his tone. I ignored him and headed into my cubicle office, wondering what the hell I was doing here. Paolo followed me. He was dressed for his upbeat mood: hot pink polo shirt, cream slacks, shiny black riding boots.

"You don't look so hot," he said. "That nose still bothering you?"

I touched it gently. My nose was still enlarged over the bridge. Carl was probably right about getting it straightened. But right now I had more important concerns. "Leave my nose out of this."

"Right, sheesh. Don't bite off my tongue. You had a couple calls. One from Frye. You ever finish that appraisal for him, from the fire?"

"Not yet." I had no intention of finishing it now. That wasn't why Frye called anyway. Eden had a hand in the fire. She would never collect her insurance.

"Also the cousin called. Wally Fortney. He's the one with the goods, eh?" Paolo grinned like a wolf. I shrugged. "Whassa matter? You should be creamin' your drawers over those Tantros." He glanced out into the gallery from the doorway as the bell tinkled. A shapely woman, dressed in expensive clothes and lots of jewelry, stepped in. "Look at the casabas on that one." He whistled discreetly through his teeth.

I felt so tired suddenly. Eden's foul conspiracy, Carl's departure, Ray Tantro's second murder. They weighed on me. I hoped Paolo would leave me alone without bringing up Martin Ditolla. That was one I could do without today.

The bell rang on the gallery door again. "Oh, shit. It's that asshole Laughlin," Paolo whispered through his plastered smile. "Hiya, Jake," he called out, waving.

I turned toward the doorway to see the two men shaking hands. We had been doing our best to avoid showing Jacob Laughlin's art for the last six years. His bugling elk, charging bears, and frisky racoons, some of them exquisitely wrought, were not our cup of tea. We all have our tastes, and the taste of Laughlin's art was sour to us. Then there was his personality.

"Paulie, you old SOB," Laughlin said, smiling. His kinky brown hair stuck up off his scalp, untamed. He was the only person I knew who got away with "Paulie."

Paolo stretched his lips. Some would call it a smile. "How's it goin', man?"

"Heard you had some Tantros in. I had to come see for myself." Jacob kept his eyes off them, small gray eyes sunk into his fleshy face. He dropped his big, soft hands into the pockets of baggy khakis that crumpled around his ankles.

"Right over there." Paolo waved his hand toward the milling crowd.

Laughlin looked quickly, then back at Paolo. I sat with my arms crossed, one foot bouncing, watching him. Silently I dared him to acknowledge my existence.

"Pretty neat, locking on to those pieces right before the poor guy gets plugged," Laughlin said, in his crude but accurate way.

"Plugged?" Paolo frowned.

"You know, lead poisoning?" Laughlin said, pointing a plump finger at Paolo's chest for emphasis. "Bang, bang, you're dead?"

"He died last week, in the fire."

Jacob's belly laugh filled the small office. "You didn't hear? He took it in the chest at his studio this morning. Somebody else was in that fire. Mighty suspish."

Paolo squinted at me, confused.

"Ray Tantro was found shot this morning," I said, leaving out the detail that I had found him. "Jake's right. Somebody else died in the fire."

Paolo still looked confused, shook his head, and stared out into the gallery. He excused himself to see to the customers, leaving me alone with Jake Laughlin. I would see that Paulo paid later for this favor.

"How did you find out, Jake?"

He propped his ass on the edge of my desk, covering a good portion. His eyes gleamed. "I have a few friends in high places. I heard *you* were there." I tried to look busy with the mess on my desk. "Some coincidence."

I glanced at him, not liking the tone of his voice. How could I get rid of him? He was settling in.

"You and Ray knew each other, didn't you? Somewhere back in your golden youth?" I asked, leaning back in my chair again.

Jacob tried to look chagrined. "Yes, old art school buddies, we were."

"I guess this makes you top banana again," I said. Jake's eyebrows twitched. "You must be glad Ray's out of the way at last."

He looked properly insulted. "I considered Ray my friend."

"That's not what I heard. The word was you were bad-mouthing his show all over town. A little professional jealousy, Jake?"

"Our work was very different. I don't know anyone who made a comparison between us."

"Even you?"

"In art school we were friends. Rivals maybe a little, yes, but friends. Great talents can't help but be rivals."

Great talent? Jake Laughlin? "Did you see him a lot here in Jackson?"

"Uh—yes, we did get together a couple of times for a drink. Talked about the art world, our work. He had nothing but nice things to say about my work. He was very happy for my success. And vice versa, of course.''

I nodded, trying to look him in the eye as he stared out the door, folding his arms across his large chest. Nice try. With Ray dead, Jake could say anything.

"What happened to him during those dark years? Do you know?"

Jake squirmed on the desk and stood up. His face was beaded with sweat. "We never discussed those years. I always assumed, well, you know." He shrugged and looked out the door at the paintings.

"No. I don't know."

"Drugs. Booze. The usual culprits. It's not something I was going to pry into. I'm not that kind of a friend," he said.

"But you had drinks together. He was drinking still."

Jacob nodded sorrowfully. "I wish I could say otherwise, Alix, dear. But some people are just destined for tragedy."

"Well, I'll see you at the funeral," I said, trying to sound final, then wondered if there would be a second service. What was his mother thinking now? Would she grieve all over again or just shrug her shoulders, baffled by life and death?

"Of course." Jake tapped two fleshy fingers on the desktop in parting. In the gallery he wrapped a huge arm around Paolo's shoulders and began a long-winded diatribe about Ray Tantro's paintings that cleared the gallery in three minutes flat.

IN THE NEXT two hours I made phone calls, including one to Wally Fortney. His wife Dixie answered. Wally wasn't home, but she'd give him the message. She didn't bring up the shooting, so neither did I.

I returned a call to a dealer in Santa Fe, a friend. She had shown some Tantros in the late '70s. Her father owned the gallery then, she had worked there summers in college. She remembered her father saying that Tantro's work had gone to hell and that everyone thought he was washed up. But the paintings still sold well, riding the coattails of his reputation.

It wasn't much help, but somehow the sound of my friend's voice on the phone was reassuring. I had to explain the newest wrinkle in the Ray Tantro story, his second death. The more I tried to explain it, the more I wondered who died in that fire—and why. If Ray had planned the scam to paint his own pictures after he was declared dead, then who had killed him? It made no sense.

I had to put it out of my mind. A calmness built through the afternoon from the familiar routine, familiar surroundings, from tying up the loose ends of my desk, of business, from explaining the gorgeous lushness of Tantro's paintings to admirers. It was good to feel good, to feel needed, productive. Grandma Olava would have been proud.

I was looking out the window at six, hoping for a glimpse of Carl's green El Dorado wandering aimlessly through the streets. Part of me hoped he was still around and hadn't taken off for parts unknown or done something stupid like kayaking the Snake by himself. I couldn't forgive myself if something happened to him. The other part of me was happy to be left alone, to have one less person to please. But I hadn't pleased Carl. I couldn't even remember trying. The night we wasted, lying side by side in misery, too wrapped up in our own heartaches to reach out for the other.

The gallery was empty. Tourists congregated on the sidewalks and curbs to watch the gunfight between a couple of sharp-shooting cowboys that the chamber of commerce sponsored each evening in the summer. It was a bit of a pain for me, being right on the street where it took place, having to hear the blanks and the shouting and smelling the gunpowder. Not to mention the obstruction of the boardwalk with nonbuyers. But it helped keep people in town. Right after the gunfight there was usually an increase in shoppers.

Through the crowd, a head taller than most, Deputy Michaels pushed his way down the boardwalk. The sun still shone on the street, but the tourists under the overhang were in deep shadow, so deep I almost didn't see the deputy in his brown uniform. I stepped back from the window, hoping he'd pass. Instead he stopped in front of our door, looked up at the name stenciled in gold on the glass, and came inside.

"Miss Thorssen." He tipped his brown cowboy hat, serious. Michaels stood six four and burly but with a teddy-bear quality. He had treated me gently this morning and I was grateful for that. But I never expected him to come calling.

"Deputy," I replied.

"I was just passing by and..." He paused, looking around the empty gallery. I wondered where Paolo had gone. God, does he want a date?

"And, well," Michaels blurted, "do you have a law-yer?"

I stared at him, my ears humming in the silence. "What?"

"An attorney. Somebody you know?"

Paolo came out of the john, singing a Spanish song he remembered a few of the words to, humming the rest. He was still tucking in his shirttail when he came through the office door, the toilet flushing behind him.

I heard Paolo's boot heels on the wood floor. "Problem, Alix?"

Michaels took off his hat, nervous. Just like an old-fashioned suitor come to ask the father for the girl's hand, I thought. For a big man he was shy, uncertain how others perceived him. "Just talking. Aren't we, Miss Thorssen?"

I nodded. "It's all right, Deputy." I put my hand through Paolo's arm. "Now, what did you say?"

Michaels looked confused. Of course I had heard him. "A lawyer, Miss Thorssen. You might think about it."

"Why does she need a lawyer?" Paolo extracted his arm awkwardly from my grasp and held my arm in his hand for a moment.

"I just thought you'd want to know. What I heard down at the station." He scratched his crew cut and sighed. "Of course, we're not on the Tantro murder. That's the FBI's show now."

Paolo looked at me, puzzled. "What is he talking about?"

Michaels stuck his hat back on his head. "The fact that you were there at the scene, Miss Thorssen. Found the body and all. The Feds been talking about that. And they found the weapon."

"*Uno minuto.* You were there?" Paolo frowned fiercely.

I ignored the question and looked at Michaels. "The weapon?"

"In the tall grass outside the cabin. A little twenty-two. Registered to you, Miss Thorssen."

"My gun?"

Paolo frowned harder, his tanned faced creased in dismay. "You have a gun?"

"Um, that one my mother sent after the break-ins. You remember, Pao." He stared at me. "I've never even loaded it." I looked at Deputy Michaels. His expression was sympathetic but wary. "I kept it in a kitchen drawer. I've never shot it or anything."

"Hmm," Michaels grunted. "Well, somebody did. And left it in the grass for the G to find it right there."

I put my hand to my forehead. "Oh, God."

"What about prints from the fingers?" Paolo asked. "On the gun."

Michaels shook his head. "Not that I heard. But they dusted the victim's truck and found Miss Thorssen's prints all over it. And the house too."

"Well, I—I was there." Everyone knew I was there. But I didn't kill him. Of all the people who wanted him dead, I was the least. I wanted him alive, to speak to me, to vindicate me, to tell me secrets and magic and lies.

"Yes, well, the lawyer, Miss Thorssen. The lawyer," Michaels repeated, as if my mind couldn't grasp the concept. In that moment, he was right.

Michaels looked around the room suddenly, eyeing the paintings. "Are these his? The deceased?" He walked to the three colorful Tantro paintings that dominated the room.

"Those are Tantros, yes," Paolo said, an edge in his voice. He looked at me strangely. "Alix got those yesterday. She is appraising them for the Metropolitan Museum of Art. *In New York City.*"

Michaels squinted at them close up, then backed away, cocked his head as if he understood art. "Nice stuff." He turned back to me. "From Wally Fortney, right?"

I refused to acknowledge him, more from surprise than stubbornness. They knew about Wally? Had the Feds talked to him already?

The deputy nodded, as if I'd replied. "One last thing. Ol' Wally told the G that you were mighty anxious to get the pictures. Mighty eager, he said." Michaels turned to look me in the face. "He said you wanted to be sure Tantro was dead."

Michaels straightened his hat back on his head. The bell rang as he pulled the door open. "Just a suggestion, you know. A lawyer with a real nice suit."

FOURTEEN

I SLEPT POORLY that night. In my dream I kneeled over Ray Tantro and he blinked his cold, blue eyes and looked at me. *Ray,* I whispered, *tell me what happened. Tell me why you went away.*

You don't know? he whispered, his voice raspy and thin. *You were there, Alix. You should know.*

But I wasn't there, Ray. I wasn't with you.

He pulled his long legs up, folding his knees. With his bad hand he touched the three holes in his chest but his fingers came away clean.

We went down the same road, Alix. You were walking beside me.

I frowned at him. *I don't know what you mean.*

Something we both wanted, Alix. Something we both still want. Everybody wants it.

He rose to his feet and looked at the blank canvas. He took a brush in his hand, and the paint on it was wet and thick. With one stroke, one magical stroke, he painted a picture of heaven on the canvas, a purple-fringed cloud that was so beautiful I felt my heart break in my chest.

Tears smeared my vision, and when I rubbed my eyes he was gone.

I woke before dawn, my cheeks wet. The room was cold with night air. My stomach hadn't recovered from the acid burn I felt when Deputy Michaels had said I wanted Ray Tantro dead.

I had turned in the gallery and faced the wall. I couldn't let Michaels or Paolo see the shame on my face, the pettiness that had betrayed me down in Star Valley, the greed, the blind avarice, the sudden need for riches and fame through the paintbrush of a dead artist—who wasn't quite dead then but definitely was now.

I hadn't killed him but I was guilty, guilty of everything I despised.

Then there was Ray again, dead on the studio floor, and I thought about the samples they took of the blood on my hands, my shoe, my fingerprints, a strand of my hair. I hadn't even known him. I wanted to, I did. I heard his voice in my dream, indistinct and low. *We went down the same road, Alix.* But he kept dying, and dying.

THE MORNING LIGHT was heavy with dew, a foggy gray. Its weight cloaked me as I looked out the window, wrapped in my yellow chenille robe with the convenient ventilation. It was Sunday again, already. The week behind was a blur of emotion, violence, anger, death, denial. And now, even in the quiet of morning, I could feel the screws begin to turn. Screws that tightened down on me.

The apartment was quiet at last, aired out of the Eden smells, rid of Carl distractions. Cleaned to the gills, down to baseboards, rugs shaken and dishes washed. If only the simple task of cleaning out the kitchen sink, stacking the plates neatly on the shelves, toilet seat wiped with Pine-Sol—if only these things would clean up your life, give you peace and order and sunshine. It may have worked for Grandma.

No sunshine this morning. On the street below, the only vehicle parked on the square at this hour, Carl's vintage emerald El Dorado, sat covered with moisture. I wondered where he had stayed. There were no motels in the immediate vicinity. Did he sleep in the damn car? I rubbed my face hard.

A movement on the grass in the square caught my eye. I strained my neck to see around the elm trees that shaded the lawn. The figure moved, then stopped and moved again.

The rhythm continued until I could see the face. Yes, it was Carl. He was doing something strange. Movements with his hands, standing like a statue. I'd seen this before, on television. In big squares in China, thousands of Chinese in stork positions. What did they call it? Not kung fu. My hazy brain refused to respond. Then, as I saw his bare foot out behind him, dangling, I thought of it. Tai chi.

I slipped on my clogs and retied the robe. I ran down the stairs and out the back alley door, trying to hold the robe together over my bare legs. I stopped, breathless, at the sidewalk, looked both ways, and ran toward the square.

It was before six and the square was deserted. High in the trees birds began to awaken. When I reached Carl's car and slowed, I thought for a moment I had the wrong guy. The man in the grass seemed different, a black-and-white bandanna tied around his head, black sweatpants and sleeveless T-shirt. He was good at the positions, concentrating hard, but he looked ridiculous. I kept hearing sounds and looking over my shoulder as I waited on his cold bumper. I was sure some burly cowpoke would come along, laugh his guts out, then beat the living tar out of Carl.

He moved into a new position, one knee high, arms out, and held it, his face turning red. Then he moved slowly, methodically, into another. After ten minutes I forgot about ambushes. There was a simple purity to Carl's movements that was beautiful. And the quiet this time of day was intoxicating. Bird sounds were all you heard, high in the branches, families of birds calling each other, feeding each other, chirping, trilling. I closed my eyes and listened, hypnotized. In my mind's eye Carl was a bird, floating in the air, his arms wings.

"You bucking for an indecent exposure rap?"

My eyes flew open. Carl stood above me, hands on his hips, a kind of sad smirk on his face as if he wanted to smile but couldn't. Sweat dripped from his stained bandanna into his dark eyes.

I stood up quickly, covering my legs. "Carl, we have to talk."

He wiped his face with his shirt and didn't answer.

"Please, Carl. I'm sorry about yesterday. I won't defend it. But they've found my gun. My mother sent it to me last year. There were some break-ins at the gallery and she was worried about me. I never touched the thing."

He stared at me a second. "I don't get it."

"They found my gun at the scene. At Ray Tantro's cabin."

"How'd it get there?"

I touched his arm. He was warm and covered with sweat. "I don't know, Carl. Help me, please."

A pickup slowed in the street behind the El Dorado. A cowboy got out, took a broom and dustpan from the back of the truck, and swept up debris from the gunfight last night. He threw in the tools, grinned at me, and tipped his hat. I raised my chin in greeting, relieved I didn't know him personally. Nothing like standing in the middle of the town square in your ripped bathrobe to bring out all your friends and enemies.

"Where was it?" Carl asked.

"In a kitchen drawer."

"Who has access to your apartment?"

"All my houseguests, of course. And Paolo, he has a key. And Megan, our evening help."

"Where does Paolo keep the key?"

I tried to think. "I don't think he keeps it on his key chain. Probably in his desk."

Carl slipped the bandanna off his head and wiped his face with it. "So anybody who was in the gallery could have taken it."

I rolled my eyes. This wasn't helping. "Deputy Michaels came by and suggested I get a lawyer."

Carl frowned and watched a bicyclist zoom around the square on a road bike. "That can wait. Just because your gun was there doesn't mean it'll match up with the bullets in Tantro."

"And if they do match?"

"Come on." He took my arm and led me back across the deserted street, eyeing my bare legs as the robe sagged in the belt. "We both need to clean up."

WE SHOWERED TOGETHER. It was the last nice thing that happened to me that day. I rubbed soap all over his smooth mocha back and chest, shampooed his hair with vigorous fingertips, and let him scrub my back with a loofah. I let him do some other things too. Nice things. If his arms were wings, his fingers were delicate, expert feathers. It was almost as good as the pup tent. I caught my breath under the showerhead as he slipped away, toweling off as I turned the water colder. When I heard him leave the tiny bathroom, I let a sigh escape me and turned off the water.

The telephone was ringing when I emerged, dripping, wearing the bathrobe again. Carl held out the phone.

"It's Danny," he said.

"Hi," I said, my mind still back in the shower with Carl.

"Shit, Alix," Danny sighed. "What the fuck have you done now?"

"I know, Danny. I never should have gone out there without you. You told me."

"No, no. It's the gun. Your twenty-two."

"I didn't shoot him. I didn't do it. I wanted to talk to him. To ask him questions. I didn't want him dead." Was I going to have to say this over and over?

"Yeah, well, tell it to the judge. I hear the Feds are making their case. They want to wrap up by Monday morning. They like to be efficient."

"Tomorrow?"

"Listen, Frye is giving them all kinds of bullshit. You don't even want to know what he's saying. It'll make you crazy."

"Tell me, Danny."

He said he'd be right over and hung up. I put on a faded green Metropolitan Museum T-shirt from a Picasso exhibit and a pair of worn jeans. By the time I'd dried my hair Danny was drinking coffee with Carl in the living room. I sat on the edge of the sofa and looked sideways at Danny.

"So tell me," I said. "What's Frye saying?"

Danny sighed. He wore a flannel shirt with the sleeves cut off and canvas climbing pants. His hair was a mess, like he'd been tugging it, and his eyes had rings under them. He flashed his blue eyes at me, still angry.

"I can't believe you got yourself into this mess, Alix."

Carl was giving me a disapproving look too. "She runs right into things," he said.

"I should have waited for you, I know," I said, feeling my back rise at the collective criticism. "But, goddamn it, I was the only person who thought Ray was still alive. Nobody believed me. I tried to tell Frye but he blew me off."

"Now he's saying that you were hunting for Ray," Danny said.

"Hunting? What's that mean?" I frowned.

"He's giving the Feds the impression that you wanted something from Tantro and were looking for him against advice of the cops."

I caught Carl's eye. "Well, that's true, I guess. But it's not a crime."

Carl set down his coffee cup on the table. "Forget all that. How did they get her gun?"

We sat a moment in silence. Street noise had begun below, a truck in the alley, a car backfiring on the square, the rattle of a skateboard on the boardwalk, the clop-clop of shod horses on asphalt. I rose and went to the kitchen drawer where I kept the gun. In the front was a pile of bills wrapped in a rubber band. The old orange cigar box where the gun had lain was still there. I lifted it out and opened it.

Inside, where the small chromeplated .22 and a box of bullets had nestled, was nothing.

"Wait, Alix, set it down," Carl said, rising. "Maybe we can get them to dust it for prints."

Danny shrugged as I put the cigar box on the counter. "I doubt the shooter left any. The gun was clean, I heard."

"At least my prints weren't on it," I mused, sinking to my elbows on the counter.

Danny stood up and stretched. "I have to get some sleep. My editor doesn't know it but I'm taking the day off," he said. "He loves a good murder."

After Danny left, Carl and I couldn't agree on what to do with the cigar box. He was in favor of popping it into a bag and taking it to the cops. I was sure that was useless, and maybe would even backfire, since my fingerprints were certainly on the box. They might use it as a further nail in the coffin.

Leaving the cigar box on the counter, we made our way out the back door and walked to Jedidiah's House of Sourdough for breakfast. Tubs of blue lobelia and spires of purple lupine nodded with dew. Cool air filtered down the grassy runs of Snow King Mountain, fresh with pine. Hummingbirds circled a clump of red monarda, buzzing as they swooped. But the shadows and the morning's pale, half-clouded sky were full of questions—and gloom.

I had grabbed my slouch hat on the way out of the apartment. I didn't want to talk to anyone. I pushed my Ray-Bans up my tortured nose and slumped along the street. Carl had his hands deep in his pockets and kept looking back over his shoulder.

Down the street a figure appeared around the corner, making headway toward us at a clip. I recognized the profile of the racing wheelchair before I saw Martin Ditolla, shoulders pumping, head down, training hard. I straightened but didn't have the presence of mind, nor the smallness of spirit, to get out of sight.

Martin looked up and spotted me. He slowed, letting his powerful arms go limp as he leaned back in the slinglike seat that hung between the oversized racing wheels. His legs were tucked into the front of the blue cloth sling.

"Alix, my gal." He panted, flashing me a huge smile. His gray ponytail was disheveled and damp. "You're a hard one to get ahold of." He rolled up the small parking lot ramp, next to the car.

"Hi, Martin."

Carl shook Martin's hand. "Nice wheels, man. You training for a race?"

"You guys know each other?" I said. My brain seemed fuzzy with other concerns.

"We met at the Second Sun. Waiting for you to arrive, Alix," Martin said, panting a little. His chest and arms were slick with sweat, his tank top soaked.

Martin apologized for the dirt on his gloved hand. He explained he was training for a marathon in three weeks.

"I got a buddy on the force. He's a wheeler," Carl said.

I looked at him. This was a side of Carl I hadn't seen. I realized there were probably many sides of Carl I hadn't seen, didn't know, and hadn't imagined. He had come down here to see me, to get to know me better, and all I had offered in return was trouble. My shoulders sagged further. When would I quit letting everybody down? I could barely look at Martin's tanned face, so trusting and optimistic.

"Yeah? Does he race?" Martin asked.

"He's just getting into it. He used to be a runner," Carl said. "He's one of the best detectives on the force. Coordinates the Crime Scene Unit."

"What happened to him?" I asked, ever the nosy broad.

"Shoot-out. A drug bust. Took a bullet in the spine."

Martin nodded, wiping his face on his already damp shirt.

Carl glanced at me. "I'm starving." He turned to Martin. "Look, we're going to breakfast. Maybe you could join us."

"Ah, sure." Martin brightened. "We need to talk. Give me half an hour."

"At Jedidiah's," I called as he wheeled off into the street. With a few powerful throws of his arms he was up to speed, cruising around the corner and out of sight.

JEDIDIAH'S HOUSE of Sourdough was housed in a turn-of-the-century clapboard cottage, added onto over the years but still retaining its frontier flavor. Painted pale green, it sat a block or two from the square and was a favorite of tourists. I hadn't been there in years. Not that there was anything wrong with it. I just could never get a table.

Today, although a Sunday, we were lucky. In high summer that means early, beating the tourists. When we arrived on the small, slanted porch and went through the ancient screen door, it was only 8:05. Jedidiah's had been open for five minutes.

We sat at a square oak table in the bigger dining room that accommodated all of eight tables. The waitress poured us coffee and we sat, silent, sipping and regrouping.

I felt Carl's hand on my thigh and looked up, surprised. I had been deep in thought about what I should do next. I needed to talk to the principals in the case again. There had to be more information, something I was missing. I had whittled the list to Esther Tantro, Wally Fortney, Dr. Miller, and Margaret Elliot.

But now Carl was moving his hand up the inside of my leg. "Carl," I whispered, looking for the waitress.

"What?"

"Stop it."

He didn't stop it until the waitress refilled our coffee cups. "I thought you were an angel sitting on my bumper this morning."

"In my bathrobe?"

"An angel in a yellow bathrobe. Why not?"

"You were so pissed last night."

"So were you." His fingers were at it again.

"Maybe we could go backpacking instead of kayaking," I offered.

"You did kinda like that pup tent." He grabbed his coffee cup with both hands suddenly, leaving me tingling. "That spill on the Big Kahuna really got to you, didn't it?" He examined my face.

"I got stuck in the kayak."

"You didn't drown. You have to face those kind of situations and know you can get through them. It's like the first time you have to draw your gun. You've been playing over the scenarios so many times in your mind that when it really happens you can't believe it. Some guys freeze."

"And the bad guys shoot them?"

"It happens."

"To you?" I asked.

Carl shook his head. "No, but I can feel this wall building inside me. One day I won't be able to draw my gun at all. When you see that coming, it's time to quit."

"Maybe you could get a different job on the force. Like your friend on the Crime Scene Unit."

Carl shrugged, unconvinced. A commotion at the front door heralded the arrival of Martin in his everyday wheelchair. I got up to move a chair out of the way at the table. He moved his wheelchair expertly into position with the waitress hovering as people tend to do.

We ordered breakfast, an omelette for Martin and the house specialty, sourdough pancakes, for Carl and me. Martin drank three glasses of water, one after another, until finally he came up for air.

"I sweat five pounds of water during those long training rides," he explained. "Gotta hydrate."

Carl smiled. "Alix and I were just saying this is our first normal meal since I got here. You know, pleasant, social."

I gave him a look. We had had a few nice dinners, hadn't we? I squirmed on the hard straight-back chair, remembering the feel of his fingers on my thigh. I had a strong desire to go back to my apartment and take another shower with him. Squeak the bedsprings with the wild monkey dance. I let the idea drift over me, a titillating thought.

Martin's eyes flicked between us and settled finally on me. "Sorry to bring up business. But if I don't bring it up now, who knows when I'll see you again."

I tried to smile. I didn't want to hear this.

"It's the paintings, Alix."

"I know."

"They've been done for three months, framed for over six weeks. I can tell you aren't ready for them—"

"It's not that, Martin."

"Just let me explain. I sold two of them."

"You what?"

"I know I promised them to you. I'm sorry. I saved the two best ones for you. The ones hanging in the Second Sun. Of course, they won't be a set like the four. But I needed the money."

I couldn't think of anything to say. Regret at losing the set mingled with relief at not being responsible for the bankruptcy of my friend. My throat clogged with emotion. The sight of Ray Tantro's blank canvas popped into my head: What was it saying? Why hadn't he painted in that room? Where did he paint? Why had I found him? I blinked my eyes and focused on Martin again. His large head was still perspiring. His hair was damp on his forehead.

"You're not mad?" he said uncertainly.

"Mad? No. Disappointed. I loved those pieces, Martin. They were the best things you've ever done."

Martin smiled modestly. "I talked to Paolo a couple of times and he never would say anything. I got the feeling there was some disagreement between you two and I hoped it wasn't because of the paintings."

"To be honest with you, Martin—" I stopped myself. Why tell him we couldn't afford his paintings? Why tell the world that we would soon be splitting the spreadsheets? Paolo could blab to his bedmates, but I wouldn't. "To be honest, it's going to put a hole in my autumn plans. But maybe we can work something else out. I mean, the season is weeks away yet. At least we can keep displaying the other two."

Martin chewed a mouthful of eggs. "I know I let you down. If you got into production of the prints right away, I could oversee that for you. Before I go to Salt Lake for the race."

"When is that again?"

"Three weeks."

Great. Now I only had to come up with five thousand dollars for the remaining two paintings, get them color separated and into production with the printer in the next three weeks. As if I had the five grand lying around, ready to slap into this good man's hand. As if I had the time to shepherd his fine works through the printmaking process, or the energy to give that they—and he—deserved.

"I—I'll talk to Paolo about it," I said, pouring maple syrup on the pancakes. Carl was shoveling them into his mouth. "Martin, I can't promise anything. You understand?"

He nodded and seemed to be finally getting the message. His eyebrows twitched as he cut a slab of whipped egg with his fork. "Whatever you guys want to do, Alix. You've been great to me."

We ate our meal, making chitchat about the dismal weather, kayaking the canyon, Carl's lack of plans since quitting the Missoula PD, and Martin's one-man show in a Sun Valley gallery this winter. When it was time to go, Martin insisted on paying.

"I owe you," he said. "And more than just—" He consulted the bill. "More than just sixteen forty-five."

We moved toward the door. "Who did you sell the paintings to? Or is that privileged information?" I held open the screen.

"Oh, Alix. I'd tell you anything." Martin spun his chair around to face us on the porch and laughed hard. "You wouldn't believe it if you heard it from anybody else anyway. I sold them to Jake Laughlin."

FIFTEEN

"WHO'S JAKE LAUGHLIN?"

We stood on the sidewalk in front of Jedidiah's House of Sourdough, our stomachs stretched from pancakes and that heavy feeling in our limbs from too much syrup. At least Martin looked alert, stretching his arms out from his wheelchair. The orange shirt he wore made him look even healthier. Carl had asked the question.

"You must have met him the same night you met Martin. Pudgy, arrogant. Bushy, bushy brown hairdo," I told Carl. "Paints wildlife scenes. What would he want with your pieces, Martin? No offense, I mean, but they're so different from what he does."

"I know." Martin nodded. "You know what I think? I think he's starting a gallery himself. He made some comments about Westward Galleries, you know, gave me the idea he wasn't happy there."

"Jake Laughlin will never be happy," I grumbled.

Carl wasn't listening. He stared, frowning, down the street to the corner. I followed his gaze. Sitting by the stop sign on the side street was the biker, his black helmet with mirrored visor making him faceless. He sat motionless, astride the big chopper, looking the other way.

"Come on." Carl grabbed my hand, pulling me down the street toward the corner.

"Nice meeting you, Carl," Martin called as we broke into a run.

"Thanks for breakfast." I managed a wave behind my back to Martin.

The biker was still a block away from us when he calmly made a U-turn, walking chained boots in a circle. He revved the motor and disappeared down the side street. Carl dropped my hand and dashed into the street. His sandals slowed him down. By the time we reached the corner, the biker was gone.

"Did you see the license?" I panted, out of breath.

Carl shook his head. "I'm not sure he had one."

The traffic, both foot and auto, had picked up. Families in shorts and sandals shivered in the morning dew, peering greedily into closed stores for replacements for the sweaters they left at home. Two bicyclists swerved around us as we stood in the gutter. We began walking slowly back toward the apartment. We were almost to the square when a silver Jeep pulled up next to us.

"You two lost?"

Paolo grinned from his open window, wearing a red turtleneck with the sleeves pushed up. "Get in, lost ones. I've been looking for you."

I got in the front, Carl in back. Paolo's Jeep was the new model, loaded with extras like gray leather seats, blaster stereo, and sunroof. I had never actually been in it. The seat cradled my backside; he had even turned the seat warmer on, an unusual but welcome summer choice for Wyoming.

"Where are we going?" I asked when Paolo did a U-turn much like the biker had.

"Just driving. The cops are looking for you everywhere. They came by the gallery and your apartment. Then they came to my house, wanting to know if I knew where you were. Luckily I didn't. I'm a terrible liar." He smiled.

"Oh, right." I turned to Carl and rolled my eyes. "What did they say?"

"They want to question you about the murder."

"Goddamn gun," I grumbled, looking out the side window. "Wait till I give my mother a piece of my mind for sending it to me."

"You didn't have to keep it," Carl said. "Especially since you never learned to use it. It's dangerous to have a gun in the house that you don't know how to use."

"I don't need a lecture, Carl." I sunk into the leather seat and pulled down my slouch hat. But inside I knew that hiding wasn't the answer to this mess. I was going to have to act if I was going to get my ass out of this sling.

"Just like Argentina," Paolo said. "Everybody has a pistol."

"Wyoming isn't much different," I said.

"That's what I liked about it, when I first came out. It reminded me of home. Cowboys, horses, mooing cows and hay and mountains. Just like home."

I watched him. *Then why don't you stay?* Why leave this home-away-from-home? His face was sad in memory, as if something good had passed.

"But it has changed. It doesn't look like home anymore." We were on the business strip west of town, filled with cheap motels, restaurants serving barbecue and fast food, car dealers and rafting companies, helicopter rides and climbing gyms. It wasn't how I had envisioned Jackson either, when I'd come. But it was America to me, a part I disliked but accepted, free enterprise, capitalism in action, the money where the mouth is. Perhaps that was something that Paolo could never understand.

I put my hand on Paolo's arm. "Can we go to your house? I have to, you know, use the facilities."

"The faculties—?"

"The toilet."

Paolo grinned and swung around toward his bungalow.

"HE SEEMS LIKE a good guy. A little glum, but a good guy."

We stood in Paolo's kitchen while he made coffee. I already had jangled nerves from too much caffeine and too little sleep. Carl was in the bathroom. I looked out over the lush backyard, delphiniums towering in the back, daylilies nodding their orange heads.

"Who? Carl?" I said absently.

"Carl, yes. Is he good to you?" Paolo poured water into the coffeemaker.

I turned. "Who wants to know?"

"Just a concerned friend. What? Do I sound jealous?"

Maybe I just imagined that hint of excessive concern in his voice. "I'm not very good to him, if you must know. I told him to go home yesterday."

"What, didn't he wash the toothpaste out of the sink?" Paolo smirked, remembering one of my pet peeves when we lived together. It seemed so petty now, but I used it as a rationalization for giving my partner the domestic boot. At the time it was too painful to admit I knew of his dalliances, or that I cared too much to make a stand.

I changed the subject. "Did you ever meet Ray Tantro?"

Paolo flipped the switch on the machine. "At Eden's opening for the show, sure. I met him there."

"You went to the opening?"

"It was your Sunday to work, I think. Speaking of which, I have to go open up in a few minutes." He glanced at the wall clock, a clever tiled number that read over a face full of cockeyed numbers: *Time Becomes Meaningless in the Face of Creativity.*

"Wait a sec, Pao. Tell me about Ray Tantro," I said, pouring myself an unneeded mug of java. "What was he like?"

He frowned. "Kind of a what-you-call-it? A jock."

"A jock?"

"Yeah, full of himself. Talking loud and basically full of horseshit."

"Like how? What did he say?"

"Like this." Paolo struck an arrogant pose, nose up, hands on hips. "Bug-heeled boots, fancy cowboy clothes. Then he says, 'This piece reflects my inner being in conflict with the tempest of life around me.' Baloney like that. Very boring."

Carl found us. "Coffee, Carl? Just made it," Paolo said, looking at the clock again. "Gotta go, guys. Hang out here if you want. Things may be a little hot around your place, Alix." He looked at me sternly. "I don't like the cops showing up at the gallery. It scares away the customers."

"Always thinking about the customers. Never mind my rear end is in a sling."

"Keep your rear end out of other people's business." He gave the anatomy in question a firm slap on his way out of the kitchen. From the living room he called, "My old Subie is in the alley. I'll leave the keys here on the table if you want to use it." The door closed behind him.

CARL AND I took the battered Subaru back to my apartment, having lost our ability to agree on anything, particularly a course of action. I had argued in Paolo's living room for a full frontal assault on all the main suspects in the case, but Carl had reminded me that the only suspect we knew of was sitting right there on the mauve leather couch. Then I wanted to go talk to Margaret, and the doctor, and Eden again, to round up anybody who knew Ray, his mother, his neighbors, his friends.

But Carl didn't agree. He had a cloud on his forehead and refused to talk about it, as if his mind was far away.

AT TWO IN THE afternoon Carl and I stood stiffly on the stoop of Danny B.'s apartment, not far from Paolo's house. The sun struggled through high clouds, turning the day a pale shade of blue cream. A clay pot of bright salmon geraniums sat on a corner of the cement stoop. The brown stained siding had weathered badly, in streaks, and the cement steps we mounted were unadorned by railings. They led to an untended commons of grass and weeds where a rusty tricycle sat abandoned.

I knocked on the metal door, painted a dark gold. On it hung a homemade wreath made from red willow branches. Inside a baby cried, a woman's voice hushed him. Carl didn't look at me as he said, flatly: "You let guys give you fanny pats?"

"I usually don't. So don't get any ideas," I tried to joke. But he wasn't in a jovial mood. He slumped against the building, dressed today more like I remembered him from last summer: hair slicked back, face tense, jeans and cowboy boots. I noticed suddenly that he had shaved his mustache.

"So he's the exception," he said.

I opened my mouth to speak when the door opened.

A slight, blond woman stood smiling with a baby on her hip. When we had called fifteen minutes earlier, Geri Bartholomew told us Danny was taking a nap but to come over anyway because she was tired of watching the kids alone. Her voice was light and full of laughter. She ushered us into the small apartment, more like a town house with bedrooms upstairs.

Danny bounded down the stairs, disheveled, black beard a mass of fur. "Sit down, please. Oh, Jesus, the papers." Several Sunday newspapers were strewn over the available seating, a matched set of fifties furniture, sofa and two armchairs in a blocky, semideco style with skinny wooden legs and brown curly upholstery. The thing about polyester, it's indestructible. You can be stuck with the same ugly couch for fifty years.

Danny rounded up the papers into a heap and dropped them on the floor. "Do we have coffee, Ger?"

"None for us, thanks. We're way over our caffeine quota," I said, sitting on the hard couch. I pulled a rubber squeak toy from between the cushions and set it on the papers. The living room was reasonably tidy for a family with two small children, sparsely furnished with a huge toy box in the corner.

"Well, I need some. Scanlon and Doc Miller had me out till two. Those two can nurse a beer longer than anybody." Danny chuckled, perching on the armchair that faced Carl's by the front window.

"What did you find out?" I said as Geri left to get coffee.

"That those two can't hold their liquor, nurse 'em all they want." Danny smiled, sliding into the bottom of the chair. He ran his hand over his long dark hair and sighed.

"Did they say anything about the fire?"

"Oh, sure." Danny sobered, seeing my face. "Scanlon still thinks it's arson, of course."

"Brilliant," Carl said.

"I know, I know. It's obvious," said Danny. "And the victim—whoever he was—was intentionally burned to conceal his identity. Doc Miller changed his tune on that. He doesn't think it was suicide now."

"Equally brilliant," Carl sniped.

I glared at him and turned back to Danny. "Will they re-open the investigation?"

"I don't know that they'll have a choice. But Frye will drag his feet, I'd guess. The election is only six weeks away. Nobody can blame him for the Tantro murder."

"And it takes the attention away from the earlier one," I said. "You've got to keep up the pressure on Frye, Danny."

"I haven't got anything new to use. Scanlon is, excuse me, a whining wreck who might have been a great investigator once. But now all he knows is that it's arson and somebody died."

"Smokey the Bear could have told him that," Carl opined. "Or the Easter bunny."

"Thank you, Carl," I said.

Geri came back with Danny's coffee. "Are you sure I can't get you something?" We assured her we were fine. She scooped up the baby from the floor where he was crawling, introduced him as Henry, and went out the back door.

"Bradley's probably out there building a bomb, the little terrorist. Three years old and heavy into sabotage." Danny smiled, shaking his head. "Yesterday I went to put on my shoes and found them filled with mud up to the shoelaces." He sipped his coffee, then set the cup on the table. "You still haven't told me why you went out there yesterday, Alix. I feel responsible. I shouldn't have called you."

"Bingo." Carl again. We tried to ignore him.

"I had to talk to him." I rubbed my forehead. "I knew he wasn't dead. I knew he wouldn't kill himself. He was such a genius with paint, and he fell so far. He was just coming up out of the darkness. He wouldn't kill himself. Not now."

"He really was big, then?"

"Very. I remember NBC News—who was on then? John Chancellor? He did a report himself on Tantro's one-man show in New York. Ray was twenty-three."

"So the drugs and liquor flowed. I can see it," Danny said. "To be so famous so young. It's hard to take that kind of adulation and keep your head on."

"At any age."

"Okay, okay," Carl said, leaning forward to finally join the discussion. "So who the hell died in the damn fire? If it wasn't suicide, then somebody killed a guy. Why? And the big question burning in my mind—why did somebody work so hard to implicate Alix?"

I looked at Danny for answers. He shrugged.

"If we find out who died in that fire, we'll find out who killed Ray Tantro. I'm sure of it," I said.

"Unless the first murderer *was* Ray Tantro," Danny said.

"Maybe he killed somebody to make it look like he was dead. So that cousin Wally or whoever could make money on those old pictures," Carl said.

"Then what happened to him?" Danny asked.

"He got into a disagreement," I said.

"With Wally?"

"I don't think so," I said. "Wally didn't kill him."

"How can you be so sure?" Danny asked. "Who has the most to gain from Ray being dead? He'll make a fortune off those paintings now."

"And who trashed you to the Feds," Carl said.

I shook my head. "Not Wally. He's like this classic Mormon dad. An Ichabod Crane with eight kids, works in a cheese factory."

"So what has he got to lose?" Carl smirked.

"Seriously, Alix," Danny said. "Just because a guy's got a family doesn't mean he isn't desperate enough to kill somebody. Maybe that *makes* him desperate. Maybe he only meant to scare Ray and something went wrong."

"Then what about my gun? How would Wally get ahold of it?"

Danny squinted, thinking. "He could have come to town. Broken into your apartment."

"I don't see it," I said. "Wally just isn't that bright. I met him."

"Don't underestimate people, Alix."

I looked at my hands. Back in Wally's garage, his pregnant wife puffing with the heavy tarp, the treasure under there. Had I overlooked something in my heady state? Had the prospect of all those Tantros blinded me to Wally Fortney's motives? Sure, he wanted the money those paintings would bring. That wasn't criminal. Ray had given him those paintings, Esther had said so. What he did with them was his own concern. He thought Ray was dead.

"So you think Wally set the fire too?" I asked.

"You mean, with Ray?" Danny asked. "He might have. Because the reason for that fire has got to be that Ray wanted everybody to think he was dead. They had to be in it together."

"Then why'd Ray come back to Jackson? Why risk it?" Carl said. None of us had answers to that. We examined our fingernails for a few minutes.

"How soon before the fire broke out does Scanlon think it was set?" I asked Danny.

"An hour. Maybe more. It wouldn't take long for the candle to burn through the balloon. Or for the vapor to cool in the attic."

"We can check alibis, then. Sort of. It would take a while to get the guy in place, squirt the vapor into the attic, set up the balloon." I paused. "We didn't tell you what we found at Eden's apartment."

"We found nothing," Carl said.

"That's right. The valuables were cleaned out, Danny. No TV, no stereo, no microwave or other kitchen gadgets. Very few clothes left." Eden's bedroom was in my mind, the mess of sheets and blankets, the pillows indented from sleep. Both pillows. "Do you know if Eden was sleeping with anybody just before the fire?"

Danny looked at Carl, puzzled. "Why ask me? She's your friend."

The phone rang in the kitchen. Danny went to get it. Carl sat back in his chair, silent. I glanced at him. "We're not getting anywhere, are we?"

"I don't think the cheddarhead swiped your gun and set you up," he said.

"I don't either. But who else would want Ray Tantro dead?"

Danny came back, standing with his arms crossed. His expression was somber. "That was Jim, my editor. The FBI is looking for the judge to get a search warrant for your apartment."

I squinted. "I've been expecting that."

Danny nodded. "Jim wants me to see if I can go along. I doubt they'll let me."

"Can they search my place if I'm not there?"

"If they have a warrant."

I stood up. "I guess I'd rather be there. So they don't wreck the place."

Carl rose. "Good idea." He looked grim, his mouth a thin line, and I could almost see the works of his brain turning. We said good-bye to Danny. He promised to call if he found out anything else. He hugged me quickly, as if to apologize for his outburst this morning, and told me to take care of myself.

Carl sat behind the wheel of Paolo's beat-up Subaru wagon, feeling around on the floor and in the glove compartment. I opened the door, reached inside my jeans pocket, extracting the keys. As I got in he snatched them from my hand. By the time I shut my door we were in the street.

"Where do you want to go?" Carl's words were measured, but his eyes were troubled.

"My apartment. I guess it's time to face the music."

I assumed Carl was concerned about me, but he nodded distractedly; his bottom lip covered the top and the newly shorn skin. I wanted to reach out and touch the soft place under his nose, but his stiffness held me back. I thought of this morning in the shower, and it seemed as far away and irretrievable as yesterday.

He stopped in the middle of the street in front of the gallery, having made record time, reached over, and opened my door.

"You're taking Paolo's car?"

"I have to make a phone call. Then I'll be up," he said, his words clipped.

"You can call from my apartment," I said, sticking one foot out on the busy street. Behind us an RV the size of Connecticut chugged fumes into the mountain air.

"Just get out, Alix," he said, looking back at the traffic.

"Is it something you want to talk about?"

"You want to talk? Okay." His temper burst through his composure for an instant. "This whole thing was a mistake. I knew that from the beginning. Last summer was a mistake."

I put my hand on his arm. "No, it wasn't. What about this morning?"

He shook his head angrily. "You don't have room for anybody else in your life. You fill up the empty spaces so you don't feel lonely. But not with somebody who might make demands on you. No. Dead artists are much less demanding."

He revved the Subaru's miniature engine, then shrugged off my hand. I climbed out of the car. Carl grabbed the door handle and yanked it shut.

I stood in the street, watching as he peeled out, squealing around the corner in the tin-can Subie that had lost its color a few winters back, not to mention its tire tread and dubious muffler. I was hurt by Carl's surliness but too preoccupied to let my mind grasp it. The Subaru screeched down the block and careened around the corner, the dull silver paint almost flashing in the weak sunlight. What had I done? I couldn't even think about it. I wondered if he'd ever be back.

Carl Mendez, I thought as I walked through the gallery and waved to Paolo in a gaggle of blue-hairs, deserved a better car than the old Subaru.

And he deserved better than me.

THE SAAB SISTER was waiting like a debutante for a dance behind the police station in city hall. Before I went up to my apartment I wanted to get her back. I watched her for a good fifteen minutes before attempting her rescue. Once away from the cops I stopped, pried off all four rust-spotted hubcaps, and checked the lug nuts. Satisfied they were secure, I chucked the hubcaps in the trunk and went to park in the alley behind the gallery. For once no one had parked in my spot.

The roar that preceded what happened next ripped up the narrow alley, bouncing off the painted brick walls of the old buildings. I stood with my key in the lock of the driver's-side door, trying not to think about what the FBI had in store for me upstairs. My shoulders hurt, my nose hurt, my heart hurt about Carl, and the roar startled me. I jerked my head up and there he was, all in black with mirrored visor on the bubble helmet, leather and chains and Harley. I fumbled desperately with the key in the lock, and by that time the motorcyclist was right there, next to me, his heavy black boot extended, knocking my feet out from under me. The pain shot through my ankles, up my back, coinciding with the terrible noise of the cycle. I opened my mouth to shout, flailed my arms, still clinging to my keys and backpack, but felt nothing but the high pitch of confusion, the falling, falling. I landed hard on my back. My spine jolted, my skull crashed on the asphalt, and the roar was gone.

SIXTEEN

WHEN I OPENED my eyes, Paolo had his hand on my forehead. He smiled at me, concern in his eyes. I struggled to sit up as he put his arm around my shoulders.

"What happened? I heard a motorcycle when I was coming back to empty the trash," he said. "You fall down?"

I did a quick body inventory and found a large bump growing on the back of my head. Twisting my shoulders, I felt my back. It was sore but not incapacitated. One ankle-bone had a large bruise, growing a lump. I stood up with Paolo's help.

"The biker from hell," I said, looking down the alley. On the street babies hollered in strollers, kids whined, blue-hairs paused to look at the flowers, all oblivious to bikers and their menace. I shivered, imagining the alley as another world, separated from the idyllic grace of vacation by some invisible wall. Had the cyclist just vanished into that crowd without making a ripple?

"A biker?" Paolo looked behind him at the street, then spun to look the other way down the alley. "Where did he go?"

I picked up my keys, slouch hat, sunglasses, and backpack from the street. "I was looking at the sky. Well, stars anyway. I couldn't have been out long."

He looked into my eyes, examining me. "We better take you to a doctor. They say if you pass out, go see the doctor."

"It's just a bump, Pao."

"Well, come sit down inside for a while."

I followed him into the gallery and sunk into my office chair while he brought me a glass of water, as if that would help my possible concussion. I drank it anyway while he told me his news.

"The cops were here for an hour, asking questions," he said.

"I'm sorry, partner." I glanced into the empty gallery. "Did they scare everybody away?"

"Everybody but one. That friend of yours, the ski bum. Pete."

"What did he want?" A picture formed in my clotted mind of Pete in the towel with his screaming white chest and that dodo look on his face. I felt sick. Maybe I did have a concussion.

"He wants one of the Tantros. He offered, swear on Mother Mary's holy grave, he offered me twenty-five thousand bucks for the one called *Gloria.*"

"Get out of here."

"On the soul of my father. I didn't think he was serious, but he sure looked like it. What's the story on him?"

"His brother's some investment banker or something. He must be making an offer for him. Those paintings aren't for sale anyway."

"They could be. The Met hasn't bought them. Maybe they won't. Maybe the cousin will sell them." He lowered his voice as the doorbell tinkled in the gallery. "Can you talk to the cousin? Talk some sense into him?" He looked over his shoulder at the customers, then got that puppy-dog-pleading look on his face. "Just think what that sale would mean to us, amiga of mine. Just think."

I told him I would try. I wanted to talk to Wally Fortney again anyway. A piece of my mind begged to be given to him, a huge, unrepentant piece. How dare he imply to the cops that I wanted Tantro dead? I hadn't said that. Not exactly.

The amount Pete Rotondi had offered was extravagant. But what was twenty-five thou to a hotshot on Wall Street who probably brought in five mil in an average year? What had someone just told me? Don't underestimate people, Alix.

DESPITE MY IMPULSE for revenge on the biker, I realized there was little I could do but report the incident to the police. And Charlie Frye was the last person I wanted to see today. So instead of waiting for the federal search warrant to come through (hopefully the judge was out fishing on this fine Sunday afternoon), I got back in the Saab Sister and hit the road.

The high mountain sun grew brighter as I traveled south. The weather in Star Valley was a good ten to fifteen degrees hotter than Jackson. I had a headache but took a couple aspirin and brought along a huge iced tea from my refrigerator. The sun shone here, relentlessly. Waves radiated off the asphalt on Cedar Street. Dixie answered the door, face dripping with sweat, holding her swollen belly. She said Wally was in the backyard and shut the door without niceties.

The sound of a mower coming to life drowned out my footsteps on the concrete driveway. I walked gingerly, with a tender ankle and a backache from my fall. The house and yard, despite toys, balls, bicycles, swing sets, and baseball bats, displayed a careful neatness that I had seen in the deliberate rows of canned food in the garage. The lawn where Wally was pushing the old mower hardly needed a mow; the edges were trimmed around the chain-link fence in the back, the picket fence in front. A pile of toys sat on the sidewalk, picked over by five kids ranging in age from five to fourteen, who were putting them away in the open garage.

The oldest child, a lanky boy with huge feet and a sun-bleached crew cut, frowned when he saw me by the chain-link gate, waiting. I smiled and pointed to his father. The boy glanced at Wally, then walked in long strides toward him.

Wally cut the motor of the mower, mumbling a few words to the boy, who promptly went back to work. Ray Tantro's cousin was dressed in old khaki slacks that hung from his bony hips, and a short-sleeved shirt that revealed his freckled, ropy arms.

"Is there somewhere out of the sun we can talk?" I asked. Even with my hat, the sun baked my face and shoulders, draining what energy I hadn't blown up in the alley. Wally led the way to a cellar door. We walked down three steps into the dark, cool air.

"My summer hideaway," he said. "Course, we all use it in August. The heat's really getting to Dixie." He looked up at the unfinished ceiling, the beams close overhead. The room was his workshop, a tool bench stretching across one end, concrete floors, no windows, but cool. "Guess you were right about Ray."

I stuck my hands in my jeans pockets, now wishing I'd worn shorts. "Not for long."

Wally pulled out a handkerchief and wiped his face. "This doesn't change anything with the museum, does it?"

I took off my hat and ran my fingers through my damp hair. The goose-egg bump hurt. "I doubt it. Ray's still dead. The paintings are still Ray's, or rather were. And now they're yours."

He nodded, businesslike. I had to wonder if he felt anything for his dead cousin. Used to working with artists and Latins like Paolo who tell you their feelings in no uncertain terms, I felt at a loss reading regular guys like Wally. Maybe mowing the lawn was how he dealt with grief. At least Grandma would have approved. There were worse ways to grieve.

"I hung the paintings in the Second Sun and somebody made an offer on one," I said. "I know you offered them to the Met, so we told him it wasn't for sale."

"How much?"

"Is it for sale?"

"Depends on how much." He looked up again as footsteps crossed the floor; muffled voices filtered down. "How much?"

"Twenty-five thousand. For *Gloria*."

Wally stopped fidgeting. He stared me in the eyes, checking. I stared back. "I thought you said a hundred," he said finally.

"I said no guarantees, Wally." He watched the children through the open door for a moment.

"Is twenty-five serious?"

"It could be. Sometimes we get wild offers if something isn't really for sale. It's safe that way." I waited for him to tell me to sell it. I knew he would. His tongue worked against the inside of his cheek, impatient to yell, to collect. "Did you discuss money with the Met?"

Wally shook his head. "I figured we'd get to that later." He rubbed his temples. This kind of transaction was clearly not his everyday cup of tea.

A wail began upstairs, muffled at first, then louder. As it rose it became "Waaaalllleeee!" The recognition transformed his face. He plunged awkwardly for the door, out into the blinding sunlight.

I found them in the kitchen. Dixie lay on the floor, clinging to an overturned chair. Wally knelt beside her, asking her over and over what was the matter. She couldn't speak, just clung to the chair, then to his arm. Big-eyed children, the same three I had seen the first day, watched from the hallway.

"Is it time? Can it be time?" Wally said into her wild eyes. Dixie wore a big flowered housedress and no shoes, her hair soaked with sweat. "It's too early, honey. Too early."

Dixie moaned, clutching her belly again, a grunting agony passing through her. I stood by, helpless, until it was over and Wally stopped his constant mumble that seemed to help her through the contraction. "Should I call a doctor?" I asked.

Wally put his arm under her shoulders, cradling her. "She's always had the babies at home with a midwife. I helped. But now...I don't know."

"I'm calling an ambulance." I looked around the kitchen for the telephone and found it by the door, on the wall. I dialed 911 and gave them the address. "They're coming, Dixie, hold on."

I WAITED WITH the children. The older ones reassured me I could go, that they would all be fine without my supervision. The younger ones dragged me onto the swing set. Rosie, the two-year-old, wore my Ray-Bans for about thirty seconds before she dropped them in the sandbox.

The call came less than an hour later. Dixie had a four-pound boy in the Star Valley clinic operating room within minutes of her arrival. He was underweight and six weeks early, but seemed to be holding his own.

The kids piled into the Saab Sister and gave me directions to the clinic. When we reached the stolid, sun-bleached brick building, they rushed to their mother's side, against the admonitions of a nattering, overweight doctor. Wally held Rosie in the hall.

"Congratulations," I said. There was so much I had to talk to Wally about, things that needed to be said. He nodded, exhausted. Little Rosie buried her face in his neck.

"About Ray," I began. "When did you last see him?"

"Ray's dead. He's gone."

"I know, but..."

"It's bad luck to talk about the dead," he said, looking through the open door at his big, busy family. Dixie was receiving pats and strokes and kisses.

I had to know something that would bring him around. Something to help me find Ray's killer. No one else cared for Ray. Esther wouldn't help. I searched my mind, staring

at the gray tile floor of the clinic, a small medicinal out-
post.

"Why did you tell the FBI I wanted to make sure he was
dead?" Thin ice here, thin ice. I held my breath.

Wally squinted at me, disgusted. "Because that's what
you said. You said, what if he's not dead? Like you knew."

"I didn't know, Wally. I felt, you know, with my intui-
tion, that he wasn't dead." I paused, taking a breath. "I
found him."

Wally said nothing. He patted Rosie's back, comforting
her. She wiggled and he set her down on the floor. She
streaked toward her brothers and sisters, squealing.

"I didn't kill him. Somebody else did. But I found him.
With three holes in his chest, clutching at the drape, his easel, his art. Clutching at life that somebody took from him."

I could see Ray Tantro again in my mind's eye. The dark,
three-day beard, the icy skin, the dead eyes that once saw
beauty, the hands that once wielded a paintbrush.

Wally paled after my tirade, slumping against the wall.

"What happened to his fingers?" I demanded, a harsh-
ness in my voice.

He blinked, a little color returning. "What?"

"His fingers. The missing digits. This and this one." I
held up my hand, covering two knuckles on my ring and
pinkie fingers with my other hand. Wally shook his head.

"You aren't really his cousin, are you?"

"Of course I am." Suddenly indignant, Wally straightened, pulling himself off the wall. "My mother and his
mother were sisters. My mother's been gone six years."

Little Rosie ran out of the room, grabbing Wally's hand.
She dragged him in by Dixie's bed where his large, happy
family swallowed him up.

AN HOUR IN the county courthouse told me that Wally was
at least telling the truth about his mother. June Emilia

Plantier Fortney had died in Star Valley six years ago. She was seventy-two years old. I looked up Esther's birth certificate and found nothing. Apparently she wasn't born here. Then I found her marriage license: Esther Louise Plantier and Anthony Raymond Tantro, married June 6, 1940. I looked up Plantier in the phone book in the lobby of the old, sandstone block building and found two. No answers at Thomas E. Plantier. The other listing, Frank Plantier, was a business line at a car-parts store on Main Street. I jotted down the addresses and numbers and found my car again.

The NAPA car-parts store sat on the far end of Main Street, across the street from one of the gas stations that bracketed the town. Faced with aqua metal panels fading in the harsh sun, the store's windows were hung on the inside with translucent gray sheets of plastic. The effect inside the store was a dim, greasy atmosphere, not unlike lying on your back under your car's engine.

Rows of mufflers, filters, steering wheel covers, cans of oil and lubricating liquids lined utilitarian metal shelves. I stood for a moment, getting my bearings, when a middle-aged cowgirl with "Patsy" embroidered on her NAPA shirt found me. I asked for Frank Plantier. She strode to the back to find him.

Frank emerged, a man past retirement age, of small stature but commanding a bulk that some would call deadly. His girth was held in by a large blue NAPA shirt with years of grease stains. A round, bald scalp echoed the bottom half of his face. He let a pair of reading glasses slide down on his nose to take a look at me.

I introduced myself. He was polite, shaking my hand, but wary in the way of small-towners. "Who you say sent you?"

"Wally Fortney. You are related, he said."

"Sure, he's my sister's boy."

I smiled. "That's what he said. I'm looking into the estate of Ray Tantro. His paintings."

Plantier shifted his weight, slowly. "I don't have any. My sis Esther's got a few, but he never give me one." He scratched his scalp and leaned against a shelf of Pennzoil. "I never held it against him or nothing. I don't have much use for paintings."

"Then you didn't know he left Wally quite a few?"

"Did he? Nah, I don't see Wally much since Junie died. I got seven kids of my own to keep track of, you know what I mean?" He laughed, shaking.

"Did you see Ray often?"

He shook his head. "Ray was a heap of heartache to Esther. First he goes off to some fancy art school and just about wipes out their savings. Then he thinks he's so whopping smart he quits! Like piss on you, Ma, I'll do what I want. Then he goes down, really down, I mean. Booze, drugs, all of it."

"That must have been hard for the family."

"Hard for Esther, sure. Tony died ten, twelve years ago. She's been propping Ray up ever since. It was bad enough he was in the hospital in Casper. That liked to kill her."

"When was this?"

"Last year, I guess. Yeah, I was doing some remodeling here in the store, I remember. Waxed the floor too. Last spring. Had to go look in on her place for her. The wife never liked Esther, if you want to know the truth. So little brother gets to do it." He smirked conspiratorially. "Not that I mind getting away from the wife here and again."

We talked some more, about the Plantier sisters, how they were famous for their party dresses when they were young, how their oldest brother, Thomas, was Stake President of the Latter-Day Saints, how the community hung together and all that good stuff. We never mentioned the three holes in the chest of Ray Tantro.

On the way out I announced Wally and Dixie's new arrival, with some pride for having helped in my own small way. Frank nodded distractedly. He had his own seven kids to keep track of.

SEVENTEEN

THE AFTERNOON SUN beat down on the hood of the Saab, bleaching out what remained of the eggplant red of the paint. I adjusted my sunglasses, wiping sand from the hinges, and checked the lug nuts again before getting into the hot car. It was five-thirty, and the heat was just beginning to fade as the sun moved westward. My head settled into a low-grade throb, tolerable but making me want to lie down in the shade somewhere.

I gave the teenage gas station attendant a little wave, saw his heart palpitate, and started up the Saab. Then I saw him.

Dressed all in black, the biker was off his Harley, drinking a can of something, his head back, draining it. Three blocks separated us, blocks of storefronts, spindly trees struggling in the Wyoming sun, one stoplight, six pickups, and one horse trailer.

He was drinking the soda or beer with his helmet still on, visor flipped up, but at this distance he could have been anyone. Bikers worship their leathers even on the hottest of days. This guy was no different: black jacket with big diagonal zippers, leather pants or chaps, driving gloves. And the same black helmet.

He tossed the can in the gutter and flipped down the mirrored visor as he swung a leg over the seat of his hog. He walked it forward a couple steps, then stomped the motor alive.

My heart thumped in my chest. I looked over my shoulder, pulled the Saab out into traffic. I wanted to follow *him* this time, not vice versa. If I moved slowly he would pull out. If not, I would at least get his license number.

I crept toward him, doing a big twenty-miles-per while I kept my eyes glued to the flash of his chrome handlebars. The light changed to red and I pulled up. A block away, he revved the engine. Just before the light changed he made a U-turn and disappeared down the side street. The chase was on.

By the time I squealed around the corner, he was nowhere in sight. I slowed at the next corner, where the stores gave way to old white houses with listing iron fences, and looked both ways. I chose right, to the north, drove a block, looked again, and went back toward Main Street.

Star Valley was mid-siesta, the sidewalks empty, a breeze blowing the streetlight hanging from cables above the street. I idled the Saab, put her in neutral, and took out the clutch. I tried not to think about what I would do with the biker if I caught up with him. At least I would find out who he was. Were these encounters intended to distract me from my pursuit of Ray Tantro and his killer? What did he want? Was he the one who had loosened my lug nuts? Was he the one who killed Ray?

Then, from nowhere, he roared by, feet up by the front wheel, hands high on the elongated handlebars, going seventy-five down the dusty highway toward points north. In the rip of noise I fumbled with the gearshift, searching for first gear, and did my best James Bond maneuver into Main Street, barely missing a cattle truck.

The '67 Saab, I hasten to admit, was not built for speed. With a body like a squat pig and the engine equipped with two squirrels, I was lucky to keep her at fifty. While I had the Harley in sight as we left town and kept on the straight highway, slowing through Freedom, as soon as we entered the Snake River Canyon, he was gone.

The narrow, winding road made me slow further. I peered ahead at the curves, looking for him. I slowed down, deciding staying on the road and out of the river was most important. I gave up on catching him and let my mind work on the puzzle of Star Valley.

I'd visited Esther Tantro after my talk with her brother Frank. She had been out in the apple orchard, a big straw hat shading her face. She was picking up rotten apples off the ground. She met me with a bland, dismissive air, then stared at the green, worm-eaten apple in her hand.

"Used to have the best apples in the county when Tony was alive," she mumbled. She wore a long blue gingham dress, circa 1940, with cheap athletic shoes and white socks. "He sprayed every spring, three times. Just the oil, not any chemicals, never believed in chemicals. Mother Nature had her ways if you could keep the worms out of 'em."

She dropped the apple to the ground, stooped, and picked up another. "Some of 'em you just don't know what killed 'em. Look at this one." She held the green apple out to me. "Looks perfect, don't it? Why would it fall off the tree, you wonder. But look." She pulled a paring knife from a basket on the ground and sliced the apple in half expertly. "Rotten inside. Looks good but it's all rotten."

She tossed the apple aside, squatting near the base of the tree. The straw hat didn't hide the creases in her face, or the sadness in her eyes.

"Mrs. Tantro, was Ray in the hospital in Casper?"

Looking away from the horizon, she nodded, throwing the knife into the basket.

"And did he get better and come home?"

"He came home," she said, standing with the basket handle over her arm, looking for all the world like Auntie Em, somewhere over the rainbow. She didn't look at me but at her toe, kicking apples aside as she went to the next tree and examined its rejects.

"Did you nurse him here?" I asked, following.

She nodded. "He quit the alcohol. He had quit the drugs a few years before."

"Didn't you think it was odd that he had killed himself with drugs and liquor in the burning gallery?"

"He was lost to me by then." She looked up, a stern frown on her brow. "You have any children?" I shook my head. "Then you can't know. Unless you have a child who you give life to, who you pray for, who could have everything, be anything, and he throws it all away. Unless you have a child, you can't know."

We looked at the diseased apples awhile, letting the emotions, the grief pass. She had lost her son after all. She was dressed in gingham in an orchard wearing a cheery straw hat but, by gum, things were not cheery. Life had dealt her a cruel blow, giving her a talented son and taking him away. Nothing could change that.

"Wally said that Ray gave him those paintings when he took Ray in, helped him. When was that?"

We began a slow stroll back toward the house. The bitterness and pain in Esther's outburst dissolved in the dry grass of the neglected orchard.

"Before he went in the hospital he was sick off and on. He was still drinking then and he had stomach trouble. Ray was ashamed to come to me sometimes, so he'd go to Wally's." She reached the back steps and hauled herself up a step before turning back to me. "Wally was always good to Ray. Most folks in the family wasn't so good, you know."

"Your brother Thomas?"

She squinted at me under the hat. "You LDS?" I shook my head. "Thomas is a pillar, you know? He's a good man, a family man. But he didn't—" Her voice broke and she stared over my head at the buff hill behind the orchard. "Ray was a special child. Thomas never understood that."

BY THE TIME I got back to Jackson it was close to seven. As I drove through town, the evening twilight turned a tarnished gold as the sun sunk below the Tetons. The gallery was dark. No sign of Feds or Paolo. I parked in the street this time, avoiding the alley. The phone was ringing as I let myself into the apartment.

It was Paolo. "I didn't let them in. I couldn't find my key," he said, breathing hard. "Is everything okay in the apartment?"

It had been such a long day since I had found Carl in the square doing his tai chi. But my place looked good, homey and quiet, so comforting I could lie down on the sofa with its frumpy linen cover and fall asleep. Would have, if company wasn't coming.

"Appears that way."

The buzzer blatted its obnoxious noise, indicating someone was at the front door of the gallery. I considered removing it many times, but since it is out of the way, over the door and reads in big red letters FOR EMERGENCIES ONLY, I've let it stay. I'd had less than a dozen prank buzzings in eight years, so what the hell. Only now I wished there was some way to disconnect the damn thing.

"Is that the buzzer?" Paolo said.

"I gotta go. It'll be all right." I hung up and looked around the apartment wildly. Damn FBI must have been watching the place. What were they looking for anyway?

The buzzer sounded again, a flatulent blare, long and tedious. I set down my backpack and went down to meet them.

The small crowd on the step straightened up as I flipped on the gallery lights. With their navy blue jackets, pressed gray slacks, and clipped haircuts, the three of them might as well have had buttons on their lapels that read FBI. The number of sightings of men in coat and tie in Jackson, Wyoming, in a year's time could be counted on one hand.

"Alix Thorssen?" The head man spoke, a medium-height guy who didn't get enough sun. His blond hair was graying over the temples, eyes blue, darting over me, then the gallery and back. "We have a search warrant for your home and business." He handed it to me, a long, folded piece of paper like a mortgage deed with official-looking signatures on the outside.

"Well, come in, then. I was just about to take a bubble bath and eat a box of bonbons. Maybe you fellows can help." I smiled at the three of them, giving them a little eyelash action. The only reaction was a cheek twitch from the youngest agent, who couldn't have been twenty-three.

They filed past me into the gallery, their proper, polished shoes clicking on the wood floors. As I closed the door, leaning against it, they circled, vultures preparing for their task.

"Your apartment is upstairs, I understand?" The head agent had still not introduced himself. Not that I cared what his mother called him, it just seemed polite.

"You're well informed, Mister—?"

"Newberg. Federal Bureau of Investigation."

"Can you tell me what this is all about?" Playing dumb just seemed to come naturally tonight.

"Homicide. Raymond Wayne Tantro." He was watching me now, his eyes missing nothing. I suddenly lost my desire to be playful. This man had my number, or thought he did. He wasn't a vulture but a bloodhound, and I was his prey. "Take us upstairs, Miss Thorssen." He and the second agent, who could have been his younger brother they looked, walked, and dressed so similarly, followed me toward the door to the office and through to the back hall. Newberg turned to the rookie. "Look around. Check behind all the paintings. There's a couple extra rooms back here too. And the desk."

I ran my hand across my warm, friendly desk, cradle of all my dreams and imaginings, as I led the men upstairs. The framed poster of the supercilious cowgirl, six-gun at her shoulder and gleam in her eye, looked all wrong. Our footsteps tapped the wooden stairs. It was going to be a long night.

EIGHTEEN

AT LEAST Pete and Re-Pete were tidy. That's the most I can say for Newberg and his look-alike. They certainly weren't courteous, friendly, or helpful, as much as they did resemble grown-up Boy Scouts.

They weren't polite when I tried a little backhanded interrogation, trying to get them to say just what they were looking for. In fact, they asked me to leave. I thought better of it, opening a bottle of white wine. I poured myself a glass, stood around in the kitchen, and watched.

Newberg did the big room, giving his partner the plum job of my underwear drawers. The lead agent took his job very seriously, as Deputy Michaels had suggested, right down to taking the slipcover off the sofa.

He picked up rugs, felt along baseboards, shined his flashlight into nooks and crannies that I was glad Grandma Olava couldn't see because I hadn't cleaned them in eons. He took out all the dishes, the pots and pans, went through the refrigerator with a fine-tooth comb, and lay on his back under the dining room table. He was methodical and impassive. His eyes missed nothing, no crack in the plaster or back of picture or top of lampshade.

"Just what are you looking for?" I asked for the tenth time. I had been racking my brain as I moved out of his way to the sofa, to the kitchen, back to the sofa in its previous life, a worn, yellow, stained beauty. They had my gun, didn't they? They could place me at the scene. I had some kind of a weird motive in their minds. Why didn't they just shackle me up then and there?

Newberg didn't answer my audible question, as he hadn't nine other times since his answer that it was policy to reveal nothing. I got out the phone book, turned the yellow pages to Attorneys, and began thumbing down the list. There was no shortage, including the infamous buckskinner Gerry Spence. I moseyed into the bedroom, leaned against the wall, and found Re-Pete working the dresser drawers.

"So how come the FBI is doing a lowly search warrant gig? Don't you guys have lackeys for this?" I smiled at the agent, twirling the wine in the glass, recovering some of my sass.

The agent, on his knees digging through my pajamas, didn't look up. In a deep voice so low that Newberg couldn't hear, he said: "We like to do things ourselves in this kind of situation."

"Oh, oh, wait, I get it. You don't trust the local cops. Did you hear about the fire where they found the man they thought was Ray Tantro? Had an inquest, pronounced him dead. And now he shows up dead again."

"I heard about it." He stood up and opened the closet, taking a visual survey before tackling it. I knew how he felt.

"I wonder who that guy was."

"What guy?"

"The guy in the fire."

The agent stepped into the closet, his polyester navy jacket with the gold button still immaculate. My closet was a small walk-in, not as big as Eden's. I plucked the postcard from Ray's off the mirror and read it again. The picture on the back featured a cowboy in midair on a bucking horse, and read: National Finals Rodeo.

"I'm thinking," I continued, wedging the postcard back on the mirror, "that whoever killed that guy in the fire, shot him up with drugs and left him to burn, also killed Ray Tantro. It's just too coincidental."

"I don't believe in coincidence," his muffled reply came from behind my coats. He was going through pockets and feeling up linings.

"So are you guys looking into the fire? Because it's got to be connected."

The agent emerged, hair askew, almost looking like a real person. His sandy hair didn't have gray yet. He had a kinder, more open face than Newberg, but not a friendly face. I imagined he had been friendly once but had learned to hide it, to be tough, to be manly, to be FBI.

He turned to the other side, patting down rain jackets and summer slacks. "It's a jurisdictional thing, Miss Thorssen."

"You can call me Alix. And your name is—?"

As if to answer, Newberg's voice boomed from the hallway. "Singleton?!"

Singleton nearly jumped out of the closet, pushing me gently aside. Wine sloshed onto my shirt.

They were mumbling to each other by the front door as I came out, wiping my shirt with a hand towel from the bathroom. Newberg saw me and turned, suddenly gallant.

"Miss Thorssen. We're finished here. Thank you for your cooperation."

I tried to read their faces, see what they had found.

"We'll just be seeing how Agent Munro did downstairs, then we'll be gone," Newberg said, opening the door. Singleton was smoothing his hair as he disappeared into the hallway.

"Wait a minute," I protested. "I've been very cooperative here. A lot more than most people would if you started going through their personal stuff. I think you owe me an explanation. Am I going to be charged with something?"

Newberg hesitated, his hand still on the doorknob. We could hear Singleton and Munro downstairs, talking.

"We can't discuss that at this time. We'll be in touch," Newberg said.

It was nine o'clock. I stood, confused, tired, hungry, listening to their footsteps on the wood floor below. Their voices were low, indistinguishable. They talked for five minutes, then let themselves out.

After going down to bolt the door and douse the lights, I tackled the mess they'd left. It wasn't much really, but I wanted to eradicate every reminder of their intrusion. Suddenly I was angry, zipping back on the slipcovers, patting down the cushions, straightening picture frames. Newberg had taken all my vintage Mighty Thor comic books out of their plastic sleeves, leaving the sleeves stacked next to the case. He had put the comics back haphazardly in a pile on the shelf.

The phone rang. I glared at the bookcase as I moved to answer it. Paolo again. "Are they still there?" His voice held the kind of strained excitement that people get from brushes with the law. I assured him they had left. "Can I bring over some beans and rice? Have you eaten?"

"No, I mean, yes, bring them over." I could use the company now, neutral company. Someone I could shout at if necessary. One tried to restrain oneself in the presence of the high-and-mighty FBI, even if one was only partially successful. I unlocked the back door for Paolo, then sat in front of the bookcase putting the Mighty Thors back in chronological order. As often happens, I began to read the comics again, savoring the plights of my hero, the Thunder God. Reading of attacks by mutants and double-crossing friends of the superhero made my woes seem more manageable.

Paolo trudged up the stairs with a big soup pot in his hands, his face flushed. "What did they do? It doesn't look like they were even in here."

"Don't sound so disappointed," I said, still sitting on the floor against the case with three comic books on my knees. "They weren't too vicious."

As he set the pot on the kitchen counter and got out some bowls, I got up and set the table. Paolo searched my face with his black eyes. "Are you okay? Did they hurt you or anything?"

I shook my head. "It was just a search warrant. Not a license to shake me down."

"Then why are you frowning like that?"

I sat at the table in front of the bowl of steaming black beans and rice. "I'm afraid if I was them I'd be arresting me tomorrow morning, no matter what I found in my apartment."

"What?"

"Never mind. Just make sure you don't have plans for the week." I felt terrible, as if the bump on my head had taken out all my fire. As if I had nothing to do but await the inevitable.

"You're not serious?" Paolo asked, sitting opposite me.

"I might be."

We ate in silence. Paolo's bean dish was warm and comforting. I wondered how many more times I would eat his mother's famous recipe from Argentina with the hint of anise and hard-charging hot peppers. I thought of asking for the recipe, but that would mean talking about his leaving and I couldn't bear that right now. I skirted the issue by bringing up his chosen successor.

"Have you talked to Eden?" I asked.

"This morning she came in. She was with Pete." He straightened, remembering. "Did Wally say he'd sell *Gloria?*"

"Probably. He had his ninth kid today, while I was there."

"Nine kids? He can use the money, then."

I shrugged. We had never really talked about Eden as my partner. Thoughts of Paolo's leaving, Eden's betrayal, Carl's disappearance, Martin's sale, Newberg's steely eyes, all swirled in my head, heavy as molten lead.

Paolo was still fixated on the Tantro. "We would charge him a fee, maybe a little discount since we don't have any agreement, eh? He'll go for that, no? He'll be making, what, twenty-two, twenty-three? What do you think? Ten percent?"

"Sounds fair." Wally probably would balk, but the money would offset his misgivings.

We finished dinner and stacked the dishes in the sink. Paolo was high with anticipation of the big sale and dragged me downstairs to look at the painting again. On the way I grabbed my old Tantro off my desk. I had never looked at it side by side with the big canvases. The comparison would probably not be favorable to my little snow scene, but I wanted to see how it held up.

Paolo held a glass of wine by his shoulder, standing back with the spotlights on *Gloria,* admiring her. I had held out for ice water. The meal had helped my fatigue, but another glass of wine would have done me in. I sat at Paolo's desk, laying the small painting in front of me.

Gloria was a curious piece for Tantro but in many ways the best thing he'd ever done. It was the painting I would most want to have in my collection had twenty-five grand come my way. The winter scene was executed with an impressionistic grace that made you feel both the biting prairie wind and the blessed blanket of warmth made by a deep, slumbering snowfall. The trees were stoic reminders of summer, of hope, and the frozen river promised tadpoles and roe. It was a vision of sleep, renewal, seasons, yearning, and trust.

"Magnificent," Paolo said. "The best piece we have ever had, don't you agree?"

"The other two aren't shabby either," I said. On their own they too were magnificent.

I picked up my junior Tantro and walked around to the wall where the three huge canvases hung. It fit in the space between *Gloria* and *Field at Noon,* almost scraping their stretched-canvas sides with its old green frame. I held it at arm's length, trying to back up to look at all the works. Paolo went into the back room, returning with hammer and nail. In a moment my small piece hung like a comma in a sentence of bold statements. I stood back with Paolo and silently compared.

The size, of course, was the first thing you saw. It was hard to get past that. The scope of the bigger works was so vast, an orchestra of color and light. By comparison the little piece was a single violin, sweet and demure but simply too tiny to make an impact.

"When did you get your little one?" Paolo asked, squinting at the signature and date in the lower right-hand corner.

"I've been trying to remember. Either in '75, or the next summer. I came home to visit and my mom took me to a bunch of galleries."

"It must have been cheap," he said, not unkindly.

"I came into my trust that summer. From my father. For me it wasn't cheap." I remembered suddenly the elation, then the grief and guilt I had felt about the trust, my last tangible connection with my father. He had died six years before, six miserable teenage years. I considered myself an adult in 1975, but dealing with his death all over again was a struggle. I could still feel the weight of his loss deep in my bones.

"It got you to New York, right? Your dad's money."

"Right." I smiled at Paolo. He put his arm around me suddenly as if he too was remembering those New York days when we fell in love. He gave my shoulder a little squeeze.

"And it made you an investment. A good investment." Paolo took the small piece off the wall and looked at the back. *"Memory of Winter,"* he read aloud, placing it back on the nail.

"I didn't buy it for an investment."

"No matter." He shrugged. "It was a good one."

I bent down and stared at the thick paint strokes of my piece. Then I moved to *Gloria,* squinting. Then back. A painting looks so different up close, like the cells of the body that when isolated appear to have so little relevance to the whole. I put my nose up to the little Tantro again, frowning.

"What?" Paolo said behind me. "What is it?"

"I don't know. Take a look at this." I pointed to a small area on the right side of *Memory.* "At the snow here."

Paolo moved close. The snow was white in that spot on my painting, tinged with violet. There was a layer of dust on it made more visible because I had rubbed a spot with my fingertip.

"Now here." I pointed to a similar snowbank on *Gloria.* He leaned into it. "See the difference?"

He looked back and forth. The snow on the big canvas held an odd green tint. For them to be identical would have been unusual. "What?" he said, stepping back. "Yours is dirtier."

"Not the dirt. They've been stored differently. Something else. The quality of the paint."

Paolo almost touched his nose to my piece, then leaned out, raising his eyebrows. "Cracks."

Where I had rubbed *Memory of Winter* distinct hairline cracks showed up, now lined with the dust I had pressed into them. I wet my finger on my tongue and smeared my spit on the whitest part of the snow. More cracks, deep ones.

Paolo waved his arm at *Gloria.* "No cracks."

"Nothing like mine." I looked at him. "What does it mean?"

Paolo was examining the other two canvases, then stood back, scratching his chin. "There is something about the colors in these big ones. They don't match yours."

"So he bought new paints. What does it prove? Why would some paints crack and not others? It's just the white."

"There used to be a white paint. I remember one of Ramon's artists used it," he said, referring to the owner of the gallery where he had worked. "This guy did a big series for Ramon. Lots of red, white, and blue stripes. All the white stripes did this." He pointed at the cracks in *Memory*. "Ramon had a fit."

"Just the white?"

"A quick-drying white. The artist tried to cut corners, get more stuff done. You know how long it takes for oils to dry. The thick ones can take months."

"Even a year," I said.

"Yes. But Ramon made him do them all over. He was a stickler for quality." Paolo examined all the paintings up close yet again. "The greens are different too. That could be explained, I suppose. But artists get used to mixing certain ways. Especially when they are working on a cycle that is similar of subject, of style. The subject matter is the same in the big ones and the little. The big three all have similar greens. And pinks. And the style, the strokes, is the same."

The greens of the big canvases were muddy, whereas on my piece the greens had a marine blue touch to them. There wasn't much pink in my little piece, but what was there had an orange cast. In the big paintings a truer pink, streaked with red, showed through.

I didn't want to believe this. A shiver edged up my bruised spine. It couldn't be true. These had to be Tantros. They were his legacy, his gift. They had to be authentic.

Paolo kneeled by *Winter Glass,* his hand on the lower left corner. "Look at this."

I bent down. In a large clump of dark green paint, applied thickly with a wide palette knife, a fingerprint was now visible. Paolo's fingerprint.

"It isn't completely dry. Just on spots where the paint is very thick, but still. *It isn't dry.*" Paolo stood up and brushed his hands together as if dismissing the whole thing. His handsome face was creased with disappointment. "They took that quick-drying white off the market in about '75. The big pieces were painted later, within the last year. I don't care if they do say '74 on them. No way were they done at the same time as the small one. I stake my reputation on it.''

NINETEEN

THE MOON SHONE an anorexic crescent directly overhead as I drove out of the sleeping town of Jackson. It was close to one-thirty by then, but sleep, for me, was not in the cards. The mountains rising on either side of the road as I headed west were thick and dark with twinkling spots of light at vacation homes. Traffic consisted of a loud carload of party-hardies and semis grinding gears as they approached the town.

Carl had called about eleven. He was halfway home. He had taken my advice and called his friend in the Crime Scene Unit about getting back onto the force. Anywhere but patrol work, he asked his friend. It turned out the captain had held up his resignation anyway, thinking he might change his mind after a good vacation. A couple hours later his friend called back and said it was set up. Carl wasted no time pointing his El Dorado north. He said just being around me made him realize how much he would miss police work, especially the detective part of it. I took that as a compliment.

I crossed the Snake River, dotted with gravel bars and stippled silver in the thin moonlight, then turned off toward Teton Village. I marveled again at the excitement in Carl's voice. He had done the right thing, I told him. I wished him well. He said he was sorry about the things he said. I told him I wished I could have shown him a better time in Jackson. He promised to call soon.

The road to the ski area was lined with expensive resorts, condominiums, a fancy golf course, and shacks that ran half a mil. Interspersed between these developments were older residences, some elaborate, some not, tucked among the firs and aspens. I found the lane to Pete Rotondi's place after slowing to a snail's pace on the highway.

Five homes sat along the gravel drive. The first two, by the highway, were the oldest, cabins that had been revamped and expanded but were still small and funky. Pete's was the last, nestled in the spruce and aspen trees. I parked the Saab near the drive and walked in the dark toward the house, around Pete's car with the kayaks strapped on top. In the dark it looked like a giant dragonfly.

The kitchen light was on. I knocked lightly on the side door. The house was not large, a newer one-story with cedar siding. Berms were covered with flowers, the white phlox bright in the moonlight. A flagstone walk curved through the lawn to the small covered porch. Sage and thyme grew to one side of the kitchen stoop.

Eden's face peered around the curtain, her brown curls in her eyes. She squinted at me, turned, and flicked on the overhead light.

"Alix. What are you doing out here? It's so late." She stepped back to let me in, looking after me to see that I was alone. She wore denim shorts and a red sweater that was probably Pete's. It hung almost to her knees.

"I have to talk to you, Eden."

She moved to the stove where a teakettle sat waiting. "Would you like some tea? I was just about to have a cup." I let her fuss with cups and tea bags until we were settled finally at the kitchen table. The kitchen had rustic pine cupboards and Mexican tile counters, very tasteful. The table and chairs were pine too, the ladderbacks sporting rush seats and plump flowered cushions.

"Nice place," I said, admiring the botanical prints of carrots and cabbages above the table.

"The whole house is wonderful. You'd never think it, looking at Pete." Eden smiled, lowering her guard a little. "He's gone to bed. He's guiding at six tomorrow."

"So you two are hitting it off?"

Eden shrugged. "He's been nice to me."

Meaning, of course, nicer than *some* people. I sipped my tea, trying to discover how to grind information out of someone you had lost respect for. She seemed so vulnerable and alone, but I remembered the way she had used me. I held down the bad feelings as Eden's small face brightened.

"I've got something for you. Wait here." She disappeared down the dark hall, returning a moment later. "The new Mighty Thor. I already read it, so you keep it for your collection."

She handed me the comic book and sat down. On the cover a large whiskered face glowered in a burst of yellow lightning. Under it read, "Odin... Awake!" Odin was proclaiming: "Thou Art Naught but a Mortal Impostor!!! Where is the True Thor?!"

"It's close to the end for the guy who's been posing as Thor," she said.

"Mmm, yeah, the architect." I opened the comic carefully, flipping to the "Tales of Asgard" in the back. It looked as if Odin had woken up grumpy and was out for Heimdall's hide.

"Right. Nobody knows what happened to the real Thor. Not even the impostor." Eden leaned over her tea, letting the steam caress her face. She looked tired, closing her eyes. "Remember way back when that other guy was Thor for a while? That lame doctor? Thor has had lots of impostors over the years. What do the Norse gods call them?"

"Doppelgängers. Ghostly doubles." I set the comic down on the table. I would read it later, add it to my collection. "I need to talk to you about Ray."

She tensed, pulling her knees up under the sweater. "What about him?"

"His paintings. The ones you were showing in the Timberwolf."

"I know. They weren't very good," she said, frowning. "But I needed something big to help the business. Something that would attract a lot of attention. You should understand that, Alix. It was business."

"Is that why you took out the extra insurance?"

Her eyes suddenly filled. She started to say something, then bit her lip, looking at the ceiling.

"Talk to me. I can help you. I don't think you meant to hurt that man in the Timberwolf. But if you don't tell me what happened, I can't help you." I reached out and took her hand. "Please, Eden."

"I knew they weren't Ray's," she choked, tears spilling down her cheeks. "But when he approached me I was so desperate. I never thought anybody would get hurt."

"The paintings were forgeries?"

She nodded, brushing her cheek with her sweater sleeve. "You don't know how I felt when they brought that man out of the gallery. I felt like I had killed him."

"Who set it up? The paintings, the fire. Who did it?"

"Ray. He said he'd take care of everything. He was so nice to me. Took me places. Out to the park, to restaurants."

"Who did the paintings, then?" The phony art studio with the dried-up palette and brushes smeared with paint for appearance' sake—it was a sad coincidence that Ray had died in there. His art was all a fake. It was already dead.

"Somebody around here, I guess. He wouldn't tell me." Her face twisted. "I just wanted everything to be right again, Alix. Like when I started. All my money was gone. I just wanted to be a success. I could feel it just out of reach. Rich out there but I couldn't get it." She hid her face in her hands and sobbed.

I touched her shoulder. "Drink some tea, Eden. You'll feel better."

She obeyed, then set down her cup with a look of horror. "Will they arrest me now?"

"I don't know. Arson is a felony, even if you aren't the one who lights the match."

"Oh, God," she cried, but the waterworks were depleted. She sat stunned, staring at the dried flower arrangement in the center of the round table, looking very small.

"Try to help me, Eden. The FBI is making a case against me for Ray's shooting."

She frowned. "What can I do?"

"Tell me everything you remember about Ray Tantro."

THE SUN DAPPLED the asphalt in the Snake River Canyon, trickling through the trees to dry the dew. Minutes before I had been shaking out the kinks at the little store at Hoback Junction. The knot on my head from the tackle in the alley had gone down. The ankle was stiff but functional. The coffee was fresh and hot and just what I needed after sleeping in the back seat of the Saab Sister. I filled her tank and mine and headed south again.

Eden and I had talked until four. Once we had determined both our necks were in a vise she talked readily, euphoric with confession. I left in the predawn, drove to Wilson to whistle at Valkyrie, give her a nose pat and a hug, then settle in with an army blanket in the back seat.

Passing through Freedom, I wound now onto the high prairie of Star Valley. I turned at the stoplight and found the Fortneys' place already bustling. Children ran around in the picket-fenced yard in shorty pajamas and diapers, chewing on graham crackers and bananas. One swung fiercely on the swing set while two others chased around, squealing. Little Rosie stood watching it all, sucking on a cracker. When I knocked, the fourteen-year-old boy I had spoken to yesterday answered the door, wearing dirty white pants and a long-sleeved white shirt.

"Is your father here? Alix Thorssen again." I smiled apologetically. He left me standing in the open doorway. Wally showed up, tucking in his shirt.

"Morning. I have some news about the painting. *Gloria?*" I said.

"I'm on my way to work. Can it wait?" Wally glanced away as a girl skipped by behind him. "Things are a little crazy around here."

"Let me drive you in," I said. "It'll only take a minute."

It took Wally ten minutes to get out of the house, shouting orders at the older children, then grouping the small ones in the yard to admonish them about good behavior. When he reached the Saab at last, climbing in, he looked beat. His thin face was flushed and sweaty, as if he'd worked his shift already.

"I think the deal's a go," I began, driving as slowly as I dared toward the cheese factory on the other side of town. It was a five-minute drive, tops.

"I've been thinking about that." Wally squirmed in the seat; his voice registered a tad higher than normal. He stared out the window at the passing houses, as if disinterested in twenty-five thousand dollars. His foot began to tap against the floor mat. "I can't sell to...to a private buyer. I already offered it to the museum."

Something was going on. Wally refused to look at me, nervous tics shooting through his body. "You haven't made any kind of deal with the museum. I haven't appraised them yet. Let me handle the Met."

He shook his head fiercely. "No. Can't sell to anybody else."

"I understand the ethics involved, Wally. But—"

"That's right," he almost shouted. "Wouldn't be ethical."

"All right. I understand." I turned the corner as if ice, not cottonwood snow, covered the pavement. "I was going to ask for a letter of provenance from you for the private buyer. But the museum will need one too."

Wally's foot stopped tapping. "What kind of letter?"

"Provenance. That means where the artwork came from. Where you got it, how and when you got it, any authenticity you can provide on it." His hands clutched his dented black lunch bucket.

"I got 'em from Ray. I told you."

"Mmm. And when was this? What year?"

He paused, then said firmly, "Nineteen eighty-one and eighty-two. Ray was sick the year before and we took him in."

I looked in both directions of Main Street and eased the car into the traffic heading south. "When Ray was sick up in Casper, did you take him in?"

"No. Aunt Esther took care of him."

"He had a liver problem?"

Wally looked at his watch. "Can you hurry? I'm late enough already."

"Was he painting in '81 and '82?"

"Not when he was sick. Listen, I was supposed to be at work ten minutes ago." Wally looked a little frantic, like he might get fired or something. I accelerated a little for the last two blocks.

"Wally, those paintings he gave you weren't his."

He looked at me hard. "Weren't his? You mean he stole 'em?"

"No, I mean somebody else painted them. Within the last year."

We were stopped in front of the factory. Wally's hand shook as he reached for the door handle, swinging the door wide without getting out. "I don't believe it."

"When did you get them, Wally?"

He blinked hard. His Adam's apple bobbed. "In '81 and '82," he repeated.

"Couldn't have. They weren't painted until last year. Where did you get them, Wally?"

As if a rocket had fired under him, Wally jumped from the car, slamming the door behind him. I called to him through the open window. "Tell me who did them, Wally, and we can make a deal."

He walked stiffly in his dirty white uniform toward the factory entrance. The lunch bucket pulled down his left shoulder, bumped into his knee. As he opened the door he allowed himself a final look back, as if to make sure I was real.

THE OLD HOUSE showed so many signs of age that it was easy to overlook its fine lines, the graceful porch with gingerbread trim, the fancy shinglework under the pitch of the roof. I sat in my car for a few minutes outside Esther Tantro's farmhouse, letting my imagination add pots of flowers hanging under the porch overhang, flower beds bright and lush, fresh paint in cheerful shades brightening the siding and trim. I wondered if Esther had plans to do any of these things with the insurance money.

I had stopped in town and made two phone calls. First I called the hospital in Casper, then made a quick call back to Maggie Barlow, my insurance agent friend. She had been scouring records and calling in favors to find out the results of Ray Tantro's insurance claims. The insurance company had refused payment after the first death of Ray Tantro because it was ruled a suicide. Now, with the second, they were a little baffled but had made motions as if to pay up soon. The beneficiary, as I knew already, was Esther Tantro.

I was parked in front of her weatherworn house, reading a comic book. I couldn't imagine that Esther had killed her son for the insurance money. A well-meaning person, loving, full of sorrow. I thought of her in her sunbonnet in the apple orchard, dressed in gingham. Yet, grandmothers in tennis shoes had been known to push their nieces off cliffs.

I closed the comic book and smoothed down the glossy cover with my hand. There was something so elemental about comics. The good and evil, the clear, bright colors, the endless fight to hold back the dark night. *With my last breath I will fight. Death will come yet still I fight on, avenging my brethren, my name, my honor.* The hero in his many incarnations, godlike yet fallible, prone to human foibles of greed, lust, vanity.

Poor Thor had been thrown out of Asgard more than once because of his unruly habit of picking fights with somebody who didn't pay him enough respect. Loki had banished him, giving his powers to a hapless human. Now Odin searched for his son, shouting at the human Thor: "Thou Art Naught but a Mortal Impostor!!!"

I set the comic on the seat beside me. Esther Tantro had come down the back stairs wearing a pair of blue pedal pushers and a man's plaid shirt, the sun hat shading her face. She hadn't seen me, turning with a pair of green garden gloves in one hand toward the apple orchard uphill behind the house. I jumped from the car, pulling my father's hunting jacket tight around me in the unexpected cool breeze. Overhead a storm was brewing, clouds darkening half the sky in the west, a violent purple morass.

I reached her as she turned to walk around the orchard, bypassing the mess of fallen apples rotting on the ground. She heard me and turned, a startled look on her face as she brought up the pruning shears as if as a weapon. Her expression loosened as I stopped and tried to look harmless.

"Mrs. Tantro. Gardening again?"

She dropped her arm. "Shouldn't run up on a person like that. Around here you might get yourself shot." She turned back in the direction she was headed. I stepped up next to her. "Pruning some of my rosebushes today. I never got to planting my vegetable garden this year. That's real gardening. Tomatoes, zucchini, and such."

"We can't grow those in Jackson. I mean, if I had a garden, which I don't," I said. "It's warmer here."

"A bit." She looked around at the sky as the wind lifted her hat brim, flapping it. "Going to storm. Ray loved thunderstorms."

"Me too. The rain clattering on the roof."

We walked silently through yellowing grass, tall and wild. On the left the apple orchard petered out, the trees at the end of the row completely dead. The dead ones were grotesquely beautiful, twisted arms shivering in the wind, gray and barren. On the right the hill swelled, a few native juniper growing in a wash. The rest of the hill was open, covered with clumps of native grass and sagebrush burned in the August sun.

Esther stopped and contemplated a row of sad rosebushes. There were ten or twelve of them in various fits of decline, thick stems cut neatly with spindly growth and dried buds hanging on. She kneeled down to the one nearest her. Of all the bushes it looked the healthiest, but she began snipping at it, whacking away its limbs.

After a moment I sat down in the grass next to her. "Did you bury Ray up here?" I said, straining against the wind.

Esther gave me a quick look, pursed her lips, and hacked off the biggest stem near the earth.

"He must have died, what, about a year ago? The people at the hospital in Casper said he left AMA—against medical advice. You brought him home to die."

She sat back on her heels, her hands in her lap. The pruning tool slipped from her fingers. Her eyes that held so much sorrow already looked up the hill and filled with tears. A loud crack of thunder shook the hillside as the storm neared.

"I did the best I could," she whispered. I could barely hear her and leaned closer.

"I'm sure you did. It was out of your hands."

"In God's hands. He's in God's hands now." Tears rolled down her cheeks and her lip quivered as she sighed. "I did the best I could."

"Did someone help you bury him? Up there on the hill?"

"It was his favorite place. He would sit and watch the storms come in. I would call and call, afraid he was going to get hit by lightning. But he never did."

"Who helped you, Esther? Who buried him?"

"Me and Wally. We buried him."

There had to be someone else. Wally didn't paint those pictures. "And the man who called himself Ray Tantro? Did he help you?"

"He talked to me. He knew Ray from somewhere, I guess."

"Did he paint the pictures they said were Ray's?"

"He was a cowboy. Ray had to tell him everything about art. He didn't know anything. Ray was so weak by then, not eating. And that cowboy kept after him, asking Ray questions till he wore out."

She got up then, leaving the pruning shears on the ground, and began walking straight up the hill, her steps long and determined. I followed her, holding her elbow as she faltered when the path got rocky. The wind was vicious near the top, whipping and whirling, lifting Esther's sun hat off her head and spinning it in the air high above us.

The old woman stopped at the crest of the hill, at a small flat area where a spindly aspen tree grew, surrounded by sagebrush. The little tree bent to the ground in the wind, then popped up, tiny round leaves quivering. We stood high and exposed, small hills all around us. The thunder rumbled again, and like Esther years before, I worried about lightning.

The sky was black now. Esther walked over to the small aspen and held the thin trunk in her gnarled hand. Her gray hair flying about her face, she gazed at the ground near its base. It had a different look than the surrounding grasses, with bare dirt and withered plant growth. This was where Ray was buried. The real Raymond Wayne Tantro. The one and only.

The thunder boomed right overhead and rain spilled from the cloud. *The Thunder God spoke. Mortals are not always who they seem.* Three human beings had died as Ray Tantro, and all three were indisputably dead. Is the identification of a man so important? Does it make him more dead? The man in the cabin, the man I couldn't stop thinking of as Ray Tantro, was just a cowboy who did a very good impersonation of somebody nobody knew.

Now he and Ray had even more in common. They shared the same fate. But didn't we all? Wasn't that Thor's message? I would never forget the face, the dead oceanic eyes, the fingers clinging to life. Who was that cowboy, the only Ray I knew?

As the thunder rolled again, speaking of distant triumphs and mighty battles, its tears drenching me, Odin spoke.

Thou Art but a Mortal Impostor.

TWENTY

WE SAT, DRIPPING, in Esther's kitchen. She made tea, brought me a towel for my hair. My father's jacket hung on the back of the chrome-and-vinyl chair, making puddles on the linoleum. Shivering, I scooted closer to the old wood-stove as Esther fed it small splits of pine.

On the way back to the house, I had to support Esther. All her strength evaporated at Ray's grave, as if she had died, at least partially, with him. But her old house with its worn memories had comforted her through much pain and sorrow, and it worked its small miracles today.

She made me a grilled cheese sandwich in a cast-iron skillet on the woodstove. Oozing with Star Valley cheddar, smeared with Star Valley butter, its sweet odor filled the large kitchen. Very little had been touched in the room since the 1940s. A small refrigerator with a huge chrome ornament like an early Plymouth hummed and rattled in the corner. Chrome-topped counters were scrubbed shiny. Chipped green cupboards screamed for attention. On the window over the sink hung apple-print café curtains with dusty red pom-poms.

The woodstove stood alone across the kitchen from the table that offered a view of Esther's fallow garden high with thistle. With its porcelain-faced warming ovens above the cooking surface, the stove was a relic that wouldn't give up. A source of heat and food and comfort, a big black mother.

Esther's long gray hair was stringy and wet, pushed behind her ears. She didn't seem to notice the way her pedal pushers were plastered to her legs, but she had taken off her socks and shoes. Her feet looked swollen. The big shirt steamed, dripping on the floor in a circle around her. I wondered if it had been Ray's. She turned from the stove, skillet in mittened hand, and set it down on a tile on the table. With the spatula she cut off the crusts of the sandwich and set it on a battered white plate in front of me.

"Thanks." I saw no more sandwiches in the skillet. She returned to the stove with the skillet, then sat down to watch me eat. "Here, you have half." I pushed the plate toward her.

"No, no, I made it for you. It's for you," she said. She set her chin in her hand, elbow on the table, as if exhausted. "I miss cooking for Ray."

I took a bite. The gooey cheese coated my tongue. It was delicious and consoling, the way the best food is. Esther brought me lemonade in a big glass, then sipped her tea.

"Why don't you go change? You must be cold," I offered.

She shook her head. "I'm fine. Don't worry about an old woman."

Her lined face with full cheeks and sad eyes drooped under her wet hair, making her look older. Outside the rain continued, beating against the roof in spurts, angry and loud.

"I always made grilled cheese for Ray when he stayed up on the hill too long." Her voice thinned and she stared out the window. "I miss the days when he was young, shooting gophers with his BB gun and building things. He loved to build things. And draw pictures, of course."

"Was he your only child?" I asked, hoping not.

"The youngest. His brother and sister are ten and twelve years older. Doctor told me I couldn't have no more kids, then Ray come along." A weak smile on her old lips. "He was a blessing."

"Forgive me—but did the cowboy come up with the idea about the paintings?"

"There was someone else Ray talked to, in the spring when he come home from the hospital. He was there almost six weeks. I spent as much time with him as I could." She looked at her hands in her lap suddenly. I figured tears were next, but she looked up dry-eyed. "I only met this man twice, at night. Ray didn't want me to know who he was. He said the secret would die with him then."

"What did he look like, Esther? Did he have a name?"

She shook her head again. "Can't tell you neither. It was dark and Ray kept him away from me. Never heard him say more than a howdy, ma'am. Ray said this was what he wanted. To help me after he died. It was what he wanted, so I did it."

"The cowboy passed the physical for Ray, then? For the insurance?" She nodded, watching her hands pick on the wet shirt hem. "You never had a number to call, any way to contact the man?"

"The cowboy, yes, the one who was . . . Ray. In fact I was supposed to call. They gave me his number, said to call anytime. But I never did. What would I say? He wasn't my son."

Esther took my dishes to the sink, squirted in some liquid soap, and turned on the water. As she stared through the curtains at the raindrops rolling down the glass, I hoped her other son and her daughter visited her, brought their children. Something about Esther's forlorn attitude, her calm despair, made me think they didn't. Maybe Esther had favored Ray too much, alienated the other two. These errors in judgment are difficult to explain or understand. Only the regret, the pain remains. The bright spot in her life, her talented son the artist, was gone forever.

Whoever the forger was, he had covered his tracks admirably. Kept contact to a minimum. And above all, done away with all the major witnesses. The only one left who knew his identity was Wally. And he needed Wally to sell the paintings. Wally was his only link to the outside world, the legitimate world.

But Wally had been found out. As I wiped my mouth on a paper napkin I worried suddenly about Wally's safety. If he told the forger that I knew the paintings were frauds, Wally's life was in danger. There had been enough murders.

BY MIDDAY Jackson exploded in tourist colors: pink halter tops, neon green shorts, black cowboy hats, brown fishing shirts, snow white legs. Mothers pulled crying toddlers into traffic, fathers carried infants in fancy backpacks, grayheads wore matching walking shoes and ate matching ice cream cones. A row of motorcycles all tilted, parked, at the same angle. Inside an RV a party was under way. Jackson Hole in August: the good, the bad, and the ugly.

The thunderstorm had bypassed the Hole so far. The skies were still blue, sunny with clouds bunching on the Tetons. I parked the Saab in the alley and felt my damp clothes clinging to me as I climbed the stairs to my apartment. I made a pot of coffee before changing into jeans and a dry T-shirt. It had been a long day and night. My head was crammed with new information, plotting the edges of the forgery scam. I stood at the sink, watching the clouds move across the sky in dark clumps, and drank coffee.

The footsteps on the stairs leading to my door were fast and hard. I tensed. Did Wally call the forger? Did Esther tell Wally that I had figured out the scheme? When would the Feds tie up their lies and charge me with homicide? And, another thought: Was the motorcyclist who foot-tackled me the forger?

The knock was tense, quick. I set down my coffee cup silently and tiptoed toward the door. The knocking started again. Then the voice.

"Alix! Open up. It's me."

Sighing, I reached out for the filigreed brass knob from the brothel days and opened the door. Paolo looked distraught, running his hand through disheveled black hair. One blue silk shirttail hung from his pleated gray pants.

"You have to watch the shop. I got to go out," he blurted, turning to go back down.

"Wait, I've got to—"

He turned, angry. "You owe me. I been working my butt off and where have you been? Running around all over the place, who knows where."

"But, Paolo."

"No buts. This thing came up."

"What thing?"

He was halfway down the stairs. "Just get down here. The place is packed." He jumped the last two steps, then paused before entering the gallery to compose himself. "I give you one minute," he called without looking back.

One minute, my ass. I found my cowboy boots in the closet, pulled them on, and grabbed a navy blazer that my sister had worn to college. By the time I carried my coffee cup and hairbrush down the stairs with me, yanking out wet snarls, I was ready to snarl myself. I hated being tied to this gallery when something was happening outside. What's more, I hated my partner ordering me around.

The instant Paolo saw me come through the back door, he left by the front one. No wave, no I'll be back, no Here's where you can reach me. I snarled at him through the plate-glass windows, watching him almost run down the board-walks, bumping into people. He crossed the square and was lost in the crowd.

Twelve or fifteen people roamed the gallery, looking at paintings, picking up cards, and spinning sun-catchers in the window. The wood floor was tracked with mud. I threw my hairbrush on my desk in the back, grabbed my messages and coffee cup, and went to sit at Paolo's desk in the front.

A message from my mother, one from my sister back east. I set them aside to remind me to call them. I took a swig of coffee and tried to ignore the customers.

"Miss? Oh, miss? Over here." A middle-aged woman wearing a white canvas hat and a flowered shirt was waving at me from the back of the gallery. "Can you help me?" She was smiling and sunburned.

I hauled myself up. "Yes, ma'am?"

"Jesse and I are interested in one of these." She waved toward three large weavings by a local artist. "But we flew out here from Chicago and there's no way we could get something like that home in the bags."

"We can ship it for you, if you'd like. You save the sales tax that way."

"Oh, really? I see." She turned her gaze back at the weavings, their mountain scenes in muted greens and browns. "I like this one with the cabin. But I'm not sure it'll go in the living room. It seems kind of, you know, cabin-ish. Not that it's not lovely. You know what I mean?"

I was picturing her living room now in yellow silk with plastic covers left on because the Pekingese sometimes jumped up on the sofa, a small, empty butler's tray coffee table, and one fake plant.

A woman squealed near the front of the gallery.

"Jesus Christ, Freddie, that is the third cone you've done that to. No more for you."

Freddie, who looked about seven, had curly blond hair and chubby cheeks and a big chocolate stripe down his shirt and shorts ending on his shoes, where the ice cream now lay melting. He stepped back, kicking the scoop off his tennies onto the floor.

"I'll get a rag," I said to the mother, who continued berating the abashed Freddie. He stared at his scoop of ice cream longingly. Within minutes I had cleaned up the mess, and Freddie and company slinked out.

During the melee the lady in the white hat had disappeared too. I sat back down at the desk. *I can't do this. I have to concentrate.* There was something I was forgetting, overlooking. Most art forgers want to be found out, want to have the world recognize their incredible talent. This forger had to rely on the unreliables, people with an emotional stake in the outcome. Esther had already betrayed the plan; it was a matter of time with Wally.

Paolo had taken down the fake Tantros. My small *Memory of Winter* lay on my desk. I retrieved it, sat back down, and cleaned it with spit and tissues. I would hang it in my apartment. I amused myself for several minutes, imagining it hanging in different places.

The front door tinkled. A rowdy crew of adolescents stumbled in, poking each other with elbows and making butt noises with their mouths. A real likely group of buyers. I surveyed the rest of my messages until my eye caught one. It was from my friend Willa in Santa Fe, who ran her father's gallery.

Willa was in the gallery when I called.

"I was talking to somebody about Tantro. One of my friends back in Massachusetts. Runs a gallery in Amherst," Willa said. "She said he used to come in there once in a while when he was in school at RISD. He was just a kid then, but cocky. Thought he had the world by the tail."

In my mind I saw Esther then, and the aspen tree struggling against the wind, the new grass struggling on the mound of earth, the thunder rumbling and rolling. But we all are young once, and we all die. Ray Tantro just lived hard and died young.

"He's dead, Willa."

"I heard. Somebody shot him?"

"No, not really. It's a long story. Was there anything else?"

The punks were getting into a scuffle back by the weavings, grabbing at each other, giggling, and punching. I stood up, ready to be playground director again.

"Did he have a wife or kids? Any family?" Willa asked.

"Big extended family. Listen, I have to go. Duty calls."

I hung up, walking around the desk trying to figure out how to break up three two-hundred-pounders in surfing shorts and high-top basketball shoes. But their friends beat me to it, seeing trouble on the way. A few 'Cool it, mans' was all it took. But I had had it.

"Okay, everybody out. Closing time."

All eleven customers looked at me, stunned.

"Sorry, closing up, here we go." I herded them toward the door with my arms.

"But it's only two-thirty," one woman protested, as if she needed more time to gather her opinions and make her purchase.

"Family emergency, ma'am. Come back tomorrow."

I ignored the dirty looks as the last of them shuffled out. I turned the sign on the door to Closed and locked up, just in time before a new group stepped up and rattled the handle. I pointed at the sign, made apologetic shrugs, and ran upstairs for my car keys. If Paolo could split, well, I damn sure could too.

DANNY *B.* WAS on my apartment line, telling me about the latest from the official side when the buzzer from the gallery front door sounded. I ignored it and kept talking. "So he never married?"

"Never that I found. Had a couple girlfriends, one in Massachusetts that nobody can find. The FBI and Frye had been doing a real rundown on him."

"Did they find anything juicy?"

"They aren't telling. I guess they've talked to Eden Chaffee. I'd like to talk to her too. She probably knew him best in Jackson. Guess they had quite a hot little thing go-ing.''

I paused. Eden had left this item out of her story last night. She said once that she might have loved him—but lovers? And now she was burning Pete's candle. Where did she find the energy?

"And Paolo too," Danny continued. "I talked to him this morning. Warned him about the search warrant."

"What—here again?"

"No, his house. Since you two are partners."

"Don't these guys have any real leads?"

"They're being careful. They've got you at the scene, and your weapon. I hear the bullets match. But something is holding them back from the arrest. Something about the time of death is my guess. Dr. Miller has him dying at least four hours before you showed up."

"I see." The buzzer went off again, obnoxious. I stuck my finger in my free ear. "Danny. I have a scoop for you. The man shot in the cabin was not Ray Tantro. He was a cowboy posing as him."

"Why would he do that?"

"Forgery scam. Somebody was painting Ray Tantro lookalikes. Then bingo, Tantro's gone, and the prices sky-rocket."

"Is this fact or theory?"

"Tantro's mother told me this morning that he died a year ago. He's buried on her property in Star Valley. Paolo and I figured out the paintings were forgeries last night. The paint was not completely dry on pieces dated 1974."

I could hear him scribbling. "Shit, this is hot, Alix. Any-thing else?"

"Lots, but—"

The buzzer went off again. Somebody was laying on it, insistent. It sounded like somebody who had buzzed be-fore.

"—I have to go." I hung up. I wondered if the Feds were watching the back. I scooped up my keys and backpack, locked my door, and slipped down the back stairs.

The alley was deserted. The Saab sat alone in the shadow from the building. Down by Deloney a UPS truck was parked with its lights flashing and motor running. The other end of the alley was open, revealing a bustling summer afternoon of foot traffic, bicycles, and heavily loaded station wagons.

I locked the alley door and hopped in the car. As I pulled out onto Broadway, watching more for darting children than unmarked cars, I saw a short-haired, sunglassed man standing at the corner by himself. He wasn't on vacation. As I passed him I held my slouch hat between us as a shield. It was a weak ploy; the Saab was easily identifiable. But the stagecoach ride, complete with four-horse team, pulled in behind me, and we both made the light before it changed.

I headed west, turning toward Wilson at the new stoplight. I still thought of it as new, though it had been around at least five years. It represented progress, traffic, and the end of smalltown Jackson to me.

The Teton Village road had lost its sun by the time I got there. Clouds from the mountains that towered just west of the valley looked threatening. The traffic wasn't as heavy as during the winter when the skiers searched for fresh powder at the ski area.

Why had Eden left out the intimate detail of her affair with Ray Tantro? Or who she thought was Ray Tantro. Did she know he was an impostor? He had told her about his relatives in Star Valley but never taken her there. I believed that part.

Pete's coupe sat in the drive, burdened by the two kayaks. As I walked up behind the car, a mockingbird dive-bombed me. I had to duck under the overhanging kayaks to avoid serious head injury.

As I crouched there, awaiting further attacks, Eden came out the front door. I stepped out into the afternoon sun, startling her.

"What were you doing hiding there?" She frowned at me, at least as wary as last night.

"Bird attacks," I said, scanning the aspens for more.

"Oh, those mockingbirds." She relaxed, moving around the car toward the trunk. She unlocked it and flipped it open, revealing wet suits, life jackets, and other gear. "Help me with this stuff, will you? Pete got a phone call and if you don't get a little sun on this junk, it'll still be wet in the morning."

Eden looked refreshed, probably from a nice, leisurely nap. She wore jeans and hiking boots with a new plaid shirt. Her hair was shiny, curling down over her neck.

"Here, take this jacket."

I took the blue paddle jacket and followed her to a red-wood picnic table that did double duty as a drying rack because of its sunny spot in the lawn. As if on cue, the sun peaked through the gray cumulus vapor hanging on the peaks. Eden dumped a pile of neoprene on the ground and began to drape them over the table and its benches.

"I think I left a pair of booties in the trunk," she said, tilting her head back toward the car.

"I'll get them."

The Mercedes's trunk was small and dark, and now wet with river water. I leaned down, feeling around in the gloom for the neoprene booties. The front corners were empty. I reached way into the far corners. That was where I found it.

Coiled up and damp, the dog leash brightened as I brought it into the light. I looked at it closely, picking a hair off it, a yellow hair. A worn red leash, just like the one hanging on Ray Tantro's back door. I held the leash long, dangling. I found the cowboy that morning, the dog vanished from her chain. Was the leash gone too? I closed my eyes, trying to picture the back door again.

The screen door slammed. I stuffed the leash back into the trunk and searched frantically for the booties. I found them at last and stood up, composing myself, as Pete came around the car.

He was dressed in ripstop shorts and rafting sandals. A perpetually sunburned nose made the rest of his face seem plain. In his eyes there was a new sharpness. His lean, hairless chest had reddened in the sun.

"I can take those." He held out his hand for the booties. I handed them over, probably too quickly. Suddenly my heart began to beat in my ears. God, I hated that.

"Eden asked me to help lay out the stuff. How was the river today?"

"Good. Damn good."

I moved toward Eden. Pete stood in front of the trunk, bringing up both hands to slam it closed. I shut my eyes. That hesitation—he had seen the leash. Knew I had seen it. He slammed the trunk. I watched him, walking backwards, so I wouldn't jump out of my skin at the sound of the trunk slamming. He turned to me and I smiled.

"I'm looking forward to my lesson on Wednesday," I said. Pete nodded, walking across the lawn with me. "I don't know why I chickened out so bad the last time. Nerves, I guess. Did you hear Carl went back to Missoula?"

"I thought he was here for two weeks."

"Some stuff came up."

"I thought he was hooked," Pete said.

Eden fussed with the wet suits, spreading them out just so on the redwood table. No sooner had she finished than the sun went behind the cloud bank. She frowned up at it, curling her upper lip. "They'll never get dry now, Pete. It's going to rain."

"Bring them in, then. Put them in the bathroom." He grabbed two life jackets, and, with the booties, went into the house to hang them up.

Eden sighed, looking at her handiwork one last time before gathering things up into her arms.

"I need to talk to you," I whispered, positioning Eden between me and the front door. I took her arm, making her listen. "It's important."

"I have to do this before it rains." Her voice was icy, shaking off my hand.

"Eden, has Pete ever mentioned a studio? A storage garage? Something like that?"

She shook her head. "If you're not going to help, get out of the way. It's going to storm."

"Does Pete have a storage locker? Think, Eden."

She cocked her head. "I don't know." She moved around me, the wet equipment dripping on her feet.

I tried to think of the one thing that would link Pete with Ray. The dog leash was something, but I needed more, hard evidence. "Does he have a motorcycle?"

She laughed. "He hates motorcycles."

"What about brushes and paints?"

"What *are* you talking about?"

"Think, Eden, did you ever see him with paint on—" I stopped, remembering the night I sat confused in front of the Stagecoach Bar after Paolo had dropped his bomb on me. Pete had smelled like turpentine, his shirt splotched with white. White paint, I realized now.

"Did you talk to Pete about Ray? About your involvement with Ray? Your romantic involvement."

Eden blinked, staring at me, then squinted. "Of course not." She picked up a wet suit and flung it over her shoulder.

"Have you talked to him about the fire?"

"Well, yeah," she conceded. "He asked me. He kind of had it figured out, that the fire was planned, and I—"

"Wait. He told you how the fire had been done?"

"Yeah, sort of."

I looked at my watch. "Don't tell him we talked. Please. He's a dangerous man, Eden. He set the fire. Don't you see?"

She stared at me, her face unflinching and hard. "You're sick, Alix. It was just on the radio. I know all about it."

I blinked. *On the radio?*

"Oh, don't tell me you didn't know about it," Eden sneered. "I don't really think you were involved, but maybe you were. You and Paolo are always so cozy. They found all the supplies, even a finished painting in Paolo's garage. And gas like the kind used in the fire. They just had it on the radio. The FBI is looking for him now."

The thunder rumbled far above. Menacing flashes of light sparked below the clouds. I felt struck already. A pain in my gut, like a knife, twisted.

"Paolo was the one who helped me figure out the paintings were forgeries."

"Good cover, I'd say. Keep it up," Eden said, turning toward the house with her arms full. "I'll tell Pete you have such confidence in him. He'll like that."

I STUMBLED BACK to the Saab and was on the highway before the outrage set in. Only my concern for Paolo kept me from marching into the house and telling Pete Rotondi I knew everything about his little scheme. Only, it wasn't little. The scheme was draconian in its planning, twists, and covers. The people he used: the cowboy, Ray number one (whoever he was), Wally, Esther, Eden. Now Paolo. He used them all in his tight web.

But I didn't know everything. I didn't know enough to take Pete Rotondi to the cops. And he knew it.

AFTER DRIVING too fast back into town, I cruised by Paolo's place. The street was more alive than usual, with neighbors standing in clumps, watching the three unmarked navy blue cars in front of the bungalow.

I eased by, ready to duck if any agents came out. But no one did and I drove back through the streets to the alley behind the gallery and shut off the car.

The act of turning the key left me immobile for a moment, as if my own key had been turned too. I wondered where Paolo was, if they had found him, if he was safe, if he'd turned himself in. He had run out of the gallery in such an uncharacteristic tizzy. I should have realized he was afraid. The sky was dark and the air smelled like rain. The sidewalk traffic thinned as people anticipated the storm.

My limbs felt like lead as I climbed from the Saab and up the stairs. A fresh pot of coffee, maybe a plate of angel-hair pasta. That was what I needed. A little food, some caffeine, and I'll be a new person.

The coffee from this afternoon had fried to a black crisp in the bottom of the decanter. I had forgotten to turn off the coffeemaker. I scrubbed it for a minute, filled the machine, put in coffee, and started it up. I filled a pan with water and set it on the stove. Before turning on the heat, I remembered the radio. I sat down in front of the stereo, flipping on the local station.

Rock music. I'd have to wait until six to get a report. I could smell the coffee now as I sank back in the sofa. Coffee and pasta and the news. That was what I needed.

I don't remember closing my eyes, or know how long I slept. My body let me down, demanding rest when I most needed to stay awake. It stole those minutes, those precious minutes when I could have changed the way things turned out. But by the time I woke up, the die was cast.

TWENTY-ONE

HE SAT IN the chair, very still. Black leather pants with silver studs down the side seam, his zippered jacket hanging open, revealing his bare chest. Biker boots, chained and dusty. My eyes moved gradually to his face, the hard eyes, the wind-tossed hair, the sunburned nose.

Pete Rotondi held a gun in his right hand, casually on his knee. It was a small gun, the kind you could conceal easily in your clothing, and it almost looked too small for his hand. He looked so much like a kayaking instructor, and yet, more like a road warrior. Even more like someone with a score to settle.

I woke up fast, pulling my legs under me on the sofa. His cold expression revealed only the depth of his disregard.

"How did you get in here?" I said when my voice returned.

"Walked." He blinked lazily, then got up and turned off the music. "Get up. We're going for a ride."

"Where?"

"You'll see. Get up." He waved the gun around. I stood up.

"On the Harley? Because I really don't like motorcycles. I've got this thing, you know. My father, bless his soul, used to say I should just cut off one leg if I was going to ride motorcycles—"

"Shut up. Get your keys."

I heard myself babbling and tried to calm the drumming in my chest. I picked up my keys from the kitchen counter. "Do you want coffee? I just made a pot."

"Get out the door." He was waving the gun again. I guessed he didn't want coffee.

Down the stairs Eden waited in the Saab. She sat in the front passenger's seat, her head down. When I got in the driver's seat, she looked up. Her face was red, streaked with tears. A nasty lump was growing under her right eye.

"Are you all right?" I whispered, as Pete got in the back seat, positioning his gun at my back.

Eden glanced back at Pete. "I can't believe this is happening."

"Shut up and drive." Pete poked the gun in my back. "You both talk too much."

I glanced at Eden. If I hadn't told her my suspicions, she wouldn't be here. Why couldn't I have waited, presented the hard evidence to the Feds? Carl was right. I can't keep my nose out of other people's business, can't let the cops do their job. As I followed Pete's directions, I slumped in my seat, my knuckles white on the steering wheel.

"Faster," Pete said. I had been going about thirty on the highway leading through the Snake River Canyon, slowing for turns, hoping for God-knows-what kind of miracle to save us.

I straightened up. "This car only goes so fast." I began to think again. Where was he taking us? To Star Valley? "Are you giving up, then, Pete? Is the jig up?"

"Just drive."

"If you kill us, and Wally, nobody will be buying Wally's paintings for a long, long time. They'll know something was funny about them. And they'll be hung up in probate."

"Wally?" Eden asked.

"Ray's cousin. Pete set him up with a bunch of fake Tantros to sell after Ray died. Pete's quite an artist."

"You did those fakes in the Timberwolf?" Eden turned back to Pete.

"Pretty bad, huh," Pete said.

"Awful," I said. "Why'd you have to make them so bad?"

"Part of the plan. You wouldn't understand."

"Try me."

"Just drive."

"How's this? You made the forgeries so bad so that people would remember how good Ray used to be, long ago, and get to wondering if there were any good ones still around. Then, bingo, the good ones show up for sale."

Eden looked over her shoulder at him. "You had to kill Ray to sell the paintings?" Her eyes filled, spilling tears down her face. "You murdered him?"

It was probably good that Pete wasn't in position to slap Eden again, because from the look on his face in the rearview mirror, he was thinking about it.

"He didn't kill Ray," I said. "He killed two people that he wanted people to think were Ray. I haven't figured that part out, Pete. Who was that first guy in the fire?"

Pete didn't answer. We were entering the tightest part of the canyon, where the steep shoulders dropped off into the river below, down long, rocky banks. It was close to here where the lug nuts had loosened; Pete's doing. A shiver went up my spine. He had almost killed us once.

"Pull off here," said Pete. "To the left, that road."

Foot on the brake, I steered onto a dirt road that disappeared into a grove of Douglas firs, hoping irrationally that a blown tire would save us. But I'd put on those new tires. Not that a flat would make any difference; Pete was a man who had made up his mind. The realization of that had a calming effect and my mind cleared. Thor, the mighty warrior god, never balked at the prospect of death. It was inevitable, as natural as breathing and babies. A warrior accepts that. The words from my old Edith Hamilton: *Men and women who go steadfastly forward to meet death, often deliberately choose it, even plan it beforehand. The only light in the darkness is heroism.*

I didn't feel like a hero; I felt mortal, my heart thumping, my breath tight. I didn't choose this fate, although it has always been there, for each of us, a bookend to our brief, tumultuous, joyful lives. As we entered the shadows of the firs, Eden began to sob, low and inconsolable.

"Stop here," Pete demanded. I braked by an opening in the trees. The sound of the river far below, out of view, was not comforting. "Get out."

I opened the car door and found my footing on the rocks embedded in the roadbed, rocks the size of baseballs, dredged up from the river bottom. Eden sat hunched over, her head in her hands.

"Come on, Eden," I whispered. "Get out with me."

"Let her stay," Pete said, slamming the car door behind him, gun pointed at me. He looked strange with a gun, this pole-and-paddle guy. He didn't look like the Pete Rotondi I had known, in skintight leathers, his placid face transformed by fury and duty.

"You stand over there." He indicated the back of the car, by a clump of yellow bark willows. As I walked around, he got in the driver's seat, one boot dragging out the open door. He put the car in neutral, letting it roll toward the sharp edge of the bank. He pulled the parking brake when it was six inches from going over.

Pete turned to get out. I could see through the oval back window that Eden was saying something, her hands in the air. She grabbed his arm, screaming, calling him names, but he was stronger. He hit her across the face again with the gun in his hand. She screamed again and slumped back in the seat. I should run, I thought. I could run now, while Eden distracts him. But could I leave her there? Would Thor run like a rabbit?

Pete's face was flushed when he emerged from the Saab, his breath fast. Good for Eden. Give him a little run for his money. I wasn't afraid of him finally. I knew he would kill me if he could. But I wasn't afraid.

Man is born to sorrow as the sparks fly upward. To live is to suffer. The only solution to the problem of life is to suffer with courage.

Courage, I thought as a shiver went up my spine. Courage. Pete could make me suffer, but he could not make me afraid.

He moved toward me, brandishing the gun. "Get in the car."

His plan came clear. Make our deaths look like accidents. He was clever, killing his victims in different ways, never leaving tracks or patterns.

"No." I folded my arms as he danced nervously in front of me, glancing at the Saab.

He moved toward me. I backed away. In his heavy boots he walked awkwardly on the rocks and I was fast. He grabbed for me and missed.

"Just shoot me, Pete. I'm not getting in that car."

He lunged at me, grabbing my ankle on his way down. I fell hard, bones hitting rocks all the way down, then scrambled to my feet. He was up too, with his big hand around my arm. "Now get in the car." His breath was heavy.

I struggled to get away, but his grip was unyielding. I groaned, unable to talk, then, by reflex, turned and kneed him in the groin. His hand loosened as he doubled over, moaning. I jumped away, running.

Then the shot rang out, near my head, my ears, sailing by me into the trees. I stopped, my breath so tight it hardly came. Down below on the river a burst of laughter from a passing raft seemed to mock me.

"Turn around and get in the car," Pete growled, his voice on the edge of patience. I turned. He stood hunched, still in pain. I was glad for his pain.

"You're going to have to shoot me, Pete. I'm not getting in the car."

Something moved in the bushes beyond Pete. I tried not to move my eyes. Pete told me again to get into the car, punctuating it with another high shot into the trees. I looked harder into the trees, hoping it wasn't a moose or a skunk or a tourist with a weak bladder.

Paolo stuck his head out from behind a fir. His face was pinched with worry and tension. Slowly he moved closer to Pete's back.

As Eden opened her car door, sticking her foot out, Paolo made his move. Pete saw me watching her and glanced away from me. Paolo jumped on Pete from behind. But Pete didn't go down, and he and Paolo did a mad dance of piggyback. They grunted and swore. The gun was still in Pete's hand, thrashing wildly. Pete backed up to the Saab and slammed Paolo into it. The car jumped forward, one tire now hanging off the edge. Eden screamed. Paolo groaned but hung on.

The gun, the gun. I knew if we could disarm Pete, between the three of us, we could gain control. But the gun in Pete's hand was his ace, waving wildly despite Paolo's attempts to reach it. I moved from one side to the other, trying to stay out of range and find a chance to grab it.

Pete bent at the waist, sending Paolo sailing over his head to the ground. I ran to him, kneeling, helping him sit up. He winced, then sprang up to his feet.

"Give me the gun, you son of a bitch."

Pete smiled through his teeth. He was breathing hard but on his feet, facing us. "I'll give it to you."

"Wait," I said, holding Paolo's arm. "You need Paolo to be the fall guy."

Pete tipped his head back, flipping his hair off his forehead. "Plans change. Just like with Gil. He never should have gone out of town."

"Gil?" I said. Was that the cowboy?

"Having some pal of his watch his place. Didn't he think that the schmuck would have to know?" Pete squinted at us, backing up as Eden joined us, sliding along the back end of the Saab. She took Paolo's hand, shivering.

"So you killed the pal in the fire?" This was the part I never understood. Gil, the cowboy, had gone out of town, presumably to the rodeo in Cheyenne. He had his friend house-sit, without checking it out with Pete. Gil must have hated being a limp-wristed artist after riding wild bulls.

"He knew too much. Burning those abstracts was a bonus."

"You killed him and burned my gallery?" Eden squeaked, her face ashen against her damp brunette curls. She slumped against Paolo's other arm.

"Don't give me that shit," Pete sneered. "You arranged it. You wanted out. You killed him as much as I did."

Eden buried her face in Paolo's shoulder. I opened my mouth to defend her but decided against it. It was useless now. Paolo stood motionless, not pushing her off but not comforting either. His eyes were glued on Pete's gun.

"Enough. Get in the car," Pete ordered.

"We're not getting in," Paolo said, his voice deep and sure. I stared at him. Somehow I never thought of him as the brave type. Arrogant, bossy, but brave? Well.

"You'll have to shoot all of us," I said, my chest so tight breathing was difficult. "Then you'll have some explaining to do. Who'd you steal that gun from, Pete? I only had one."

Pete reddened, his temper rising from his neck onto his smooth, tanned cheeks. It occurred to me, in that moment, that making him angry was the wrong thing to do. But I would not go easily. No, I would have courage, with my steadfast friend at my side. *Courage to the end, amigo.*

The three of us stood watching him, frozen to the ground. He brought the gun up level to his waist. The squeeze of the trigger rippled his hand muscles as the sound burst in the cool forest air, a hot streak. I stood still, waiting for the pain. When my ears stopped resounding from the shot, I heard Eden wailing.

She was kneeling over Paolo. A crimson stain on his blue silk shirt grew, spreading from his stomach. He lay on the ground, gasping for breath, staring at the sky.

"God, no!" I dropped to my knees. "No, Paolo." I pressed on his wound, trying to stop the bleeding. I felt a fresh breeze come up from the river, a smell of brine and fish and newly melted snow. All the things I loved paraded across my mind. Here on the ground, this reality was too true to grasp. Too awful to think past. My hands pressing into his lifeblood, I wanted to tell him how I had loved him, how the best parts of my life were with him, how I had missed him. I felt the tears on my face, watched them fall onto his chest.

My hands were wet with blood. I could feel his pulse against them, the surging of life slowing. *No, no, Paolo, hang on. Please, God.*

Paolo looked at me, his eyes focusing for a moment.

"Don't leave me, Paolo. I need you. Stay with me. Stay, please." My eyes clouded with tears.

He tried to say something. His lips twitched, then his eyes closed. I panicked. "Go get an ambulance!" I shouted at Eden, kneeling on the other side of him, weeping. "Quick, run to the highway!"

But I had forgotten about Pete. Eden rose to her feet, ready to run but on the verge of hysteria. Pete stepped up to her. "Stay where you are. Get in the car, Eden."

"You killer! Murderer! How could you do this?!" She screamed, flailing at his chest. She lurched forward, catching Pete off guard as she scratched his face. She was no match for him. Pete outweighed her by a hundred pounds. But Eden was mad, and she clung to him, pulling and clawing while he tried to get her off. They moved around the Saab toward the river, Pete swearing, Eden screaming.

I watched Paolo's chest for breathing. The movement was very slight, but still there. My hands had disappeared into a puddle of blood on his abdomen, drenching his best gray

flannel slacks. Later I would always remember his clothes,
his black Italian shoes dusty with road grim, his exotic Swiss
watch that never stopped, even the five o'clock shadow that
graced his strong jaw. The fine, sweet line of his lips and his
mink-dark lashes.

Pete shook Eden loose in the shadow of a fir that stood
on the high bank above the river. She groaned, rolling to the
ground. Lying on her back, she came up on her elbows,
grimacing until she saw Pete's gun.

"Pete, don't. It's me," she cried.

"Yeah, you. Worthless twat." He raised the gun a little
more, aiming for her chest.

"Please, Pete. I—I—I won't tell. Honest." Tears
streamed down her face.

He laughed. Starting with a small chuckle, he looked
down the barrel of his gun and laughed at her. That laugh
was what got me. I was kneeling only twelve or fifteen feet
behind him, trying to keep my friend alive. Life came and
went so casually, on a whim. Before I could think, my blood
was in my ears again and I was on him in the kind of foot-
ball tackle that my big brother used on me all the time, an
ankle strangle.

Pete toppled toward the river, still laughing, then making a gulping, drowning noise. His arms began to windmill
wildly, out of control. His legs slipped out of my bloody
grasp. The gun went off as he fell, tumbling down the steep
bank. Head over heels, over weeds and wildflowers and
boulders, flailing, bones against rock. The gun was knocked
from his hand as he bounced off three trees before coming
to rest fifty feet down on the sand.

Eden pulled me up and clung to me as we watched him.
He lay at an awkward angle, facedown, a leg and arm
pinned under him, the others sprawled. We waited for him
to get up. But he was still.

Over my shoulder Paolo wasn't moving. I ran to him, cradling his head in my bloody hands. His eyes were closed, his deep, black eyes, hot with the passion of life.

"It's over, Pao. Stay with me." I leaned down and kissed his forehead. "Stay, love."

His eyelids fluttered. "Alix," he whispered. *"Mañana."*

I closed my eyes, laying my cheek on his. Eden began a wail that expressed all the regret, all the pain, all the grief deep in my Nordic heart.

TWENTY-TWO

THERE WAS no wind. The sky was azure, perfectly clear. The scent of flowers from bouquets and roses blooming nearby hung in the air. Behind us the Tetons scraped the blue pyramids of granite carved by glaciers. So close you could reach out and touch them. Tombstones for the prairie. Their silence, their permanence, comforted me in an odd, irrational way that I would always remember and associate with the spirit of my friend.

My dark-haired Thor, who faced death for me. There was nothing rational about Paolo's death. Of all of us involved in Pete Rotondi's twisted scheme, he was the least likely. He had nothing to do with it except through me. Of course, I blamed myself. If not for my incessant curiosity and snapping-turtle sense of justice, Paolo would be alive. Justice seemed such a hollow motive today.

Eden stood beside me, dressed in my black blazer and khaki pants. Her dark curls shone in the sun. On her face pain was a live thing to be tamed. How different we were. Her shoulders shook with sobs through the service, especially when she tried to sing a hymn.

Paolo had specified in his will that he wanted to be buried here in Jackson. He had named me executor, among other things. I was left with the duties of selecting a plot at the local cemetery and making funeral arrangements. For the last three days I had had few moments of rest, never more than an hour or two at a time. I had so much to do. And my dreams were not happy ones.

Carl came down right after the shooting and was a comfort. One night I even told him so. It was hard to let him hold me in his arms; the pain seemed to multiply inside me at the touch of a male. But Carl persevered, and understood in his own way the unbearable pain of losing someone you love. I would have liked to have Carl Mendez here beside me under the Teton sky, but there was a murder in Missoula and he was needed.

Only now that Paolo was gone could I admit to myself my unchanging fondness that burst into passion at times, and at other times, into boundless pleasure at his company. I remembered his apartment in New York that he had painted the color of the sea. I remembered sitting on a rock by Taggart Lake, kissing his salty neck in the wind. I remembered the feel of his fingers on my face. The realization of how deeply I cared for him, now when it was too late, made me crazy if I thought too long about it. So I concentrated on details, meetings with lawyers and undertakers, and kept the sink clean.

Paolo's mother and sister came from Costa Rica, where they had been living in exile. They were handsome women, just as he had been, with golden skin and long, dark hair. His mother, who had never come to Jackson until now, let silent tears run down her round face as she tugged on a black crocheted shawl. Death had come to many in their family before their time. But that was Argentina. She thought in America her boy was safe from crazy *pistoleros*.

A priest Señora Segundo had found led the service. Paolo had not been a practicing Catholic, but she was. And I was more than willing to let her arrange things. I felt so very tired, standing in the still, silent cemetery with the bees humming in the field.

As the priest droned on, some in English, some in Latin, my mind wandered. I thought about the man I knew as Pete Rotondi. The FBI identified him posthumously as Daniel Holland, a promising art student at the Rhode Island School of Design at the same time as Ray Tantro. He had dropped out of RISD and made a living in forgery, along with odd legitimate jobs. The FBI's Art Unit in Chicago had already linked him to two other major forgery cases over the last fifteen years, maybe several more, it always being convenient to pin unsolved cases on dead guys.

It was difficult to imagine the man I had dismissed as a dim-witted ski-and-kayak bum with a trust fund as a forger and killer. I had trusted my life to him on the river. I could think of that first debacle on the Snake impassively now, underwater in a panic, trying to roll. My nose still needed to be tweaked back into shape. But it didn't matter. The vision of Paolo with his life oozing away before my eyes while I could do nothing—that feeling of helpless terror superseded all others. My enthusiasm for kayaking, what was left, had evaporated. When I thought of it, I thought of Pete and how much I hated what he had done to Paolo.

In the stillness Ray's voice from the dream came back. *Everybody wants it.* What did he want that we all wanted? Now I understood. Immortality. If only I could have it today for Paolo. But even heroes die. Thor taught me that once, years before. In case I'd forgotten, he'd taught me again today.

Paolo's sister, Luca, touched my arm. When I looked up I saw the service had ended. Paolo's friends were milling in groups, holding each other. The turnout wasn't large, not more than thirty or forty, but Paolo was well liked. A number of former girlfriends were in attendance, all blond, lissome, and teary.

"Come to the house with us, please?" Luca was well educated and spoke decent English. Her mother did not, so Luca did all the talking for them. His sister was so pretty, so like him. "We make some dinner for everybody."

"That's not necessary, Luca. We can just—" Just what? My mind was blank.

"No, is made, all ready. Mama and me spend yesterday making traditional food. Paolo would like that," she said earnestly.

My eyes began to sting. I thought of my last meal with
Paolo, and how it had felt like a last meal, how I had begun
missing him that night. I hadn't cried at the service, or all
day, but it seemed there was a time each day that I couldn't
hold back the tears. It was unlike me to cry in public. I remembered my mother again, at my father's funeral, dry-
eyed and spine of steel.

I took a breath. "Sure, okay."

I SPENT AS long as I had to at the supper. It was no Irish
wake, no jovial recounting of the exploits of the departed.
Just good food and lots of it, and plenty of shoulders to cry
on. I couldn't stand being in his house, seeing his things. His
garden was at its peak, blue-violet delphiniums six feet tall,
Shasta daisies in starry multitude, the empty stepping-
stones. The only thing missing was Paolo. It didn't help that
he had left the house to me. I intended to remedy that by
giving it to Luca and her mother. I didn't want Paolo's
house where his spirit was everywhere, smiling as if nothing had happened.

Nothing but a fire that started it all. The man in the fire
was identified as a rodeo cowboy named Toby Dubs, who
had disappeared from the circuit on July 23 after a rodeo in
Worland. He was a drifter, no ties, family unknown, an ac-
quaintance of Gil Taylor, the cowboy Pete had recruited to
be Ray Tantro. Gil asked Toby to watch his place. Between
Eden's and Esther's insurance and Wally and Pete's prof-
its, there was plenty of money at stake. Hiring Toby was
only one of Gil's mistakes.

WHEN THE GALLERY reopened after the funeral, I took up
my post as chief salesman to the masses with the enthusiasm of Job. But the funny thing was, I didn't mind the
tourists anymore. I cleaned up bloody noses and bubble-
gum, broke up marital spats, gave directions to the public
rest room, and recommended more restaurants than you

could shake a stick at. Sold some art too. And it felt good.
I missed Paolo awfully but was too busy to dwell on it. If I
did, I cleaned. Second Sun Gallery had never been cleaner.
But the strangest thing was I enjoyed it. All of it. It was as
if Paolo's love of the great, unpredictable mishmash of hu-
manity had been left behind like a suit of clothes for me to
try on for size. The clothes may not have fit, but they were
warm. Comforting and warm like an old friend.

CRIMINALS ALWAYS HAVE SOMETHING TO HIDE—BUT THE ENJOYMENT YOU'LL GET OUT OF A WORLDWIDE MYSTERY NOVEL IS NO SECRET....

With Worldwide Mystery on the case, we've taken the mystery out of finding something good to read every month.

Worldwide Mystery is guaranteed to have suspense buffs and chill seekers of all persuasions in eager pursuit of each new exciting title!

Worldwide Mystery novels—crimes worth investigating...

 **WORLDWIDE LIBRARY®**

THE IRON GLOVE

First Time in Paperback

RONALD TIERNEY

A Deets Shanahan Mystery

THE NAKED LADY WASN'T YOUR AVERAGE FLOATER

She was, in fact, Sally Holland, wife of Indiana senator David Holland, half of Washington's Golden Couple. Within hours, a suspect is arrested—a young Latino boxer believed to be her lover. Though not at all convinced the police have the wrong suspect, private investigator Deets Shanahan nevertheless agrees to do some digging for the defense.

Another dead body later, along with some answers that just seem too easy and pat for a P.I. who has been around long enough to know the difference, Shanahan dives into the dirty side of politics and the dark side of passion—and the hideous secrets a killer is desperate to hide....

"A series packed with angles and delights."

—Publishers Weekly

Available in December at your favorite retail stores.

DEADLY ADMIRER
CHRISTINE GREEN

First Time in Paperback

A Kate Kinsella Mystery

ILL WILL

Nurse Vanessa Wooten is being stalked. Desperate and terrified, she consumes a fatal overdose but manages to get to the hospital and into the capable hands of Kate Kinsella, part-time nurse and private investigator. Kate is intrigued—though she is warned that Vanessa has a history of mental illness.

Kate agrees to investigate, albeit somewhat skeptically, until she observes the figure shadowing not only her client...but herself. Murder adds a deadly spin when one of Vanessa's patients is smothered. But elderly Mrs. Brigstock will not be the first to die...and Kate fears it will be Vanessa—or herself—who may be the last.

"This is a superior mystery." —*Focus on Denver*

"The story is engrossing, with a nice double twist at the end." —*Mystery News*

Available in December at your favorite retail stores.

To order your copy, please send your name, address, zip or postal code along with a check or money order (please do not send cash) for $4.99 for each book ordered, plus 75¢ postage and handling payable to Worldwide Mystery, to:

In the U.S.

Worldwide Mystery
3010 Walden Avenue
P. O. Box 1325
Buffalo, NY 14269-1325

Please specify book title with your order.
This title is not available in Canada.

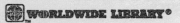 **WORLDWIDE LIBRARY®**

ADMIRER

HARLEQUIN®
I N T R I G U E®

WANTED
12 SEXY LAWMEN

They're rugged, they're strong and they're WANTED!
Whether sheriff, undercover cop or officer of the court,
these men are trained to keep the peace, to uphold the
law...but what happens when they meet the one woman
who gets to know the real man behind the badge?

Twelve LAWMEN are on the loose—and only
Harlequin Intrigue has them! Meet them one per
month, continuing with

Sam Moore
#401 MAN WITHOUT A BADGE
by Dani Sinclair
January 1997

LAWMAN:
*There's nothing sexier than
the strong arms of the law!*

HARLEQUIN®

I N T R I G U E®

THAT'S INTRIGUE—DYNAMIC ROMANCE AT ITS BEST!

Harlequin Intrigue is now bringing you more—more men and mystery, more desire and danger. If you've been looking for thrilling tales of contemporary passion and sensuous love stories with taut, edge-of-the-seat suspense—then you'll *love* Harlequin Intrigue!

Every month, you'll meet four new heroes who are guaranteed to make your spine tingle and your pulse pound. With them you'll enter into the exciting world of Harlequin Intrigue—where your life is on the line and so is your heart!

Harlequin Intrigue—we'll leave you breathless!

INT-GEN